TRUTH UNVEILED

A DR. SAMANTHA JENKINS MYSTERY

STEPHANIE KREML

HIPE BOOKS PUBLISHING

Copyright © 2021 by Stephanie Kreml

Library of Congress Control Number: 2021911709

ISBN: 978-1-955921-00-8 (ebook), 978-1-955921-01-5 (paperback)

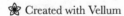 Created with Vellum

Dread. Not the feeling Samantha Jenkins expected as her friend's wedding day approached, but there it was. Claire Johnson was one of Sam's oldest friends, and Sam had eagerly agreed to be one of Claire's bridesmaids just a month after she had become engaged herself. But now, Sam dreaded going to Claire's wedding, and she felt guilty for that dread.

Claire's upcoming nuptials brought visions of Jeff into her mind. Ugh, Jeff—her former fiancé. She pushed the thought of him aside, but invariably he crept back into her mind just by the very nature of the wedding about to take place.

Fortunately, the guests at Claire's wedding were mainly people Sam had known in high school, along with a few of Claire's friends from college and later. None of them knew Jeff, since Sam had met him when she was in medical school. None of them except for Claire and Emily.

Claire had been so excited when Mike proposed to her. She told everyone she and Sam would get married almost at the same time, and Sam did the same, until … Well, so much can change in a year.

Everyone knew everything about everybody these days. Facebook allowed Sam to share her excitement when she accepted Jeff's proposal, but when they broke things off, she quietly retreated from the platform, not wanting to deal with false sympathy gushing from people she barely even knew.

There would be questions, maybe not spoken directly to her, but sideways glances, whispers when people thought she wasn't looking. Wasn't she getting married too? Did she bring someone with her to the wedding? Had she started dating again?

However, as Sam typically did when putting others first, like her patients—especially her patients—she boxed up those thoughts. She had a duty to fulfill. She would just deal with it. That's how it's done.

Before she reluctantly rushed into the events of the weekend, she had to wrap up things at work. It was Friday afternoon after a busy week, each day packed with patients at the clinic where Sam practiced in Austin. She had to admit, a break would be good for her.

Sam could have taken the day off and gone to the spa with Claire and Emily. Maybe she should have. But Sam made an excuse and told Claire that she didn't have a lot of vacation days saved up (which was true) even though she really wanted to spend the day with them (which was only half true). They meant well, but she just didn't want to talk about how she was feeling.

Just a few more patient notes, then Sam could leave the clinic and be on her way to the rehearsal. Maybe being around old friends would help her remember when times were simpler. But were they really? Or had she just been naïve back then?

As Sam tapped away on her keyboard, Cynthia, one of the medical assistants, handed her a message slip. "Dr. Taylor called while you were with a patient."

Sam felt a touch of apprehension. Dr. Peter Taylor was Sam's boss, and he rarely called unless a problem came up. "What did he want?" she asked.

Cynthia shrugged. "I don't know. He said he would email you."

"Okay, thanks." Sam turned back to her computer.

"And there's a new injury going into room two."

She pursed her lips. Cynthia knew Sam needed to leave an hour earlier than usual. "Can you tell Jerry? I have to get going soon."

"He's in room one," Cynthia said.

Rooms one and two were the procedure rooms, which meant Jerry Reid, the physician assistant who worked with Sam, was probably taking care of a case more complicated than the sprains and strains they usually treated.

"What's he working on?"

Cynthia shrugged again. "I don't know." And she walked away.

Sam closed her eyes for a moment. She liked Cynthia, but sometimes …

A trio of voices drifted over to Sam from the hallway, and she peered around the corner to see who was coming into the back office. Laura, another medical assistant, led two men in blue work clothes to the empty procedure room. An older man, whom Sam recognized as a patient she had taken care of recently, had a rag wrapped around his hand with an ice pack, his face pinched in pain. His companion looked fresh out of high school, eyes wide, like he had wrecked his dad's car.

Sam sighed and checked the electronic medical record. John Campbell. Now she remembered. She had treated him for a medial collateral ligament sprain. The chief complaint for this visit read "I smashed my finger."

She checked the chief complaint for room one, where Jerry was working. It read "I hit my head on an open filing drawer."

Sam needed to leave in fifteen minutes, which was just enough time to get things started for Mr. Campbell. However, if Jerry was almost done with his patient, she could leave without guilt. She headed over to room one, rapped on the door as she cracked it open, and leaned in.

A man in a polo and khakis was reclining in the procedure chair, his head illuminated by the lights mounted on the ceiling.

Jerry's silver hair glinted as he leaned over his patient. He wore a mask, goggles, and a disposable paper gown to protect his clothes. Grasping a needle driver loaded with suture, he threw a stitch into a two-inch gash on the man's forehead, the surrounding skin tinted brown from iodine.

Jerry pulled the suture taut, then looked up and said, "What's up, Doc?"

Sam's face softened. Jerry always knew how to put everyone at ease. "There's a new injury, but I see you're still working here. It looks like he might need X-rays, so I'll take a quick look at him before I leave."

Jerry glanced at the clock on the wall. "You should go, Doc. I can take care of it."

"It's no big deal. Should only take a minute. I'll see you Monday, okay?"

"Thanks, Doc. Have a good time at the wedding."

Sam closed the door and moved to the adjacent room. As she opened the door, Mr. Campbell was saying, "So then the bartender says ..." He looked at her with a jovial smile even as he cradled his wrapped hand against his chest. "Hi, Dr. Jenkins. I was just trying to cheer up Frank. He works with me at the garage."

Frank, the same young man Sam had seen with Mr. Campbell in the hallway, sat in an office chair against the wall, bouncing his leg, blank face staring straight ahead.

"Hi, Mr. Campbell. It's good to see you again, but I wish it were under different circumstances." She turned to Frank and extended her hand. "I'm Dr. Jenkins."

The young man stayed seated, frowning as he slowly shook Sam's hand and looked her up and down.

"I can't seem to stay away from this place, Doctor," Mr. Campbell said. He looked at Frank. "Dr. Jenkins took real good care of me when I messed up my knee a while back."

"Oh, thanks, Mr. Campbell." Sam motioned toward his hand. "Tell me what happened today."

"I was trying to take a lug nut off a wheel, but it wasn't budging, even when I maxed out the torque on the air wrench. Must have been stripped." He tipped his head toward the young man. "So I used a tire iron and asked Frank here to bang it with a mallet. It slipped, and my thumb got in the way."

Frank hung his head and said, "Man, I'm so sorry."

Mr. Campbell reached over with his good hand and patted Frank's arm. "Don't worry about it, kid. I shouldn't have asked you to do that."

Sam gloved up and started unwrapping Mr. Campbell's left hand. "Let's see what we have here."

He squirmed in the procedure chair. "Sorry, but it really throbs."

"That's okay, sir." Once Sam removed everything, a swollen thumb with a collection of blood under the nail revealed itself. Mr. Campbell sucked in through his teeth as she gingerly examined it.

"You have what we call a subungual hematoma," Sam

said. "You've broken a blood vessel under your thumbnail, and that's caused all this swelling. The pressure has built up, which is why it's painful. But I'll take care of that for you."

She discarded her gloves and hung her white coat on the hook on the back of the door. She went to the counter along the back wall behind the procedure chair, and as she opened drawers to get what she needed, Frank whispered something to his colleague.

Sam turned to catch Mr. Campbell elbowing Frank. "Show some respect, boy."

She clinched her jaw. Focus on helping Mr. Campbell.

Sam took her supplies to a stainless steel tray on a stand against the wall, then she wheeled it over to Mr. Campbell and gloved up again. She glanced at the digital clock above the TV on the wall, the red numbers mocking her. She was going to be late. But in a few seconds, Sam would alleviate Mr. Campbell's pain.

"Here's what I'm going to do," she said as she opened a blue Chux pad to cover the tray and then adjusted its height. "I'm going to relieve the pressure that has built up under your thumbnail by burning a small hole through your nail with this cautery. Place your hand down here." She switched on the procedure light mounted on the ceiling, aiming it at Mr. Campbell's injured hand, then swabbed his thumb with pink antiseptic.

"Is this going to hurt?" Frank asked, squinting at her. "You know what you're doing, right?"

Sam flared her nostrils as she concentrated on her patient's hand. "Not any more painful than what Mr. Campbell is already feeling. In fact, he's about to feel a lot better soon."

She opened the paper autoclave package holding the butane-powered cautery, chunky and plastic like the cordless curling irons that were popular when she was in high school. She clicked on the cautery and the tip glowed bright orange within seconds.

Frank's eyes widened. "What are you doing with that thing?"

"I'm just burning a tiny hole into Mr. Campbell's nail."

Mr. Campbell winked at Sam and smiled. "Don't worry, Frank. She's a pro."

"Okay. Hold still." Sam gently touched the glowing tip to the center of the nail, releasing dark red blood through the newly formed hole.

Mr. Campbell let out a long breath, his body relaxing. "Wow, you weren't kidding. The pain's gone." He raised his eyebrows. "That's amazing!"

Frank pinched his nose. "Yuk! It smells like burnt hair in here!"

Sam dabbed up the blood with clean gauze and nodded. "Yeah, not very pleasant. And you're right. Hair and nails are both made of keratin, so that's why it smells like burnt hair." She loved educating her patients, but when she looked up at Frank, anger glared back at her. She'd seen that look before, but she really didn't understand why. Didn't everyone want to know more about how the world worked? Maybe he thought she was lecturing him. Or maybe … maybe he was mad at her, because she was a woman fixing a problem he caused.

She blinked, clearing her mind and focusing again on Mr. Campbell. As the blood flow slowed, she wrapped Mr. Campbell's thumb with a clean roll of gauze. "Now we'll get an X-ray to see if it's broken. We'll put a splint on your thumb to protect it anyway, but if it's broken, we'll need to start you on some antibiotics."

"Whatever you say, Doc."

As she washed up, she couldn't help but think that she

was glad Frank was not her patient. She glanced in the mirror above the sink and eye wash station. Sam did look young, but Mr. Campbell seemed to have full confidence in her. Why not Frank?

Then she scrutinized her image, her thoughts shifting to the rehearsal she was about to be late to. She had put her hair neatly in a ponytail for work this morning, but after a long day, small chestnut tendrils had escaped, framing her face with frizz. She quickly patted them back in place with her damp hands. No time to fix it better than that, and the ponytail would have to stay—if she let her hair down, she'd have a lovely dent in her layers.

As Sam turned around, she said, "I'll have one of the MAs give you supplies along with instructions on how to care for your thumb, and I'll let—" She stopped because Frank leered at her, with a grin that bordered on menacing, the anger in his eyes replaced by hate.

Mr. Campbell looked over from the game show on the TV and slapped Frank on the leg. "Stop it, boy."

Sam came around to the front of the procedure chair to address Mr. Campbell, hoping he didn't see the flush in her cheeks. "I'll put in the order for your X-ray, and we'll get you taken care of as soon as possible."

Mr. Campbell smiled apologetically. "Thanks, Doc."

She nodded curtly, ignoring Frank in her peripheral vision. She grabbed her coat and rushed out of the room, taking deep breaths to slow her heart. What was Frank's problem? At least she didn't have to be in that room anymore.

By the time she found Anthony, the X-ray tech, and asked him to perform a thumb series on Mr. Campbell, she felt more composed. Then she went to the work area to put in the order.

Jerry was back at his computer. "You're still here?"

Sam laughed half-heartedly, her unease dissipating. "Yeah, the new injury was a subungual hematoma, so I trephinated it. Anthony's getting him ready for X-ray. Just need to put in the order."

"You should get out of here, Doc. I can do that and follow up on those X-rays."

"Thanks, Jer. You're the best." She patted him on the shoulder. "And please apologize to Mr. Campbell for me."

"What for?"

"Because … because I had to leave."

Jerry grinned. "Oh, I'm sure he'll understand."

Sam texted Claire as she walked out to her car: *Leaving now. Sorry I'll be a little late.*

Now she just needed to survive Claire's big weekend.

2

S am made it to the bed-and-breakfast fifteen minutes late, but the only thing she missed was the small talk before the rehearsal actually began. That was fine by her. After parking her car, she weaved between the main house—an old ranch-style with a broad wrap-around porch—and one of the limestone and stucco buildings housing guest rooms. She brushed past a mountain laurel, its grape-like clusters of flowers enveloping her in its sweet scent, and stepped onto an expansive lawn filled with rows of white wooden folding chairs on either side of a pathway leading to a vine-covered gazebo.

Everyone had lined up in their places for the processional next to the main house's back deck, so she quietly slipped behind Emily Daniels, the matron of honor. Claire stood over to the side, waiting for her turn to practice walking down the aisle. Sam made a small wave and the bride beamed.

Clear blue sky arched over them, but in the distance thunderheads billowed up in the afternoon heat, emitting an occasional rumble, like combatants ready for battle. As

Sam took in the other members of the wedding party, her eyes locked on to Claire's older brother Brad for an instant, and he smiled at her. She looked away. Maybe the anticipation of being around him this weekend had contributed to her apprehension about the wedding in addition to her breakup with Jeff.

When she was younger, she had had a crush on Brad, the popular football player who got everything he wanted. He still had that charm, but Sam knew better now. Unfortunately, the way Claire had lined everyone up, Sam would be paired with him during the recessional. Sam took a deep breath. No problem. She could deal with it.

The group completed two passes through the ceremony before they had to leave, since the venue had a wedding scheduled for that evening. A couple of minor blooper moments happened, small things like Claire's forgetting to take back the bouquet prop from Emily, and the ring bearer sitting down in the middle of the aisle, having to be coaxed along with the promise of a lollipop. The jovial mood helped Sam relax, and when it was time for her to take Brad's arm, he was polite, even addressing her as "Dr. Jenkins."

Afterward, the group went to a small restaurant in a remodeled old house specializing in Texan cuisine, with appetizers like rattlesnake cakes and various game for entrees. As they ate, the storm clouds opened up outside, releasing the pent-up energy within. The members of the party sat at the table as they had been at the rehearsal, with the bride and groom at one end of the table, their friends and family flanking them on either side.

Between bites of pistachio-crusted rattlesnake, Emily said to Sam, "I feel so bad for the couple whose wedding is going on right now." She grimaced. "So much for the lovely outdoor setting."

"That is a shame," Sam said. "I guess they had to move it indoors."

"Claire said that's the backup plan. The venue can set up for the wedding ceremony on the dance floor of the reception space if they need to."

"Hopefully, the weather forecast is better for tomorrow," Sam said as fat raindrops battered the windows, like a small army trying to get in.

After the rattlesnake, Sam opted for a massive boar chop. She was starving. She'd skipped lunch because she felt bad about leaving early. The other ladies opted for pecan-crusted snapper, which looked just as delicious and was much lighter, but Sam didn't care. Who was she saving her figure for anyway? And when dessert came, a decadent pecan pie completely encased in chocolate, she savored it without guilt.

She sat quietly through most of the meal and listened to the conversations around the table, glad no one really cared about her predicament. Sam had recently reconnected with Emily when they became members of the bridal party after Claire's engagement, and as Emily excitedly explained her plans to open a bath products boutique with Claire, Sam felt a pang of envy. She wished she had that kind of freedom.

The year before, Emily had started an online craft business, selling soap and other bath items on Etsy. After a while, the business grew to the point where she had enlisted Claire's help, and since so many of their friends loved the products they made, Emily and Claire decided to open a storefront.

During the bachelorette party, Emily had asked if Sam could help with the orders that were constantly streaming in from Etsy while Claire was away on her honeymoon. Sam had agreed. It sounded like fun, making soaps and packaging them in pretty papers, selling brief moments of respite to relieve the stress of life. Sam could use that right now.

After dinner, the staff cleared plates and offered coffee, and Sam stole a second to check her phone, peeking at the email message from her boss.

He had forwarded a company-wide memo, which had gone out earlier in the day, announcing the launch of an ad campaign highlighting how their doctors were board certified. The problem was Sam wasn't board certified. And since she had left residency before completing her training, she was not eligible to sit for any board exams.

Above the announcement of the new ad campaign, Dr. Taylor's email simply read "You may have seen this. Let's discuss during our meeting next week."

Sam's mind churned, trying to figure out what it meant. She couldn't shake the sinking feeling in her gut. She had left residency for many reasons, but she hadn't had a plan. After years of schooling and training, Sam was adrift. And now she was afraid she might lose her job.

Then Brad's boisterous voice drew Sam's attention across the table to his conversation with Todd, Emily's husband. "Then Mr. Volker told me, 'If you can do that, I'll come to you the next time I need to move property!'" He smacked his hand on the table, his broad shoulders bouncing as he laughed.

Todd tipped his wineglass toward Brad. "That was strong, Brad. I'm glad I brought you on board."

Brad smirked, his blue eyes sparkling with a hint of mischievousness. "I'm glad we're on the same team again. You set up the play, and I closed it, just like in that championship game." Brad's voice softened. "I wish things were always that easy."

As he talked, Brad's eyes met Sam's for a moment.

Though she felt uncomfortable around him the few times she'd crossed paths with him since they'd been in high school, she suddenly felt her unease fade. Maybe it was because of the wine, or maybe it was because she was beginning to believe he had changed. He wasn't drinking wine or any other kind of alcohol. Instead, he had a glass of iced tea.

"Well, stick with me," Todd said, "and we'll keep making deals. Austin's booming right now, and I've got more prospects in the pipeline."

"Thanks for giving me the chance. I needed it."

"You're welcome. I'm glad to help an old friend."

Brad slapped Todd on the back. "And this deal couldn't have come at a better time, right?"

Todd's face flashed with annoyance, then he cocked his head and said, "Yeah, so how do you feel about your little sister getting married?"

"Claire's always talking about Mike, gushing about how wonderful he is, so I guess he's okay." Brad threw his arm around Claire's shoulders and squeezed.

Claire squirmed out of his clutch. "Come on, Brad. I'm not a kid anymore." She turned to Mike and put her hand in his. "Mike is more than okay. He's perfect."

Mike locked eyes with Claire as if they were alone. "So are you."

Brad and Emily, who sat closest to the happy couple, both rolled their eyes and turned to give them a modicum of privacy.

Emily tugged on the blonde strands framing her face and leaned toward Sam. "Did I tell you? Todd has promised me a trip to the Caribbean."

Sam patted Emily's forearm. "That's terrific! Tell me about it."

"We'll fly into Puerto Rico, and we'll spend a few days there before we head over to St. Thomas."

"So when do you leave?"

"Well, we haven't decided." Emily lowered her voice. "Even though Brad is boasting about the Volker deal, it hasn't closed yet. There's always a possibility it'll fall through."

"Then you might not go on your trip?"

"We'll see." Emily shrugged. "Right now, things look good. But you never know. Plus, Claire and I need to get the store up and running first." Then she glanced over at Mike, who still had his head tipped toward Claire in intimate conversation. "Hey, did you know that Michelle Hayes is Mike's cousin?"

"No, I didn't. What a small world." Sam vaguely remembered Michelle from high school. She might have had an art class with her.

Brad looked over from his conversation with Todd. "Michelle is Mike's cousin? I didn't know that."

This drew Mike's attention and he nodded.

"I haven't seen her in forever," Brad said. "How's she doing?"

"She's …" Mike paused, then smiled. "She's doing fine now. She moved out to California last year."

Brad smiled in return. "That's great, man." He turned back to Todd. "Hey, that reminds me of that time we all went out to Inks Lake. You remember that weekend?"

As Todd laughed and started telling a story how he finally got the better of Brad with a prank, Emily shook her head and smiled. "He tells that story all the time." Then she leaned toward Sam, lowering her voice. "Hey, Sam, how are you, you know … with everything?"

Here it comes, Sam thought. She squeezed her eyes

closed for a moment and took a deep breath, then said, "I'm doing okay."

Emily raised an eyebrow. "Are you sure? I mean, it's fine if you are uncomfortable right now. Since you were supposed to be walking down the aisle too. It must bring up bad feelings." She put her hand on Sam's. "You can always talk to me if you need to."

Sam smiled and squeezed Emily's hand. "I'm fine, really. Sure, I'm still trying to figure it all out. But I'm fine."

"Okay," Emily said, "I won't bug you about it anymore this weekend. I can't promise Claire won't say anything, but she'll be busy with everything tomorrow, so you don't need to worry."

Sam smiled, surprised that Emily backed off so quickly. Emily had been much pushier in the past. Perhaps that's why Sam felt closer to Claire than Emily, but now Emily seemed to be more understanding.

"I'll be okay," Sam said. "Let's focus on Claire's happiness this weekend." She looked over at the glowing couple. "That's what is important right now."

AFTER DINNER, Claire and Emily rode back to the bed-and-breakfast with Sam. By then, the storm had abated, leaving the streets glistening in the headlights. As Sam pulled into the parking lot, Claire said, "There's James!"

Once Sam stopped the car, Claire hopped out and ran over to James who was laden with photography gear. Because his aunt owned the bed-and-breakfast, James got a steady stream of referrals for weddings. And when he wasn't shooting weddings, he would do freelance work for the local newspapers, including coverage of the countless bands performing around town.

As Sam and Emily approached, James and Claire were discussing last-minute details for her wedding. "After the ceremony and everyone has moved to the reception hall, I need you to go back to the gazebo, so we can do the bridal party pics," James said.

Claire nodded. "And then during the reception, can you make sure you get a picture of each table?"

Headlights washed over them as James said, "Of course."

Emily swiveled her head to look at the car. "Is that Mike or Brad?" She squinted. "I can't tell."

The rumble of the engine stopped, and the lights switched off, allowing them to see the driver. "Oh good, it's not Mike," Emily said.

When Brad got out of his car, James looked toward the reception hall and said, "Look, I gotta go. I just came over to grab an extra battery pack before the cake cutting. I'll see you tomorrow." He started walking away.

"Hey, James," Brad called out.

James glanced over his shoulder, then turned to continue walking. Brad caught up to him. "Hey, James, I wanted to let you know I'm really sorry for how I treated you."

"Sure, whatever, man." James kept walking away.

Brad put his hand on James's shoulder to stop him. James shook him off.

Brad showed his palms. "No, seriously. My little sis is getting married, and you are one of her best friends. We've avoided each other until now. But for Claire's sake, let's be civil." Brad extended his hand. "I'm truly sorry for how I treated you. I've been a selfish prick, but I'm working on it."

James narrowed his eyes, skeptical.

Brad continued, "Look, if nothing else, let's put on a

good front to make Claire's big day be the best it can be." He smiled, showing his perfect teeth.

"Why don't you just ignore me like you usually do?" James looked at the ground.

"I'm a changed man," Brad said. "I'm doing my twelve steps, and I want to make amends."

James looked up and glared at him. "The problem is when you act on your need to show dominance."

In high school, everyone had thought James had a huge crush on Claire. Sam and Emily were there when James had asked Claire to the spring formal their sophomore year, but he hadn't realized Brad was standing behind him in the hallway.

"So you finally worked up the nerve to ask her out, dumbass?" Brad had chortled, as his gang of jocks joined in. "Why would Claire ever go out with you?"

Darts had shot from Claire's eyes. "Shut up, Brad!" She'd turned to James, who was trying to slink away. "Of course I'll go with you."

Even though Claire, James, and the rest of the group had had a good time at the dance, mostly making fun of the couples who were too serious, James had spent less and less time with Claire until recently, when Claire had moved back to Austin and reconnected with him.

"I'm sorry for all those times I picked on you," Brad said.

"So you say."

"C'mon. Let's be civil, for Claire's sake."

James held up his camera. "Hey, I'm a professional, so you don't have to worry about me. You won't even notice me."

Brad lowered his voice. "I'm sorry. Really." He extended his hand again.

Laughter drifted over from the reception hall,

drawing James's attention. Then he looked down at Brad's hand then pumped it once. "Fine. For Claire." He stalked off.

Brad turned around and saw Claire watching. "Hey, Claire."

"Thanks for apologizing to James."

Brad shrugged, "All I can do is try, right?" Brad swung his arm up and playfully tapped Claire's shoulder with his fist. "But I'm serious. I've turned a new leaf, and I'm on step nine, so I'm doing what I'm supposed to do: make amends."

Everyone stood silently for a moment. Did he really mean it? Or was this just for show?

Then Brad said, "Well, I'm so glad you found Mike. He's a great guy, and tomorrow will be your dream come true." He beamed as he gave her a bear hug, lifting her off the ground, swinging her like a doll. "I can't believe my little sister is getting married!"

"Thanks, Brad. I am a bit nervous, though," Claire said, as she escaped his grasp and smoothed out her clothes.

Sam took Claire's hand. "It's okay to be nervous, but you glow when you're around Mike. It's obvious how you make each other feel." Sam thought she knew what that felt like once, but now she wasn't so sure. Claire and Mike really did seem to adore each other.

"Sam's right," Emily said.

Sam smiled. "Just think of how Emily and Todd are together."

Claire turned to Emily. "So how is married life? Any advice?"

Brad backed away as he held up his hands. "Okay, ladies, I'm going to let you continue your conversation without me."

"Sure, Brad. Remember, we're having breakfast with Mom and Dad in the morning."

"No problem, sis. I gotta grab something, then I'm going to catch Chris's band. They're playing at Maggie Mae's. See you at breakfast."

After he went inside, Emily said, "Brad's still hanging out with Chris?"

Claire wrinkled her nose. "I don't think he's seen Chris in quite some time. I'm sure he'll be fine. Brad has changed a lot lately." She squeezed Emily's hand. "Thanks again for convincing Todd to give him a chance. I'm sure he won't do anything to jeopardize that."

"You may be right, but … Brad has his moments."

The night was cooling off now that the sun had set, and they heard cheers and clapping from the wedding reception. Another set of headlights shined on them, this time it was Mike's car.

Emily tugged at Claire's arm. "We need to go somewhere else. Mike can't see you the day of the wedding." She looked at her watch. "It's only a few more hours!"

"It's so nice tonight. Why don't we go hang out on the balcony in my room," Claire said. "But let me see Mike just one more time."

Sam thought the whole superstition was old-fashioned, just a way to cope if things went wrong. As Claire ran over to Mike, she noticed Mike and Brad had the same car model. "Isn't it funny that the main men in Claire's life have Mustangs?"

"Figures," Emily said. "Boys like muscle cars."

Sam chuckled. "Yeah, all men are the same, aren't they?"

After Claire and Mike shared one last hug and kiss, and he disappeared into the building, Sam said, "I'm pretty beat. I'm going to turn in for the night."

"C'mon, Sam. Let's catch up."

That's what Sam was afraid of. What did she have to say that they could catch up on? She hadn't done much outside of work for months. What Claire would really want to know is if Sam had gotten over her breakup with Jeff yet.

"No, that's okay. It's been a long week."

Claire grabbed her hands. "Please, Sam? This is my last night as a single woman."

Sam didn't answer. She was exhausted and didn't think she could deal with the questions Claire would inevitably ask.

"Please? For me?"

She took a deep breath. If her broken engagement came up, she would just say it's off limits, exactly because she didn't want to lower everyone's mood. "Okay," she said, "let's go."

They settled on Claire's balcony overlooking the Hill Country. Stars dotted the deep indigo sky as crickets chirped, and an owl hooted in the distance. Claire opened a bottle of wine, and they all sipped as the summer breeze, cooled from the passing storm, fluttered through the live oaks around them.

Claire picked up where she left off with Emily. "Do you have any advice, since you're the one with marriage experience? How has this year been?"

"I won't lie. Not every day is a cakewalk. We have good days and bad days, like we did before we got married. But our lives are intertwined now, and I have to consider Todd when I make decisions about anything." Emily tilted her head. "Sure, I did that before we were married, but now it's not an option, because I've made him the most important part of my life."

Claire stared out into the night, appearing to contemplate things. "Mike is the most important thing to me." She turned to Sam after a moment. "And how are you doing? I hope all this wedding stuff isn't stirring up bad memories."

Here it comes again, Sam thought. Emily was right—Claire couldn't resist asking. She leaned back and crossed her arms. "Don't worry about me, Claire. This weekend is all about you. I don't want to be a downer."

"You won't bring me down. We're your friends and we want to help." Claire glanced at Emily. "What really happened between you and Jeff? I'm about to get married, but you called off your engagement. That's got to be uncomfortable." Claire shifted in her chair to lean closer to Sam. "Be honest. Emily and I are here for you."

"Yes, Sam. We want to do whatever we can for you." A warm smile blossomed on Emily's face. So much for not bugging Sam again. "Sure, this is Claire's big weekend. But we love you too. We know this must be hard for you."

Sam gazed at her lap. "It's difficult to explain." She grimaced, her jaw tightening. Why couldn't they just drop it? Why did they have to keep pushing? She would need to deal with these painful things at some point. But not right now.

They wouldn't back off unless she gave them something. She looked at each of them, their faces laced with concern. They really wanted to help her.

The anger that had started percolating up inside because they wouldn't stop pestering her suddenly subsided. She hadn't been taking care of herself. Med school and residency had beaten out any self-compassion she had. Her life was all about service to others—her patients. They came first, no matter what.

And then her mother's illness had knocked Sam off-kilter. Her mom was her emotional anchor, giving her the motivation to keep going in residency. Her mom had said, "You don't have much control now, but you will later."

Now her mother was gone, and everything was unraveling.

"You've been through so much recently," Claire said.

She was right. It wasn't just her breakup with Jeff that Sam needed to deal with. Had she really mourned her mother's death as she needed to?

"Seriously," Emily said. "We're here to support you."

Sam picked up her wine glass and rolled the stem between her fingers. Now was not the time. But her friends needed something, needed to feel they were helping. So she said, "Jeff and I just grew apart. Being in residency didn't help and then Mom ..." Tears welled in her eyes as she peered up at Claire. She shook her head. "But really, this weekend is about you. So let's not dwell on my issues. It's a time for you and Mike to celebrate your love."

Claire hugged Sam. "You always put everyone else before yourself." Then she put her hands on Sam's shoulders, so she could look directly at Sam. "Thanks for not wanting to dampen our spirits, but we're strong, and we want to help you. We're not done here. You need to talk about this."

Sam closed her eyes. "I know."

Emily squeezed Sam's hand. "We will discuss this more. We can have a girls-only weekend. But we'll do it when you're ready."

"Thanks, guys." Sam wiped away the tears.

3

The next morning, Sam awoke to knocking on her door. She looked at her phone. Almost nine o'clock! Wow! She hadn't planned on sleeping so long. Maybe her body needed it.

Sam stumbled to the door, wiping away the sleep from her eyes. She peeked through the peephole. Seeing it was James's aunt, she opened the door.

"Hi, Carol. What's going on?"

"Oh, Sam, it's awful!" Carol was near tears. "Something's wrong with Brad!"

"What?" Fully awake now, Sam turned to find her shoes. "What happened?"

"He was supposed to have breakfast with Claire and their parents this morning. But when he didn't show up or answer his phone, they asked me to check on him." Carol sobbed. "He wasn't answering, so I unlocked the door, and he looked like he was in a deep sleep. But when I touched him to wake him, he was cold."

"Oh!" Sam couldn't believe it. She took a deep breath,

then put herself in physician mode. "Is he breathing? Did you check for a pulse?"

Carol shook her head rapidly. "Can you help?"

Sam slipped her tennis shoes on her bare feet, then followed Carol out the door. "Have you called 911?"

"Yes, they're on the way. But you know what to do, right?"

"Sure, but the paramedics will have the equipment and meds. I can at least assess him and start CPR."

They navigated around the common room furniture to the stairs. Claire's frantic voice spilled over the railing. "Brad, wake up! WAKE UP!"

Sam ran up the stairs and to Brad's room. James stood outside the door, looking shocked. Inside, Claire hovered over Brad's bed, shaking him and yelling, tears streaming down her face. Standing next to the bed were their parents. Claire's dad had his arm around her mom, her face buried in her hands as she sobbed.

Sam put her hand on Claire's shoulder. "Let me look at him, okay?" Sam placed her fingers under the angle of Brad's jaw, on his carotid artery. She could not find a pulse. And Carol was right. His skin was clammy.

But just because she could not feel a pulse did not mean he didn't have one. If she had the right equipment, she could see if there was still a signal, a heartbeat. She called to Carol, who stood outside the doorway, "Do you have an AED?"

Carol frowned. "What's that?"

"It's an automatic electronic defibrillator. They usually have them at airports, sports arenas …"

"No, I'm sorry." Carol looked down. "I don't have one."

"That's okay." Focus on the ABCs—Airway, Breathing,

Circulation. Sam quickly evaluated Brad, checking his airway, putting her ear on his chest. No movement. No sounds. Nothing. She opened his eyelids, and her heart sank. Brad's pupils were dilated. She looked for a penlight, flashlight, anything she could use to check for reactivity. She wasn't optimistic, but maybe there was another explanation.

As her gaze scanned the room, everyone's faces gave her hopeful looks. She straightened up, knowing one thing she could do. Start CPR until the paramedics got there. But the bed was too soft. She needed Brad on the floor. She looked at Claire's dad. "Mr. Johnson, can you help me move—"

Then voices from outside the room heralded the arrival of the paramedics.

A tall, dark-haired man wearing a black button-down shirt with the emblem of the Juniper Shoals Fire Department entered the room, carrying a case in one hand, a defibrillator in the other. "Hi, everyone. Can you tell me what's going on?" he said as he knelt beside Brad.

"This is Brad Johnson," Sam began. "He's thirty-two years old and in good health." She glanced at Brad's parents to confirm.

They looked at each other for a split second before Mr. Johnson said, "He had used drugs in the past—"

"But he's been clean for almost two years now," Claire interrupted through sobs.

The paramedic looked at Mr. Johnson and asked, "What drugs did he use?"

"Oxycodone, mainly."

The paramedic nodded, issuing orders to his two colleagues, one blond, one with curly brown hair. "Get the Narcan ready and then start bag masking," he said to the blond one. "Help me put the pads on," he said to the other paramedic.

Everyone moved out of the way to give them room.

The lead paramedic put his fingers on Brad's neck, then used his pocket light to check Brad's pupils. "No pulse. Pupils are dilated, nonreactive." He looked at the curly-haired paramedic. "Let's see if there's anything on the EKG." He opened a package from the case he brought, revealing two large foam pads with wires attached. The two paramedics rolled Brad on his side. The curly-haired paramedic pulled Brad's shirt up.

"Wait," the lead paramedic said. "There's lividity."

"What?" Mrs. Johnson said, eyes wide. "What does that mean?"

"I've heard that on TV before. Does that mean—" Claire sobbed—"does that mean he's ... dead?"

Sam shuddered. She hadn't thought to check for lividity, the pooling of blood in the gravity-dependent parts of the body once the heart stopped pumping. But she rarely dealt with dead patients.

Of course she had seen plenty of death in med school and residency, and it was always a sad experience. But this was someone she had known since she was a kid. He was almost family to her, despite ...

The paramedic stood and approached Brad's parents. "I'm sorry, but he's no longer with us."

Mrs. Johnson burst into tears, burying her head into her husband's shoulder. He wrapped his arms around her as tears streamed down his own face.

AFTER THE MEDICAL examiner's office took Brad's body away, Sam sat with the others in the breakfast room. Claire had a blank look on her face as Mike rubbed her back, occasionally offering a tissue to blot her tears, his face just as shocked-looking as hers.

Then Carol loaned her office to Sam and Emily so they could call the wedding vendors, letting them know the wedding was canceled. They were all terribly sympathetic, offering to work out arrangements to credit the couple for a future event. But those details could be worked out later.

Finally, Sam packed up her bags to head home. As she loaded her car, Claire came to meet her. Sam hugged her again for what seemed like the hundredth time that day.

Claire used the back of her hand to wipe away lingering tears. "I still can't believe he's gone."

Sam closed the trunk of her car and leaned against it.

"I mean, he's so young. And healthy. Even after high school, he continued his workout routines," Claire said.

Sam turned to look at Claire. "You know, Brad said he was meeting Chris last night. Weren't you surprised?"

"As far as I know, Brad has avoided Chris. So it was a little confusing. Brad had too much to lose." Claire crossed her arms and hugged herself. "He's strong, so I know he would have been fine."

Although Brad was the consummate athlete, he had suffered a shoulder injury that had healed but left him with an addiction to opiates. Eventually, he started hanging out with Chris Baker, who somehow had connections to get whatever substance anyone could want.

Even though Brad completed a rehab program last year, Sam wasn't sure Brad could resist any temptation Chris might offer. When she was in med school, Sam learned addiction is a lifelong illness of the brain. The pathophysiology remains after recovery, and even so-called clean addicts are forever fighting temptation driven by biology.

If Sam bought into Claire's rosy view of Brad, she would believe he had turned a corner recently. But she knew relapse was likely based on statistics alone. "I guess we'll see what the autopsy and toxicology reports say," Sam said.

"That's what I wanted to ask you. Could you look into this? I think something else was going on. That someone wanted him dead."

Sam's eyes widened. "Why do you say that?"

"Well, I overheard Brad on the phone when we had dinner at our parents' last month. He was saying, 'I will not let you scare me!'"

Sam relaxed. She loved Claire, but she overanalyzed situations sometimes.

One time, Claire had thought Sam was mad at her because Sam hadn't returned her call by the next day. Sam couldn't really remember why Claire thought Sam was upset, but she remembered it was during her finals one year in med school, so she wasn't calling anyone back until her exams were done. And Sam remembered other instances when Claire made something out of nothing.

Claire saw Sam's expression. "You don't believe me, do you?"

Sam took a deep breath and smiled. "Of course I believe you." But did she really? Claire was probably in denial, but if Sam pushed back, Claire would just dig in. She put her hand on Claire's arm. "Let's see what the medical examiner says."

"They already think Brad died of a drug overdose. They found an unlabeled prescription bottle in his bag."

Sam dropped her shoulders. "Oh, Claire."

Claire looked at her, pleading. "He's been clean for almost two years. He turned his life around." She paused. "I know something else is going on."

"You're right, Brad made some big changes. He had a different attitude." A melancholy smile crept onto Sam's face. "He even started acknowledging me as Dr. Jenkins. He didn't act like I was just another one of his little sister's anonymous friends like he used to." But Sam wasn't sure if he'd just been sarcastic.

"Yeah, I know. He was a real jerk growing up. But when his girlfriend died of an overdose, it was a big wake-up call for him. He wanted to right the wrongs of his past." Claire took Sam's hand in hers and looked directly at Sam. "I know you're skeptical, and you think Brad died of an overdose. But promise me something? If the medical examiner's report comes back and shows he didn't over-dose, will you help me figure out what happened?"

Sam blinked. "How am I supposed to do that?"

"You're a doctor. You'd be able to understand what the report says."

"I suppose. But I'm not trained in forensic pathology, and you're assuming the tox report won't show anything." Sam thought for a moment. "What about Mike? He knows people at the hospital through work, right? At least he could reach out to a pathologist. That would be a better person to look at the autopsy report than me."

Claire traced her finger along the edge of the car trunk. "Mike says I'm too soft on Brad—that I make too many excuses for him."

Sam agreed with that assessment but didn't say so.

Claire stared at the pavement. "You're probably right. Brad did struggle with addiction." She looked up at Sam, taking her hand. "But if it doesn't look like he overdosed, will you help me figure out what happened?" Claire squeezed Sam's hand. "Please?"

Sam bit her lip as she contemplated this. If the medical

examiner's report showed Brad did overdose, then that would be it. And if nothing else, Sam could help Claire through her grief. Finally, Sam said, "Yes, of course I'll help you."

4

S am continued to think about her conversation with Claire, even as she tried to get work done after she made a cup of coffee and settled down at her desk in her small apartment the following morning. Patient notes, which she hadn't finished because she'd been busy taking care of Mr. Campbell before she'd left for the rehearsal, sat waiting for her in the electronic medical record system. Focusing on them, she pushed the events of the past day out of her mind. Once she completed the last note, she stood and stretched. She needed to talk to someone.

James. He lived one building over, and when she had moved back to Austin, she reconnected with him. In some ways, she was now closer to James than she was to Claire. He always put things in perspective.

Sam knocked on his door, and James answered after a few seconds. "What's up?"

"I'm not bothering you, am I?"

"Nah, I've always got time for you."

"I didn't know if Kyle was over." Kyle was James's

boyfriend. Not long after the incident with Brad where James had asked Claire out, James confided in the girls that he was more attracted to boys, but he'd felt pressure to conform to his religious parents' expectations. Over the years, he had become more estranged from his parents, but his Aunt Carol, who owned the bed-and-breakfast, accepted and supported him fully.

"He went to Houston for the weekend, since I had these weddings to shoot."

It was a splendid morning, so they grabbed a couple of cups of coffee and sat on his balcony overlooking the greenbelt behind their apartment complex.

"How are you taking this?" James asked.

"Okay, I guess. How about you?"

"I'm shocked." He rubbed his neck. "I can't believe Brad is gone. Sure, he was a complete ass, but I've known him pretty much all my life."

"Me too." Sam paused a moment. "I'm trying to remember when I first met him. It was right after I moved here in junior high. Claire had invited me to a slumber party at her house, and Brad kept trying to prank us." She gazed out over the greenbelt. "We were watching *Nightmare on Elm Street*, and he would wait until a quiet part of the movie. Then he'd jump out in front of the TV, wearing a hockey mask, like the one Jason wore in those Halloween movies."

James rolled his eyes. "He always knew how to give everyone a hard time."

"Have you talked to Claire?"

"A little. I feel so bad for her. Yesterday was supposed to be her happiest day, and now it's her saddest."

They sat in silence for a moment and listened as chatter from hikers on the trail below drifted upward, mingling with calls from songbirds. "So what do you think happened to Brad?" James asked.

"Honestly, I think he overdosed."

James cocked his head. "It makes sense."

"Claire and her parents did an intervention with him the year before last, and he finally agreed to go into a treatment program. Claire is adamant he was clean."

"So you think he fell off the bandwagon?"

"Well, after the rehearsal dinner, he left to see Chris's band," she said.

"And Chris is the one who kept Brad supplied."

"Claire swears Brad wouldn't do that, though. She's been super-hopeful about Brad this year. Frankly, he was different in the little interaction I had with him last night, more respectful."

James frowned. "I think it was all for show, for Claire's sake."

Sam sipped her coffee, then said, "Perhaps, but he started working for Todd."

"Jocks stick together."

"During the rehearsal dinner, I overheard Brad talking about how he just closed a big deal. Maybe he celebrated too much." Sam leaned forward. "But Claire thinks someone wanted to hurt him."

James looked skeptical. "Really? Who?"

"She doesn't know exactly. She overheard a conversation that made her suspicious." Sam sighed.

"Well frankly, there were quite a few times I wanted to kill him."

James said this with such force that Sam glanced at him. His jaw was set, anger burning in his eyes. And at that moment, she thought he really could have killed Brad.

"But you didn't, did you?" Sam said with some trepidation.

The anger on James's face melted into something else, something more akin to sadness, to lost innocence.

"No. Of course not. But if I wanted to kill him, then I'm sure there are others." He sat back, looked up at the ceiling, and blew out a long breath. "Honestly, having Brad out of Claire's life is a good thing. I know it's not good form to speak ill of the dead, but he took advantage of her love."

Sam pinched her lips. She couldn't argue with that. After a moment, she said, "Claire's in denial right now, which is perfectly natural. But she asked me to help her figure out what happened to Brad."

"Really? You're not an investigator."

"I know. She just wants me to look over the autopsy report when it's available. I'm sure the toxicology tests will be positive for some substance or other."

"So then, there's nothing to it, right?"

5

S am returned to work the next day. If the weekend had gone according to plan, this wouldn't have been extraordinary, but under the circumstances, Sam found work was a way to focus on something else besides Brad's death and Claire's ruined wedding.

Frustration soon replaced her sense of shock. After seeing several of her typical cases, mainly patients with back injuries from strained muscles, Sam sat at her computer typing up her notes and reviewing imaging studies.

She saw in the EHR that Mr. Campbell's X-ray was negative, and that he had already seen Jerry for his follow-up this morning. She didn't see anything for Mrs. Rodriguez, one of her other patients. Sam had ordered an MRI the week before, and she thought it wouldn't be a problem to get the MRI approved, but maybe there was a hold up for some reason. She would need to look into it.

Then Cynthia's voice interrupted her focus. "Dr. Jenkins, there's a call for you on line three."

"Thanks, Cynthia." Sam picked up the phone and

introduced herself. It was an insurance adjuster who was calling to deny the cervical MRI for Mrs. Rodriguez. Speak of the devil.

Many of Sam's patients had musculoskeletal injuries, and physical therapy was the best treatment for them. The clinic had a physical therapy center, so patients would go a few times a week, and Sam would see them occasionally to monitor their progress. But sometimes patients didn't improve, so she would order studies to see if the injury was worse than a pulled muscle, like a herniated disc.

This was the situation for Mrs. Rodriguez's case—the focus of the adjuster's denial. As Sam listened to the adjuster ramble over the phone, going on about all the reasons she was denying the MRI Sam had ordered, Sam could feel her blood pressure rise.

"Okay. I think I understand where you are coming from." Sam sighed. "The problem is Mrs. Rodriguez was complaining of shoulder pain immediately after her injury."

Sam had pulled up Mrs. Rodriguez's medical record on the computer and scrolled through it. "So the initial treating provider gave her a diagnosis of 'shoulder pain'. But Mrs. Rodriguez still has weakness in her right arm. Based on her mechanism of injury, it's possible she hurt her neck along with her shoulder."

Sam reviewed the original note and found the section she was looking for. "Let's see. It says here Mrs. Rodriguez was reaching overhead to take a box of paper towels off a shelf when another box fell on her. Her right shoulder was hurting, so that was the focus of the initial exam. And unfortunately, the initial treating provider didn't add a neck injury to the diagnosis."

Jerry had seen Mrs. Rodriguez she she first came in, but they had both seen her during her treatment. Sam was the one who saw her last and ordered the MRI. She didn't fault Jerry, and she probably would have approached the case the same way. In fact, he had tons more experience than she did, and she definitely had learned a lot from him.

Sam leaned back in her chair. "Please try to understand. Immediately after an injury, we can't always tell what the exact injury is from the exam alone. Sometimes injuries to the nerves in the neck cause shoulder pain. Because most of her pain was over her shoulder blade, I'm thinking she's pinched her C6 nerve."

"I'm sorry, but I'm not a doctor," the adjuster said. "I just have to follow the rules spelled out here in our policy."

The heat rose in Sam's neck and face. Why are non-medical people allowed to tell doctors how to practice medicine?

The adjuster droned on, "It says I cannot approve the MRI because there is no documentation of an injury to the neck. But I can have Dr. Harper call you so that you can explain the case to him."

Sam closed her eyes and let out a deep breath. "Okay, please have him call me as soon as possible. Every day that we don't get to the bottom of Mrs. Rodriguez's problem, we're wasting time. I want to help her get better. She wants to get back to work because she's saving for her daughter's college tuition."

Sam hung up the phone and ran her hands through her hair. They don't care, she thought. These insurance companies just keep stalling until they wear us out.

As she looked at the board to figure out her next patient, her cell phone buzzed. Normally she didn't answer her phone while she was seeing patients, but it was Claire.

"Sam! When I was talking to the medical examiner's office today to make arrangements with the funeral home,

I found out they finished the preliminary report for Brad. I don't know what it means. Can you help me figure it out?"

"Sure, but I'm a bit busy right now."

"All right. Can you come over after work?"

Sam glanced at the board, the schedule on the computer, and then her watch. It was a little after 3:00 p.m. There was a new injury, plus a half dozen more patients, assuming no one else walked in. "Yeah, I can do that."

"Thanks, Sam."

After she hung up with Claire, she checked her email. No new messages from her boss, so she supposed no news was good news. She would just have to wait until her meeting with him later in the week to find out what he meant in his last message. Maybe she was reading too much into it.

She looked at the board. The next patient was a new injury in an exam room instead of a procedure room. Probably something minor. She checked the chief complaint on her computer, then went to the room.

Ed Mason was a man in his mid-forties, who looked like an office worker instead of the manual laborers she usually had as patients. He was sitting in the chair next to the examination table, tapping away on his phone.

"Good afternoon, Mr. Mason. I'm Dr. Jenkins." Sam pulled over a rolling stool. "Why don't you tell me what's going on."

Mr. Mason held up a finger, then continued tapping away on his phone.

Sam held her composure—she sat only a couple of feet in front of him, wanting to make sure their relationship got off to the right start, even if he was being rude.

Mr. Mason took a few more moments to finish what he was doing on his phone before he looked up. The smell of cigarettes emanated from him. He squinted at her name embroidered on her white coat, then said, "Well, Samantha, I scratched my leg, and now it's infected."

Sam clinched her jaw, then relaxed. Let it pass. These situations came up every once in a while, where patients— usually men—tried to undermine her authority by calling her by her first name. Correcting people with this mindset usually did no good, resulting in an escalation, giving them the fight they wanted. Don't give him that satisfaction. She didn't have to like him to take care of him. "Sorry to hear that, sir. How did it happen?"

Mr. Mason explained he had been on a business trip a couple of days before, when he scraped his right calf on the runner board of the SUV he had rented. He pulled up his pant leg, exposing the injury.

"Damn piece of metal on the edge was rough," Mr. Mason said as Sam gloved up to inspect his leg.

He had a small abrasion surrounded by an area of redness about the size of a drink coaster, the skin was warm and slightly thickened. "Is this tender?" she asked as she gently pressed on it.

"Yeah, it hurts when you do that."

Sam stepped back, took off her gloves, and tossed them in the trash. "You're right. It does look like you have a skin infection, or what we call cellulitis. Do you mind if I draw on your skin?"

Mr. Mason furrowed his eyebrows. "Sure … but why?"

"So we can see if the antibiotics we start you on are working." She pulled a Sharpie from her coat pocket. "This is the easiest way. If the redness recedes, we're good. If the redness expands outside the line I draw, we know we need to reconsider things."

Sam drew a line with the marker at the edge of the redness. She checked his other leg for comparison. The injured calf was slightly bigger, so she got a disposable paper tape measure out of the cabinet drawer. She measured both calves and compared the circumferences. About two centimeters difference.

"Have you ever had a DVT? A blood clot in your legs?" Sam asked.

"No. Is this a clot?"

"Possibly. I can't really tell just from looking at it, and the infection alone may cause swelling too."

"What should I do?"

"To be safe, we should get an ultrasound."

He narrowed his eyes. "Are you sure I need to?"

"I'd hate for us to miss it. We worry about DVTs because they can break off, travel up from the leg, through the abdomen to the chest, then go through the heart to lodge in the lungs."

Mr. Mason was silent for a moment, then said, "So that sounds like it could be bad." He shrugged. "But I feel fine right now."

"I understand. However, if you do have a DVT, as long as it stays in your leg and doesn't cause your leg to swell up too much, you would feel fine. And even if it's small and it travels to the lungs—in which case we would then call it a pulmonary embolism—you might not notice anything. But if it's bigger, you might feel short of breath or tired because you aren't getting enough oxygen in your blood, since the clot would be blocking the blood from traveling through some parts of your lung. But if it's really big, it can completely stop the flow of blood through your lungs. And you could die."

"Are you trying to scare me?" Mr. Mason flared his nostrils. "You said 'if.' So tell me, Samantha, what's the probability that I even have this clot?"

Sam sat back. "I can't give you the exact probability. I

would have to look up what's reported in the literature. But I know it's greater than zero." She sighed. "I admit, it's likely pretty low, but the consequences of not catching a DVT could be devastating."

He squinted. "Devastating for you."

She frowned. How could she get through to him? "No, for you, sir. You could die."

He crossed his arms. "So a small probability I could have a clot, and if I do, a small probability it could kill me. Sounds to me like the risk I take driving in traffic every day. I think I'll take my chances, Samantha." He looked at his watch. "I have meetings all afternoon that I can't miss."

Sam spent a few more minutes trying to convince Mr. Mason to get an ultrasound, but in the end, he refused.

Back at her workstation, she rubbed her eyes before she unlocked her computer. The best she could do was document in his chart his refusal to have an ultrasound, even though what she really wanted to do was tell him off for his own good. But then he might complain or give her and the clinic a bad rating. That's what medicine had come to —a service business, where the customers are always right, even if being "right" could send them to their graves.

6

The board filled up after Sam saw Mr. Mason, so all the rooms had patients. She and Jerry barely stopped until the clinic closed. With the lobby doors locked, there were still two patients left to see. She sent Jerry home—against his protests—because she felt bad about leaving him on Friday, so she didn't leave until an hour later.

The setting sun highlighted wispy clouds against the indigo of dusk, thickening the shadows around Sam as she walked up to the bungalow Claire and Mike called home. As she approached the door, it opened, and Mike walked out with their Jack Russell terrier.

Mike turned and saw her. "Hey, Sam. Claire said you might be coming over. I'm just taking Kerbey for a walk. The door's open. You can go on in."

"Thanks, Mike." She paused, reaching down to scratch Kerbey behind the ears. The pup was named after a cafe that served Austin comfort food. "How's she doing?"

He sighed. "As one can expect, I suppose."

Mike had a haggard look to him. This couldn't be easy

for him, since he thought he would be on his honeymoon right now.

"And how about you? How are you doing?"

"Oh, I'm fine."

"But surely this has affected you too. You were supposed to get married, but now …"

He let out a long breath. "Oh, we'll still get married—this is just delaying things a bit. Then we'll get our lives back on course, after Claire … you know … when she's done mourning."

Kerbey started whimpering and tugging at his leash.

"Anyway, Kerbey wants his walk. I just picked him up from the kennel." Mike smiled wistfully. "He doesn't even realize I just sprung him from a week-long stay."

As he walked off, Sam rapped on the door and entered.

She found Claire curled up on the couch in the living room. Sam joined her and gave her a big hug. "How are you doing?"

Wet streaks covered Claire's cheeks, and she dabbed her eyes with a tissue. "I'm doing okay, I guess. Sometimes I think none of this is true and Brad's off on one of his crazy adventures with his buddies. But then reality sets in, and I can't stop crying."

"It's perfectly normal to have those ups and downs." Sam patted Claire's knee. "And how are your parents doing?"

"They're taking it hard. I spent most of the day with them, but I had to get out. Mom spent the day in bed. She's not eating, and Dad paces around like a caged lion." Her shoulders slumped. "Dad always told us to 'suck it up, buttercup,' Brad especially, but I think he's trying too hard to follow his own advice."

Sam squeezed Claire's hand. She really didn't know what to say. Part of her wanted to talk about what she'd learned, what she had seen in practice, about grief. But she didn't think it was appropriate. Her mother had told her once, "Sometimes you can't analyze everything, and you just need to feel."

After a moment, Claire said, "I should do more for them."

"You should take care of yourself too." Sam took a deep breath. "Everyone deals with grief in their own way. Give your parents some time, and you'll figure out how you can help them. Has the pastor from your church talked to them?"

"Yes, he visited yesterday. My parents seemed like they were doing okay while he was there. They were even talking about funeral arrangements with him. But today both of them seemed worse."

They sat in silence for a few minutes. Claire stared blankly at her lap, occasionally dabbing her eyes.

The TV was on, but muted. News headlines flashed across the screen. Then a police officer appeared behind a microphone. Sam recognized him, and her heart fluttered, even though she hadn't seen him in a decade. "That couldn't be …" she murmured.

Claire looked up at the TV. By then, the text on the screen identified the police officer as Dylan Myers. "Oh yeah, that's him. I thought you two were going to be an item sophomore year. What happened?"

Sam shrugged. "I just decided to focus on school more."

Claire squinted at Sam. "Sure."

The doorbell jolted them. Claire looked over her shoulder. "That's probably the delivery guy. I ordered some dinner."

Sam got up. "You can stay there. I'll get it."

"Thanks. There's money on the table by the door."

After Sam paid for the food, she brought it to the dinette table next to the kitchen. The smell of Chinese takeout made her stomach grumble. She had worked through lunch to catch up on her charts, but she needed to take care of Claire first.

As she approached the couch again, she noticed a folder and a legal pad covered in Claire's handwriting on the coffee table. Sam pointed to it. "Is that the information you got from the medical examiner?"

Claire leaned forward and picked up the pad. "Yes, let me see what I wrote." She flipped the pages over to the right spot. "I talked to someone at the office about arrangements for the funeral home, and when I asked if they knew how Brad died, she said something about his heart."

Sam narrowed her eyes. "You got them to tell you that?"

Claire cocked her head with the hint of a smirk. "I can be rather persuasive. But that means he didn't die of an overdose, right? Does that make any sense?"

Sam thought for a moment. "Maybe." She wanted to be careful here, especially since Claire was pretty adamant that Brad was clean and sober. Sam knew some illicit drugs, like cocaine, could make the coronary arteries spasm and cut off the blood supply to the heart, causing a heart attack. But there could be another reason. "Claire, do you know if anyone in your family has heart disease?"

"What do you mean by that?"

"Well, young people sometimes can have heart attacks from heart disease, which is a buildup of fatty deposits in the blood vessels supplying the heart. It's not really common at such a young age, but it runs in families. Do you know if anyone died at a young age unexpectedly in your family?"

"Uncle George had a heart attack a couple of years ago. But he's in his sixties. I thought only old people had heart attacks."

"Yes, most people at risk of having heart attacks are older. But some families have super-high levels of cholesterol that cause fatty deposits to build up faster, and in those families, some members die at a younger age—even in their thirties."

"Oh, I didn't know that."

"Yeah, I didn't either until I went to medical school."

Claire stared at Sam in disbelief. "But Brad is ... was very athletic. And healthy."

Except for the drug use, Sam thought. Instead she said, "I know. But shortly after I learned that even young people can have a heart attack, I remember reading about a Major League Baseball player who died of one in his hotel room. I think he was in his early thirties."

"So do you think that's what happened to Brad?"

"Possibly." Sam thought for a moment. "If I could see the medical examiner's report, it might show if he had signs of heart disease."

"I bet Dylan would know someone in the medical examiner's office. You could ask him to put you in touch with someone."

Sam's chest tightened. "No, I can't talk to Dylan. I haven't talked to him in years, and I wouldn't even know how to get in touch. Plus, there are usually other family members who have heart disease at a young age. So that's why I was asking."

"I only know of Uncle George. Everyone else in our family—on both Mom's and Dad's sides—are all pretty healthy, as far as I know. Of course, there are older people in our family, like Great Aunt Jane. She had a stroke. And my grandparents are doing okay, I think. Except Nana, she had some kind of blood cancer, but she's in ... what do you call it?"

"Remission."

"Yeah, she's in remission." Claire wrapped her arms around a pillow. "Maybe you should ask my parents. They would know more about this."

"Okay, I'll do that, if you think they're up to it."

"They would want to see you. They adore you. You're like a daughter to them."

A faint smile came across Sam's face. "Yes, they're like family to me too." Claire's parents filled a void her own had left. Sure, her mom was always proud of her. But her dad ...

Claire started weeping, and Sam sat, remaining silent as she held her hand. After a few minutes, Sam's mind drifted to work. She thought about Mr. Mason. Cellulitis or a deep vein thrombosis? Man, was he rude, but she wished she had convinced him to get an ultrasound. How could he question her judgment?

Sam squeezed Claire's hand. As much as she wanted to stay and comfort Claire, Mr. Mason's case gnawed at her. She really needed to check on him, but she felt guilty about leaving Claire alone.

The doorbell rang again. "I'll get it." Sam opened the door to find James with a vase of flowers. She exhaled. At least James could comfort her now, and Mike should be back from walking Kerbey soon.

"Hi, James. Come on in." She held the door open and gave him a hug as he stepped through.

Claire looked over the back of her couch and waved at James. He held out the flowers as he walked over to her. "I stopped by your parents' house, and they said you had already come home."

"Yeah, I had to leave. As much as I love them, they

were dragging me down." Claire took the flowers and hugged James. "Thanks so much for bringing these."

"You're welcome. A little something to cheer you up. I think they need some water, though."

"Here, Claire, I'll take care of that." Sam took the flowers from Claire and brought them into the kitchen. She turned on the sink and started filling the vase. She could hear them talking.

"Where's Mike?" James asked.

"He's walking Kerbey."

"So how are you holding up?" James sat next to Claire.

Claire grabbed a tissue and blotted her eyes. "I'm doing as best as I can. I'm more worried about my parents. They're pretty devastated."

"Yeah, your dad seemed lost when I was there. How is your mom?"

"She wouldn't come out of their bedroom."

His voice became quieter. "I'm so sorry, Claire."

Sam wiped off the excess water from the vase and set it on the dinette table, next to the takeout food. Her stomach grumbled again. Since James had arrived, she saw an opportunity to leave politely. She walked behind the couch and placed one hand on each of her friends' shoulders.

"I put the vase on the table for you." She squeezed Claire's shoulder. "I'm sorry, but I really need to get home. I have to check on a patient I saw today."

Claire leaned her head on Sam's arm. "Thanks for coming over."

Sam kissed her on the top of her head. "You're welcome. And call me if you need anything." She patted James's shoulder. "Take care of her, okay?"

James winked. "Of course."

Then Sam saw the legal pad with Claire's notes from

the medical examiner's office on the coffee table. Claire had written "HEART ATTACK?" and underlined it twice.

As Sam walked out to her car, the initial finding from the medical examiner's office bugged her. Did Brad really die of a heart attack? Now she had more questions than answers.

7

S am logged into the electronic health record system from her laptop once she got home. Now she was really worried about Mr. Mason, especially since he'd blown off her recommendations. There was an area of redness, warmth, and induration—the clinical term for swollen skin that's slightly thickened and firm. The induration was clearly a sign of an infection, but things could happen concurrently. Plus, Mr. Mason smoked, and he'd just flown back from Seattle. Being immobile during a long flight could increase blood pooling in his legs.

Sam grabbed a bowl of cereal—her typical dinner. Figures, here she was, a doctor who rarely followed the advice she doled out to her patients: to eat balanced meals with fresh vegetables. But she didn't have much else to eat in her apartment.

She did a quick literature search, looking at academic articles and studies to answer some of the questions Mr. Mason had brought up. How often do DVTs and cellulitis happen concurrently? Since she could only answer his questions with vague approximations this afternoon, she wanted to have hard numbers when she called him, so she could be prepared to answer his questions with confidence.

What really bothered Sam was the increase in diameter of his calf in his infected leg. Sure, Mr. Mason had a decent-sized area of cellulitis, but to increase the swelling an extra two centimeters in diameter? And his whole leg looked swollen too.

Maybe the lymphatics—the drainage for the lymph nodes, the infection-fighting centers—were backed up, causing the swelling. Or it could just be Mr. Mason had a DVT, blocking his large veins in his leg, just waiting to break off and shoot through his heart.

Sam typed her query into PubMed, the search engine for medical articles run by the National Institutes of Health. She found a fairly recent article from 2013 out of McMaster University's Department of Medicine in Canada. The reviewed previous articles on this topic—in what's called a meta-analysis—found the reported incidence of DVT in patients with cellulitis ranges from 0% to 15%.

Great. That doesn't help much.

She read on. The authors calculated the rate of DVT in patients where doctors were actually looking for DVTs, and that rate was just under 3%. Okay. So pretty low. The authors recommended that there wasn't a need to treat prophylactically for DVTs with blood thinners or to order studies in low-risk patients. But in patients with a high pretest probability or risk factors, DVTs should still be considered.

So Sam needed to figure out Mr. Mason's pretest probability. There was bound to be a set of criteria to figure that out. And sure enough, there was. She found an online calculator for Wells' criteria for DVTs. Just the fact that his whole leg looked swollen put him at moderate risk for a

DVT. He didn't quite meet the criteria for the change in diameter, which was that the calf swelling needed to be greater than three centimeters compared to the opposite side. Therefore, at a minimum, Mr. Mason needed some blood work done, a D-dimer to see if his body was making a lot of clots. If the test was negative, then all was good. But if it was positive …

Sam leaned forward, placing her head in her palms, rubbing her eyelids. Then she sat up, squaring her shoulders. Fine, if he's going to be pissed at her for calling, so be it. She would do whatever she could to help him, even if this turned out to be nothing. Even if he was a jerk.

She looked at the clock and called him.

The phone rang twice, and then a husky voice answered. "Hello?"

"Hi, Mr. Mason. This is Dr. Jenkins from the clinic today."

"Yes?"

"I just wanted to check on you. How is your leg doing?"

His tone softened slightly from how he'd spoken to her in the clinic. "It's a little more swollen, actually. And my wife thinks it's nutty you drew on my leg."

Sam chuckled at that, but if he thought it was more swollen, that made her more worried. "I know. Doctors do some crazy things sometimes. Did you get your prescription for the antibiotic filled?"

"I got it after work."

"That's great." Sam cleared her throat. "The reason I'm calling, though, is that I'm still concerned about the possibility of a blood clot. You have a lot of swelling in that leg, a little more than I would expect. Have you reconsidered getting an ultrasound?"

"Could I just get it tomorrow?"

"Well, if there is a clot, and it's big enough to cause the swelling in your leg to have increased in just a few hours, we don't know if it might break off and lodge in your lungs. Then you might have serious complications." Sam took a deep breath. "And if you have a clot, we can't predict the timing of these events, so it could happen tonight."

In the background, Sam could hear a woman's voice ask Mr. Mason who was on the phone. After Mason told her, Sam could hear her say, "Listen to the doctor."

"What should I do?" he asked.

"Go to the emergency room. They'll probably run a blood test to see if you are forming clots first, then they'll decide if you need an ultrasound." She said "probably" because she didn't want to presume what the doctors would do in the ER. Even though there are guidelines, everyone practices medicine differently.

Mr. Mason grunted. "I was about to go to bed. Now you want me to go in the middle of the night to the emergency room?"

Sam heard the woman say, "It's only 9:30, Ed. It's not the middle of the night. Listen to the doctor."

Sam waited for Mr. Mason to say something else. When he didn't, she said, "Please, sir. It's the best thing to do. It's an inconvenience, but I don't want anything to happen to you."

"Fine. I'll go," he said in a huff before hanging up the phone.

Sam hoped she was wrong. She knew if he went to the ER and he didn't have a clot, he'd complain about how she freaked him out and how he ended up with an enormous emergency room bill for no reason. On the other hand, she might have just saved his life.

SHE MADE a cup of tea and tried to settle down. Her mind wandered to her discussion with Claire. Sam could come up with explanations for how Brad had died of a myocardial infarction—the clinical term for a heart attack—but none settled well with her.

If Brad had heart disease, there would be other evidence. The autopsy would show plaques in his coronary arteries, and lab tests would show elevated cholesterol and triglycerides.

Claire's parents might know more about their family's history of heart disease. Before she went to medical school, Sam knew little about these things, so why would Claire?

Then there was Brad's drug problem. Some drugs, like cocaine or amphetamines, could cause heart attacks. They could cause constriction of the blood vessels feeding the heart, and other problems too.

Sam remembered a twenty-five-year-old patient named Doug who was triaged to the surgical service in the emergency department when she was in residency. He had horrific abdominal pain, but his pain didn't fit the profile of the usual cases of belly pain, like appendicitis or gallstones.

His pain was diffuse, not localized to areas of the abdomen associated with surgically treatable causes. Sam asked Doug what he was doing before his pain started. He was reluctant to answer the question, but then she saw it. His pupils were huge.

She looked at his vitals again. Elevated blood pressure and heart rate. At first she thought these elevations were due to his severe pain. And as people bustled around the busy ER, Doug glanced around nervously, so Sam thought he was just overwhelmed by the place. But then she realized *he had a massive sympathetic response,* which meant his body had maxed out his "fight or flight" system. He was acting agitated for another reason.

"Have you been doing any drugs?" Sam asked.

Doug looked away from her, mumbling. "Yeah. Maybe."

"What kinds of drugs?"

"I don't do drugs. Not normally. This is my first time."

Sam squeezed his hand. "I believe you. But I need you to tell me what you were doing. So I can help you."

Doug picked at the sheet covering him, his eyes flicking around. "I might have done some lines."

"Of cocaine?"

He nodded sheepishly.

"Thanks for being honest with me, Doug." She added a drug screen to his urine tests and teed up a beta-blocker to slow down his heart rate and relax the muscles around his arteries.

Doug had mesenteric ischemia—another fancy medical term, which meant a decreased blood flow to the intestines. It wasn't a common problem, but it usually happened in older folks who had bad vascular disease with a buildup of artery-clogging plaques in the blood vessels supplying the intestines.

In Doug's case, cocaine caused those arteries to spasm, which led to the pain in his abdomen. Some residents called this presentation "crack belly".

And the way cocaine kills is by affecting the heart, causing the coronary arteries to spasm, cutting off blood flow, leading to the symptoms of a heart attack.

So Sam had two big questions, which the medical examiner's report might answer. Did Brad have heart disease? Or did he have drugs on board?

She would just have to wait. But then her phone rang.

8

Sam didn't recognize the number, but she answered anyway because she was still thinking about Mr. Mason and thought it might have something to do with his case.

"Hi, Sam. It's Dylan."

Sam was taken aback. When she didn't reply, Dylan said, "Are you there?"

She blinked a few times. "Oh. Dylan. I wasn't expecting this."

"I heard you were back in town. And Claire called me."

Sam let out a short bark of laughter. "She did, did she?"

"I was surprised to hear about Brad. It's awful that he died on her wedding day. But she had an unusual request. Do you think she's okay?"

"Yeah, Claire seems to be handling it as well as one could, except for pushing me to find answers. She said her parents are taking it pretty hard, though."

"That's understandable. I can't imagine being a parent

and losing a child." Dylan cleared his throat. "So Claire asked if I might know someone you could talk to. I do know a few people at the ME's office."

"Honestly, I think Claire is in a bit of denial. You knew about Brad's drug problems, right?"

"Yeah, sure. He had that injury in high school, then got hooked on painkillers. How has he been doing since? I haven't really kept up."

"He was actually doing pretty well, which is why I think Claire is trying to find answers that may not be there. Brad completed a rehab program last year, and Claire said he's been drug free since. But the night before he died, he went to see Chris Baker. You remember him?"

"Sure do. It's amazing he even graduated from high school with the amount of dope he smoked."

"Personally, I think Brad may have returned to his old habits."

"That might be the case."

Sam switched her phone to her other ear. "Anyway, Claire asked me to look into what happened, to help her understand. And she found out something confusing today. When she talked to the medical examiner's office to make arrangements for the body, someone told her that there was something with his heart, that maybe he died of a heart attack."

"A heart attack? But Brad was pretty young. That doesn't make sense, does it?"

"Well, it could in a couple of different ways. But I need more information to really understand what happened."

"Ahh. So that's why she thought you should talk to someone in the ME's office." He paused, then said, "I don't know, Sam, I could get in trouble for messing around with this. It's not my case. In fact, I think the medical examiner's office is handling it right now. It's a suspicious death, but like you said, with Brad's past drug use, I think they'll focus on an overdose."

"But that's the thing. Brad's drug of choice was prescription painkillers. Those usually cause respiratory failure, not heart attacks. Of course, it could be true that Brad was using other substances, like cocaine or meth. Those could cause a heart attack." Should she tell Dylan about Claire's concern? That someone may have wanted to hurt Brad? Now was probably not the right time.

Sam sighed. "I guess Claire's calling you was a mistake. I don't want to cause any problems."

"Look, Sam, I do want to help. But they scrutinize everything we do in law enforcement. It's best to wait for the medical examiner to complete the report."

"I agree. Well, thanks for calling."

"You're welcome, Sam. It was good hearing your voice again. I guess I'll see you around."

THE NEXT AFTERNOON while Sam was suturing up a laceration, Cynthia poked her head into the procedure room.

"Dr. Jenkins, a Dr. Harper is on the line to discuss a case with you."

"Please let him know I'll call him back."

"I'll do that."

"Thanks, Cynthia." Sam turned her attention back to her patient. "How are you doing, Mr. Cross? Is your finger still numb?"

"I'm fine. I feel stupid for slicing it open."

"You shouldn't feel stupid, sir. I've had quite a few patients who've done exactly the same thing."

"Yeah, I know. But still. It's stupid. I'm under a lot of

pressure to clear out the loading dock quickly, and I just lost focus for a split second. Someone called my name while I was cutting the straps that were holding a bunch of boxes on a pallet."

"Well, at least it's a pretty superficial cut, so it will heal just fine. I'm almost done with the last stitch. You'll have a small scar, but again, it should heal nicely."

He chuckled. "Ah, I don't care about scars."

Sam tied the last suture and set down the needle driver. "Make sure you keep it clean and dry," she said as she applied a dressing. "Leave this bandage on until you come back in two days. I won't give you any antibiotics, but if it hurts, gets really red, and oozes pus, you let me know, okay?"

"Sure thing."

"I'll have Cynthia give you some supplies and more instructions. See you in a couple of days." Sam walked out the door and found Cynthia waiting for her. "I'm finished with Mr. Cross. Could you give him the usual stuff for a lac?"

"Yes, Doctor. Also, I wanted to let you know that Dr. Harper said if you don't call him back by 4:30 this afternoon, he's going to deny the authorization for Mrs. Rodriguez's MRI. I left a note with his number on your desk."

Sam frowned. "Fine. I'll call him back now." She went to her workstation and sat down. While she started typing up her procedure note for Mr. Cross, she dialed the number for Dr. Harper.

After a few rings, she heard, "Dr. Harper speaking."

"Hi, Dr. Harper. This is Dr. Samantha Jenkins returning your call regarding my patient, Rebecca Rodriguez."

"Yes, Dr. Jenkins, I have her case right here." Sam

heard a couple of clicks through the phone line, then he continued, "I understand you ordered a cervical MRI for her, but the primary diagnosis is 'shoulder pain'."

"Yes, sir, that was her primary diagnosis initially, but it has become evident she might have a cervical injury as well." Sam gave the same explanation she'd given to the adjuster the day before—that what seemed like shoulder pain from a shoulder injury at first may actually be shoulder pain from an injury to the nerve roots in the neck. "So I've updated Mrs. Rodriguez's diagnosis to 'cervical strain with radiculopathy'. She has findings suggestive of impingement on C6 on exam, and I'd like to rule out disc pathology."

"Hmm ... I don't see that here in her chart. When did you examine her last?"

"Tuesday last week."

"It looks like the latest exam notes I have are from two weeks ago. Could you have your office fax the notes from your most recent visit to me for review? Then I'll call you back tomorrow."

Sam rolled her eyes. She was glad he couldn't see her. Yet another delay, but she would jump through these hoops to take care of Mrs. Rodriguez. "Okay, I'll have someone fax it over to you as soon as possible."

Ha, she thought, everyone believes medicine is so advanced, but my patient isn't getting care because we're stuck in the last century with fax machines, since they're supposed to be more secure.

Sam finished her note for Mr. Cross and headed to the next room on the board. Mrs. Rodriguez. Well, her ears must be burning. She rapped on the door and entered.

"Hi, Mrs. Rodriguez. How are you today?"

Mrs. Rodriguez sat on the exam table, her legs hanging over the side. She was in her late forties, dressed comfortably in leggings and a large boat neck shirt. "I'm still the same, Doctor. I thought I would have the MRI by now."

"So did I. I scheduled you to come back today so we could discuss the MRI results along with your treatment options. Unfortunately, I've been dealing with the insurance company instead. In fact, I just got off the phone with one of their doctors. The adjuster denied the MRI because the protocols say you don't need one of your neck for a shoulder injury."

"But I hurt my neck and my shoulder."

"I know," Sam said, nodding. "However, when you first came in, was your shoulder bothering you more?"

"Yes, that's true."

"Unfortunately, Mr. Reid put 'shoulder pain' down as your primary diagnosis."

"Oh, that Mr. Reid. Such a nice man."

Sam smiled. "Yes, he is. And I don't fault him at all for focusing on your shoulder. It's hard to tell what's happening right after an accident. Your symptoms evolved over the last few weeks, and since your progress was slower than we'd expect with physical therapy, I updated your diagnosis based on that and my findings on exam." She rubbed the back of her neck. "Anyway, they had me talk to their doctor who reviews these cases, but he didn't have the notes from our latest visit."

"Why not, Doctor?"

"I don't know, but I'll make sure everything gets faxed over as soon as we're done here."

"So what does this mean? What's going to happen?" Mrs. Rodriguez hung her head and fiddled with the hem of her shirt. "I need to get back to work. I can't do anything else right now."

Sam leaned on the table next to Mrs. Rodriguez and put her arm around her.

"It's just going to take a little longer for us to get you through this."

"But I need to get back to work. They won't let me do my job because … well, they stack things up so high, and it's hard to get those boxes down. There's no light duty, so they sent me home."

"I'm sorry, Mrs. Rodriguez. I'll do what I can. I'll have the front office send over your records as soon as we're done here, and then I'll talk to their doctor again tomorrow."

"Thanks, Dr. Jenkins." She wiped away tears. "I feel so helpless right now. I'm not getting any better, and it's hard for me to take care of my family. Thank goodness my daughter Christina helps with the cooking and cleaning, and she has her job after school, but she needs to focus on her schoolwork. She's graduating, and she's the first one to go to college in our family. This couldn't happen at a worse time."

"I'm so sorry, Mrs. Rodriguez. We will get you taken care of." Sam pulled out her reflex hammer. "Let me examine you and thoroughly document the neurologic changes in your right arm yet again."

"Okay, Dr. Jenkins. I really appreciate everything you're doing. It must frustrate you too."

"Thanks, Mrs. Rodriguez. I am frustrated—I just want to help you, so you feel better and get back to your life." Sam squeezed her hand. "And we'll get it done, even if it's taking longer than we'd like."

As Sam examined her, the opening of Mrs. Rodriguez's shirt slipped below her left shoulder. "I hadn't noticed that before. That scar below your collarbone—did you have a central line at one time?"

"What's that?"

"It's like a really big IV that goes into the large veins leading to your heart."

Mrs. Rodriguez's eyes widened. "Oh yes, Dr. Jenkins. Right after my daughter was born, I got really sick with an infection. I almost died." She tapped her scar. "They put this thing in so they could give me strong medicine to fight it. But something happened, and they kept my feet up for a while."

"I'm so sorry, Mrs. Rodriguez." Sam thought Mrs. Rodriguez's doctors must have worried about an air embolism. "Were you septic?"

"I don't remember much. They gave me medicine to put me to sleep for most of it." Mrs. Rodriguez smiled. "But I'm here now, and my daughter is almost grown. So it's all okay."

"I'm so glad," Sam said. "And I promise we'll get you better soon."

AFTER SHE FINISHED with Mrs. Rodriguez, Sam found a pink message slip resting on her keyboard. It was from Mr. Mason. Sam had a call to check on him on her list of things to do, and to be perfectly honest, she was dragging her feet. Hopefully he wasn't calling to complain about going to the ER for no reason.

Sam dialed the number, not realizing she was holding her breath. Mr. Mason answered almost immediately. "You were right."

"I'm sorry?"

"You were right. I went to the ER, as you and my wife told me to. Even though it was late, everyone was pleasant, and it wasn't crowded."

"That's good, Mr. Mason. What did they find?"

"Just what you thought, I have a clot in my leg. They ran those tests and did the ultrasound. They told me it's a decent size but they've seen worse." He hesitated, then cleared his throat. "My wife told me to say you saved my life."

Sam smiled. That was probably the closest she'd get to a "thank you" from him. But it didn't matter—he got the care he needed. "I'm glad you caught it. Let's see, when do I see you again?" She pulled up Mr. Mason's chart and found his next appointment. "We have you coming in next week. That's about right. I'm sure they started you on some blood thinners in the ER?"

"Yes."

"What else did they tell you?"

"That I needed to follow up with my doctor—I suppose that's you—and I would need another test."

Sam figured they started him on Coumadin, the standard treatment for DVTs when she was training.

"Did they give you a prescription?"

"Yes, but they said I need another one from you."

"Got it. Do you have enough to last you until next week?"

"Yes."

"Great. Can you stop by and fill out some paperwork so that the ER will send your records to us? I'll review them so I know what we need to do for you."

"I can be there in an hour."

"Okay. You can stop by anytime that's convenient for you. I'll let the front desk know."

"I can be there in an hour," he repeated.

Did he think she was going to be the one to meet with him to fill out paperwork? Sam moved on. "Sounds good. If your swelling or redness gets worse, or if you have problems breathing, go back to the ER immediately or call 911, okay?"

"Okay."

"I'll see you next week, sir."

As Sam hung up, she felt her cell phone buzz in her pocket. A text message from Dylan: *I have something for you. Dinner tonight?*

Sam wrinkled her nose. She wanted to help Claire and figure out what happened to Brad, but did she want to deal with her past to get it? Plus, what happened between her and Dylan was sophomore year of high school. They were really just children when they had dated, and she was a different person now. She sighed. Fine, she could handle this. She texted back: *Sure. Where do you want to meet?*

9

S am pulled behind Chuy's Tex-Mex on Barton Springs and found a spot under the tall trees creating a canopy over the parking lot. The restaurant's casual vibes were typical of Austin's demeanor and calmed Sam's nerves. She entered through the back door, but before she got to the steps leading up to the bar, she heard her name. Dylan sat in a booth, an open file spread out in front of him next to bowls of chips and salsa. Her heart fluttered and she blinked hard. Like it or not, he instilled a reaction in her, even though they'd last dated so long ago.

Since it was midweek, the adjacent booths were empty. Pop music played overhead, and most of the other patrons sat at the bar underneath a sea of brightly painted wooden fish.

Dylan stood as she approached. "It's good to see you." He looked the same as Sam remembered. Short, wavy brown hair, and with a broad smile that caused her knees to wobble. He was striking in his department uniform.

"Hi, Dylan." Sam took a breath to slow her heart.

A waitress walked over, and Dylan quickly closed the file as he squeezed back into the booth. "Can I get you something to drink?"

"I'll just have iced tea."

Dylan raised his longneck. "And I'm good for now."

"Great. I'll give you a minute to decide what you want to eat."

As the waitress walked off, Dylan said, "How have you been?"

"Pretty good." Sam settled into the bench seat across from him.

"You've joined a practice, right? How's that?"

"It's okay. I mainly see worker's compensation and urgent care." She rubbed her chin. "Actually, it's better than okay. The patients really seem to appreciate the care I give them, and that makes it worthwhile. How are things with the police department?"

"Good. But we've been getting busier as the city has grown." He picked up a chip and broke it in half. "Unfortunately, our budget hasn't grown with the population."

The waitress returned and set a large plastic glass of iced tea in front of Sam. They placed their orders. Shrimp tacos for Sam and fajitas for Dylan.

After the waitress left, Dylan said, "You used to always order that when we came here."

"Wow, that doesn't seem that long ago." In fact, sitting with Dylan felt comfortable—maybe too comfortable. Like no time had passed at all.

Dylan smiled. "Don't I know it."

Sam looked at the file he covered with his hands. "So is that why you texted me?"

"Yeah. It's the preliminary autopsy report for Brad."

"You won't get in trouble, will you?"

"This will be public information eventually, anyway."

He smirked. "The girl I've been dating works in the medical examiner's office and got it for me."

Sam felt some relief mixed with a pang of jealousy. This would not be an attempt at reuniting. "Oh, is it serious?" She raised an eyebrow. "Seems like it might be, if she got you the report."

"Well, you know." Dylan looked up. His eyes bored into her. Her stomach tightened. "What? You didn't think ..."

"Oh no. I'm not ..." Sam shook her head vigorously. "You know, I broke off my engagement with my fiancé, so I'm definitely not looking for anything right now."

Dylan leaned back and tilted his head. "I'm sorry. What happened?"

"Well, it's a long story." Sam picked at the napkin under her tea, the beads of condensation soaking it, plastering it to the table. "I'd rather not talk about it right now."

Loud cackling drifted over from the bar. "Must be pretty funny, or the margaritas are pretty strong," Dylan said. He seemed ready to change the subject too. "Right. So this report. I saw the cause of death was a—" he flipped open the file—"myocardial in ... I don't know how to say this."

Sam peered at the report. "Myocardial infarction. It's a heart attack."

"Don't old people have heart attacks?"

"Yeah, usually. But there are a couple of reasons someone young might have a heart attack. I'm hoping the report enlightens me." She reached for the folder.

Dylan put his hand on top of the report. "Okay, so yeah, you're right. I could get in trouble, and so could Sally, the girl I'm dating. I'll let you look at it, but you can't keep it." He cleared his throat and looked directly at Sam again. "I trust you. You want to help Claire, and I know you'll use your discretion with this information."

Sam swallowed as she nodded. "Thanks for doing this."

"You're welcome." He turned the file around so she could see it. "What are you looking for?"

"Well, cardiovascular disease is one reason for a heart attack. Let's see if the medical examiner found evidence of this." She looked at the file. The report summary was on top. "You already saw this part. The immediate cause of death appeared to be a myocardial infarction."

"Yeah, the only part I understood was 'immediate cause of death'. Everything else is all medical stuff that's like another language to me."

Sam looked up and smiled. "That's okay. It was all completely foreign to me at one time too. It really is like learning another language. I'm sure there's lots of lingo you use I wouldn't understand."

A bemused look formed on Dylan's face. "Yeah, but everyone thinks they know it all because of the cop shows on TV."

"Just like everyone thinks they know what's wrong with them because they Googled it." Sam chuckled then used her finger to guide her eyes on the report. "It lists the cause of death. But the next section is 'Underlying Cause' and that's blank."

"I guess that makes sense because this is just a preliminary report."

"Yeah, they've probably sent off specimens for lab and toxicology testing, and those results take a while." She wondered exactly why, though. In the hospital, results came back quickly. Perhaps it was because there is more urgency with the living than the dead.

She flipped through a few pages, scanning them. "I

want to dig into the details and find answers to my questions. Here's the page with the gross examination."

"How do you know all this stuff? Did you have to do autopsies in medical school?" Dylan asked.

"No. Unless you're doing pathology, you rarely get involved with autopsies. They gave us opportunities to observe autopsies, though. Once, a patient died on our service, and our attending said we could go to her autopsy if we wanted. I had too much work, but another student who planned on specializing in pathology went and said it was interesting."

"So have you seen any autopsies?"

"Only before I went to med school. The premed club set up a schedule where we could observe autopsies at the medical examiner's office. So I know the basics of what happens." Sam tapped on the file. "I'm not super-familiar with autopsy reports, though. But it doesn't look much different from what we do for the clinical history in other areas of medicine. And the examination section looks similar to the pathology reports I've reviewed."

Dylan pointed to the top of the page. "So what does 'gross' mean? I assume it doesn't mean 'gross,' like 'disgusting.'"

"It's the part of the pathology examination that looks at the whole organ. I remember 'gross' means 'large' in German, so I guess that's where it comes from."

"Ha, I remember that. You were taking German when we were …"

Sam blushed.

Dylan cleared his throat. "I remember you took German."

"Yeah, my dad insisted on it, since he considered it a 'scientific language'." Sam rolled her eyes. "A lot of good it's done for me as a doctor here in Texas. I only use it once a year at Wurstfest." As she said this, she remembered family trips down to New Braunfels each fall, how she and her mother would sit along the banks of the Comal River, the breeze carrying polka music to them from the festival tents. She missed her mother so much.

Sam pushed that memory aside and smiled at Dylan. "I should have taken Spanish. That would have been more useful."

"I took Spanish because it was supposed to be an easy A." Dylan laughed. "But it wasn't, really. My mom and aunts didn't teach me all the grammar I needed for the class."

"That's right—your mom's family is from Mexico."

Dylan nodded, then looked at the report. "So what else does this thing say?"

"The next section is the microscopic description. So I guess you could say 'gross' is like 'macro.' It's looking at things from a distance."

"That makes sense." Dylan smiled. "You always had all kinds of random facts in your brain."

Sam let out a chuckle. "Yeah. Don't know how I remember all this stuff." She looked down at the file again. "So for the gross examination of the heart, let's see ... 'no chamber hypertrophy or dilatation' ... 'valves appear unre-markable' ... 'coronary arteries widely patent with no evidence of plaque or calcification.' That's what I was looking for."

"What does that mean?"

"His heart looked normal, and there's no sign of heart disease, which is what usually causes a heart attack. People with high cholesterol can have a blockage in the arteries supplying the heart. The coronary arteries."

"Sounds like coronation."

"Yeah, it's the same root. Those arteries form a circle

around the heart like a crown. When people have high cholesterol in their blood for a long time—usually years—little deposits get left in the coronary arteries, forming a plaque. Kind of like how grease can build up in pipes under the kitchen sink."

"Oh, I get it. If it's clogged, then blood can't get through."

"That's right. Blood can't get through, so the heart muscle starts to die. If doctors don't remove the blockage and open up the blood flow quickly enough, then that person has a heart attack. And if the blood flow to a big part of the heart gets cut off, that person can die."

"So how did the medical examiner know Brad had a heart attack?"

"That's a good question." Sam looked at the report again. "It says, 'a section of myocardium was stained with NBT to identify acute necrosis.' I'm not familiar with NBT, so I'll have to look that up." She flipped through the other pages. "And it says he has a patent foramen ovale. That's interesting."

Dylan squinted. "What's that?"

Sam shrugged. "It's just an incidental finding of a type of 'hole in the heart.' We all have this opening between the two sides of the heart when we're fetuses in utero to let the blood bypass our lungs because we get the oxygen we need from our mothers through the placenta. It's called the foramen ovale because it looks like an oval window. There's a little flap over it, and when we're born, the pressure changes between the two sides of the heart to keep it closed. In most people, that flap fuses with the wall of the heart to stay closed. But in a good number of people, that flap never fuses closed, which is what happened in Brad's heart. In that case, they say it's 'patent', which just means 'open'."

"You used that word when you were talking about the heart arteries, right?" Dylan asked.

She tapped the report. "Yeah, the report said the coronaries were 'widely patent'. So they were wide open."

"Did this oval-whatever thing have anything to do with Brad's death?"

"I don't think so. Most people live their entire lives with a PFO and never know it. The medical examiner was just being thorough by mentioning it in the report."

Just then, the waitress walked up with their food. Sam quickly closed the file and put it on the seat next to her. The waitress asked if they needed any refills on their drinks. Both Sam and Dylan declined.

Once the waitress left, Sam tilted her head toward the file next to her. "There's a lot here. I'd like to look at this more closely, so I don't miss anything." She looked at the light hanging above the table. "I could snap some photos with my phone so that I could read it more carefully. But this light isn't great."

Dylan put down his fork. "Oh no. I know what you're going to ask." He sat back and crossed his arms across his broad chest. "No. You can't take pictures, and you can't take it with you."

"Come on, Dylan. Please? You trusted me enough to share it with me." She looked at her watch. Still pretty early. "Just for a couple of hours?"

Dylan remained silent, flaring his nostrils.

Sam chewed on her lip, then said, "How about this? I have my laptop in my car. We could go to the Starbucks down the street." She scrunched up her face. "That way, you can keep an eye on me."

"How long do you need?"

"Maybe an hour."

He looked at his watch, then he finally nodded. "Fine.

There's something I need to do, but you can go over there, and I'll meet you around 9:30."

They ate quickly, with only an occasional word or two about long-lost friends they had in common. After dinner, Dylan insisted on paying. He walked Sam out to her car, and she gave him a quick hug.

"Thanks, Dylan." She held up the file. "I've got some studying to do. See you soon."

10

S am spent the next hour reviewing the autopsy report while sipping a latte at Starbucks. She had found a high-top table in a corner with a modicum of privacy from the other patrons, mainly students from the university. As she flipped through the report again, she confirmed what she saw initially with Dylan. Brad did not have any evidence of heart disease, but the medical examiner used various techniques to determine what appeared to be the primary cause of death: a myocardial infarction, commonly known as a heart attack. Using her laptop, Sam found out that NBT stood for nitro blue tetrazolium, a stain used to detect necrosis, or cell death, in heart muscle. But what caused it? If not heart disease, it could be drug-related. That's what the medical examiner seemed to think too.

The preliminary drug screen only showed positivity for benzodiazepines, a type of sedative used to prevent seizures in epilepsy patients, but commonly used to decrease anxiety in everyone else. There was no interpretation, but the ME noted that samples had been sent for further toxicology analysis. No opiates, though. Could someone overdose on benzos? Sam didn't think they suppressed respiratory function like opiates did, but she wanted to check.

A quick PubMed search showed it was unusual for benzos to cause death by themselves, but using them along with opiates increased risk of death.

But the drug screen showed no opiates, which surprised Sam given Brad's history. She found an article from CAP Today, the newsletter for the College of American Patholo- gists, saying that urine drug screens do not help in deter- mining whether a drug contributed to death and that designer drugs like fentanyl can't always be detected on drug screen. Sam remembered the push to use fentanyl to treat surgery patients postoperatively when she was in medical school. That, and the declaration that pain is the sixth vital sign, really paved the way in the rash of over- doses lately. Unlike morphine, made from poppy plants, fentanyl is synthetically fabricated in the lab and is a hundred times stronger. No wonder people were overdos- ing. Sam recalled a news story about a police officer over- dosing from fentanyl after a bag of the powder accidentally burst while he was arresting a dealer.

Okay. So no direct indication that Brad died of an opioid overdose, but the screens don't always show that. She wondered if someone could have a myocardial infarc- tion due to an opioid overdose, so she did another search. She found a couple of case reports out of India. In one case, it appeared the MI was due to direct toxic effects of heroin on the coronary arteries. Since there were only a few case reports, it meant this wasn't common but it was possible.

The report also said Brad had mild pulmonary edema, or swelling of the lungs, based partly on the fact that his lungs weighed more than expected. Sam looked up what an autopsy might show for an opioid overdose. Findings could include pulmonary edema and possibly cyanosis. Cyanosis, or a blueness of the skin, usually occurred after someone did not have enough oxygen for a prolonged period. The report specifically stated the ME did not see cyanosis. It also noted that the pulmonary edema could be caused by drugs, which may or may not be related to the pathology found in Brad's heart.

The report noted that based on interviews with Claire and her parents, Brad had a history of substance abuse, and it noted the unlabeled prescription bottle found in Brad's belongings. The bottle contained two round white pills marked with a "C" and a "2," but no interpretation, yet. The ME just stated toxicology results were pending and should help determine the cause of death.

Sam pulled up an online pill identifier and entered the information. She sifted through the numerous results to find two possible candidates. Clonazepam, a benzodiazepine, had a "C" and a "2" on the same side of the pill, and Fentora, a pill version of fentanyl, had a stylized "C" on one side and a "2" on the other. She looked at the prelim report again—did it say if these markings were on the same side? No, it didn't mention that detail. She wished she could ask someone, but she wasn't supposed to be looking at this report in the first place. Plus, it was a preliminary report, so it was incomplete. And the report was probably dictated, so the ME had yet to proofread it. She would just have to take the info she had, that either the pills were clonazepam, which would explain the drug screen, or that they were fentanyl, which could ultimately be the cause of Brad's death.

Sam found one more unusual thing in the report. The medical examiner identified two venipuncture wounds in the left antecubital fossa, the technical name for the fold in front of the elbow. She thought Brad had only used prescription opioids, but he may have switched to heroin, which could be injected. A good deal of heroin users have track marks on their arms where they inject or, if they wanted to make it less obvious, they might inject between their toes to hide the injection sites. The report did not mention any other puncture marks or injection sites on Brad's body.

As Sam packed up the file, Dylan entered the coffee shop. She waved to him, and he perched himself on the stool across from her.

"Did you find anything interesting?"

"It looks like the medical examiner is waiting on the toxicology report to determine the final cause of death. Seems like they expect it to be drug-related since Brad was healthy otherwise."

"Hmm. So case closed, then."

"Well, from what I remember, Brad started abusing prescription opioids after he tore up his shoulder in high school. But opioids cause respiratory failure, not heart attacks." She tapped the file. "And the report doesn't show evidence of respiratory failure."

"What causes heart attacks, then?"

"Cocaine and meth, which I don't think Brad used, and they didn't show up on the drug screen. Of course, I could be wrong. They found an unlabeled pill bottle in his room, though." She then explained the other details in the report and what she'd learned from her web searches.

Dylan listened attentively, but sometimes Sam sensed he was nodding even though he probably didn't understand everything she was saying.

"There's something else I want to check out." Sam flipped to the right page. "The medical examiner noted two fairly recent venipuncture marks in the left antecubital fossa."

"Anti-what now?"

"The antecubital fossa." Sam pointed to her arm. "It's this crease in front of the elbow. The basilic vein runs through there, and it's a pretty good size, so that's where they usually draw blood for tests."

"But if Brad was using prescription opiates, he could have switched to shooting up heroin, right?"

"How d'you know that?"

"It's part of the training we get in law enforcement."

"That makes sense. When I was a med student and resident in the ER, they gave us a list of the street names of drugs, so we'd know what our patients were taking, since they wouldn't know the actual names of the drugs sometimes."

Dylan smiled. "Yeah, funny how we all have to stay on top of the latest street lingo."

"But back to your point about heroin. The medical examiner didn't mention any track marks, which is what you usually find on chronic heroin users."

"Yeah, we learned about that too. So what do you think the marks in his arm mean?"

"He may have had blood drawn recently. I'll ask Claire about it. And I want to find out if Chris Baker knows anything."

"That's right. You said Brad met up with him the night before he died?"

"Yeah, I should talk to him."

"Wait." Dylan put his palm flat on the table. "It's the department's job to interview people if the ME determines this is a homicide."

Sam furrowed her brow. "What's the harm in talking to him? He's just a guy we knew in high school. He may have been a destructive influence on some people, but it's not like he's a criminal mastermind."

"Do you really want to do this? Dig things up so you can prove Brad died of an overdose?"

"You can't stop me from talking to Chris, right?"

Dylan crossed his arms. "No, I can't stop you from talking to anyone. But you could wait for the toxicology report. So why don't you?"

"Because now I'm curious—" she paused—"and Claire will keep bugging me."

"So? Just tell her she needs to wait too."

Sam didn't want to seem like she was a pushover, like her friends could tell her what to do. Should she tell Dylan about Claire's suspicions? She tapped the side of her latte. "You know her. She won't accept that as an answer."

"Why not?"

"I ... I can't tell you why."

Dylan raised an eyebrow.

Sam let out a long breath. "You're right. What am I doing? I should focus on my own life."

"Hey, it just means you want to get to the truth."

Sam looked at her watch. "I need to get home. I still have a bunch of charts to do." She handed the file back to Dylan. "Thanks for letting me get a peek at this."

"You're welcome." He smiled. "It was good hanging out this evening, even if it was to talk about death."

Warmth bloomed in Sam's cheeks. "Yeah, it was good seeing you too."

Then he pointed at her. "Just stay out of trouble."

11

On Wednesday, Sam faced another clinic filled with patients. But before she started off, and before the onslaught began, she had a few moments to chat with Jerry. Her meeting with Dr. Taylor was the next day, and she was still concerned about what his cryptic email message meant. She told Jerry that she thought she might be let go soon.

"Ah, Doc. I think you're fine. I've worked with plenty of docs who are just GPs over the years and they've been great."

GP stood for general practitioner, someone like Sam, who had completed at least one year of residency and had their license. "Are you sure? What if ObraCare has decided to change their policy toward hiring GPs?"

"I'm sure you'd be grandfathered. Plus, your patients love you, and you're easy to work with."

Sam smiled. "Thanks, Jer. I guess I'm overthinking it, and I'm just worried." She bit her lip. "Now that I've left a residency program, can I get back in if they let me go here? What would I do then?"

Jerry patted her on the shoulder. "You're a doc, Doc. You'll always be able to practice somewhere."

But Sam wasn't so sure about that. By then the board had filled up, and they needed to get to work.

Sam and Jerry rushed from room to room all morning, keeping the flow going to avoid negative reviews for long wait times. Even though she enjoyed taking care of her patients, the main purpose of her life seemed to be making sure that the clinic's net promoter score stayed high—at least as far as the clinic owners were concerned.

Fortunately, most patients had follow-up visits, and these were usually pretty short. Most of the time, she just made sure her patients were steadily improving, so she could decrease work restrictions to keep the patients and their employers happy.

Since her clinic also had an attached physical therapy center, she'd occasionally go over to the therapist treating her patients to get a quick update on how they were doing before she would enter the room. On the schedule, the clinic's staff usually booked patients' physical therapy and medical appointments back to back. Ever since she started working closely with physical therapists, she learned they were actually much better at diagnosing and treating musculoskeletal injuries than many doctors. Plus, they spent much more time with patients, often seeing them for three hours a week, which allowed the therapist to learn much more about the issues patients dealt with—much more than Sam ever could learn in her brief visits.

As she exited a room and headed back to her workspace, the office manager intercepted her. Jill was an energetic woman with a bob cut who relished managing the staff, something Sam was realizing she had no aptitude for.

"Dr. Jenkins," Jill said, putting her hand on Sam's elbow, pulling her closer to the wall, then bending her head toward Sam before speaking with a lowered voice. "There's a police officer here to talk to you. Do you want to see him?"

"Uh, sure." Must be Dylan, she thought. Why was he there?

"Okay. I'll bring him back." Jill disappeared and returned moments later with Dylan.

"Hi, Sam. Something's happened, and I need to talk to you."

Sam noticed the medical assistants trying not to pay attention, with Jill lingering around the door to the front office. Sam looked over her shoulder and spotted an unoccupied room. "Let's go in here."

Dylan followed her. "Don't you have an office?"

"No. There's only one office back here, and the sales guy uses it."

"What? There's a sales guy at a clinic? And he's more important than the doctors?"

"It's a long story." Sam she rolled her eyes. "Don't get me started ... So what brings you here?"

"It's about Mike Davis. He's been in a car accident."

Sam's spine twitched. "What happened?"

"Well, it appears he passed out while he was driving this morning. The doctors at the hospital think he suffered from carbon monoxide poisoning."

"Is he okay?"

"I think so. Fortunately, he wasn't going very fast, and another car was on scene when it happened. The other driver called 911. The EMTs pulled him out and started him on oxygen en route to the hospital."

"How is he?"

"He's awake and answering questions, which is how they know he passed out."

"Wow. I'm glad he's okay. How did you get involved?"

"Claire called me, so I guess she thinks I'm her guy at the department now. Anyway, she wanted me to come tell you, since you weren't answering your phone." He looked her in the eye. "And she thinks you may be in danger."

Sam pulled her phone out of her coat pocket and saw five missed calls from Claire. "She could have called the clinic." She glanced at her Apple Watch—for some reason, the calls hadn't transferred. She squinted at him. "But you're here. What do you think?"

"I think she's pretty shaken up right now. Her brother just died, and now her fiancé's been in a car accident. That's a lot to handle over a few days." He shrugged. "But I don't see any reason you would be in danger, even though she did tell me about Brad's suspicious call that she'd overheard. And now she thinks someone tried to hurt Mike." He paused. "So is that why you insisted on talking to Chris? And is that the reason why she got you—and me —involved?"

Sam looked down as she shoved her hands in her coat pockets. "Yeah, it is."

"Why didn't you tell me last night?"

"Because I didn't want to share Claire's crazy idea. I think she's come up with it as a way to cope." Sam hesitated. "So do you think I'm really in danger?"

"No. I don't. But Claire was worried about you, so I agreed to stop by. And she is going through a lot right now."

Sam wondered then if there was another reason he delivered the message in person. He said he was dating someone else, but perhaps … Instead she said, "Yeah, that's true. But do you think she's right? That maybe someone is behind this?"

"One of my mentors told me he never believes in coincidences. But on the surface, these events seem to be completely unrelated."

"I hope you're right." She paused. "So you think I'm okay, then?"

"Yeah, I guess I could have just called you, but I wanted to let you know before you heard about it on the news or some other way."

"Thanks, Dylan. I'll give Claire a call and let her know I'll be over there as soon as I can." Sam opened the door. Jill and the medical assistants scattered like cockroaches. "Bunch of busybodies," she muttered. "They all mean well, but everyone is always in everyone else's business."

Dylan smirked. "You'd be surprised how much that happens in the police department too."

12

Sam couldn't leave the clinic immediately. The patient stream continued, and it was always hard to get coverage. If she needed to take a day off, or even a few hours, she had to get approval well in advance so her boss could find another doctor to fill in for her. After her last patient, she drove straight to the hospital. Claire had texted Sam the information for where to go, and she climbed the stairs to the second floor where the ICU was located. Claire came out of the restroom as Sam exited the stairwell.

"How is Mike doing?" Sam asked as she hugged Claire.

"The doctors told me he's going to be okay. Fortunately, he wasn't driving that fast and just ran off the road into a ditch. He's banged up and bruised, but he seems to be in good spirits."

"Oh good. Is he awake right now?"

Claire nodded. "His grandparents are visiting him right now."

Sam recalled Mike had grown up with his grandparents after his mom died. "Does he remember what happened?"

"He thinks he passed out briefly. Says he was feeling dizzy and nauseous right before he blacked out."

"Goodness, Claire, what a few days it's been." Sam squeezed Claire's shoulder. "And how are you doing?"

"Honestly, I'm pretty rattled. I told Dylan the same thing I told you—that I think someone wanted to hurt Brad. And now it seems like Mike is a target too."

"But what if these are unrelated incidents?"

"They could be, but why would these happen within a few days of each other to two people I love?"

Sam sighed. "Maybe you're right." She lowered her voice as she glanced at Claire's parents sitting in the waiting area near the ICU doors. "So, Claire, you can't tell anyone this, but Dylan let me see the preliminary autopsy report on Brad."

Claire's eyes grew. "He did? What did you find?"

"The same thing you learned from the medical examiner's office. That Brad died of a heart attack." She walked Claire through her thought process for what might explain the ME's findings.

Claire crossed her arms. "You still think he died from drug use."

"It's a possibility."

"He was clean." Claire looked directly at Sam. "That's what he told me and I believed him."

Sam didn't want to argue with Claire right now. It wouldn't be useful, and it would frustrate Claire more. So Sam simply nodded and said, "The report also mentioned a venipuncture wound on his left arm. Did he have blood drawn recently?"

"He told me he went to the doctor last week. I don't

know why, but my parents probably know more about it. Do you think that might be important?"

"It could be. I'm not sure."

Claire motioned toward the ICU waiting room. "You could ask them about it now."

They walked down the hallway to Claire's parents. Claire's dad stood up and gave Sam a bear hug, as Claire's mom squeezed her arm. "How are you doing, Mr. and Mrs. Johnson?"

"Oh, Sam," Claire's mom said, "we don't know what to think. First Brad and now Mike ..."

Sam wrinkled her nose. "I don't know either. Thank goodness Mike's injuries aren't too bad." She paused then she pressed forward. "If it's okay, I have a question about Brad."

"Sure, honey, but please sit." Mrs. Johnson patted the seat next to her. "I know you've had a long day taking care of patients."

Sam suddenly realized how her feet ached, and sitting down felt good, even if it was in a hard waiting room chair. "Claire told me Brad had a doctor's appointment last week?"

"Yes, he did. He was having headaches and wanted to get checked out."

Claire raised her eyebrows as she sat on the other side of her mom. "Really? He didn't tell me about this."

Mrs. Johnson patted Claire's hand. "Brad didn't want to bother you because of the wedding."

"Could you tell me a little more about these headaches, Mrs. Johnson?" Sam asked.

Mrs. Johnson gazed toward the hallway as she spoke. "Well, they started around the time Brad came clean. He'd only get them every couple of months. Sometimes he would feel nauseous and couldn't do anything except lie down and let it pass. Other times he said the headache would only last a few minutes."

"Sounds like it might have been migraines or cluster headaches. It makes sense the doctor would run some blood tests to rule out other things."

Mrs. Johnson's voice trembled as tears welled up. "I guess it doesn't matter now." She pulled a tissue out of her purse and dabbed her eyes.

Sam placed her hand on Mrs. Johnson's. "Do you know which doctor he saw?"

"What's the point? He's gone." She started sobbing and covered her face.

Claire subtly shook her head.

Sam glanced at Mr. Johnson, who stared straight ahead, paying no attention to their conversation. She took a deep breath. "I'm so sorry." They sat in silence for a moment, then Sam said, "Is there anything I can do?"

Mrs. Johnson squeezed Sam's hand. "No, dear. Just visiting us is enough. You're like family. And we know how busy you are with your patients." She stared at the floor. "I can't believe everything that's happened. I thought we would gain another son after the wedding, not lose our only son." She gave a brief nod. "At least Mike is going to be okay."

Claire leaned over and hugged her mom. She looked up at Sam, motioned toward the hallway with a tilt of her head, and stood.

Sam followed Claire. Once they were out of earshot, Sam said, "I'm sorry, Claire. I shouldn't have pushed your mom. I'm just curious, and it could answer more questions. Maybe the headaches and his cause of death are linked."

"That's all right, Sam. I'll find out who he went to see, and I'll let you know."

"I'm sure the medical examiner's office will want that information too."

Footsteps echoed down the hallway, followed by James's appearance around the corner. "Claire!" He gave her a hug. "I got your message. I'm so sorry. How is Mike?"

"He's going to be okay. Just banged up a bit."

James lifted his chin at Sam and patted her shoulder. "Hi, Sam. And how are you doing?"

"I'm fine. This is pretty crazy, though."

"Yeah, how could all these horrible things happen?" James ran his hands through his hair. "Instead of being on your honeymoon, you're here in a hospital."

A weak smile crossed Claire's face. "This morning Mike and I were talking about how we can still get married, just maybe without the big ceremony, since the certificate is good for ninety days. After the funeral and everything settles down. Give us time to grieve. But now …"

"So what are you going to do?" James asked.

Claire looked down. "I don't know. I just feel numb." The three stood without speaking for a moment.

A loud series of clanks broke the silence as the ICU doors opened. Mike's grandparents walked out. Claire asked, "How's Mike doing?"

Mike's grandfather put her hand on Claire's arm. "He's feeling better. The headaches are improving. He's just tired now. They said we should all go home and get some rest."

A tall man in scrubs and a white coat came out of the ICU door and stopped next to the group. Sam immediately recognized him from residency.

Mike's grandmother asked, "Dr. Crawford, are you sure he's going to be okay?"

"Yes, ma'am. He's stable now, O2 sats are good. After

some rest, he should be better in the morning, and I should be able to discharge him from the ICU then." The doctor looked up and noticed Sam. "Hi, Sam. Fancy seeing you here. I didn't know you were in Austin."

"Hi, Alex. Yeah, I moved back last year. When did you move here?"

"I started my critical care fellowship last summer. I suppose you know these folks?"

Sam put her hand on Claire's shoulder. "Claire is one of my best and oldest friends. We've known each other since junior high. But it's been a crazy few days."

Alex's brow furrowed. "Why, what else has been going on?" He looked at Claire. "Mr. Davis mentioned you were supposed to get married this weekend, but there was a death."

Claire's eyes welled up. "My brother died right before the wedding."

"I'm so sorry to hear that. And now your fiancé's in our ICU." After a beat, he stood up straight. "Well, he's looking good, and we'll monitor him overnight. We have the best nurses in the hospital right here. So go home and get some rest."

"Thanks, Dr. Crawford."

"You're welcome." He started to walk off, then turned back and said, "And Sam, we should grab coffee sometime and catch up."

"Yeah, that would be good, Alex." She turned, hoping he wouldn't see her blush.

As he left, James raised his eyebrow and muttered, "He's a tall drink of water. And I didn't see a ring on his finger." He poked Sam in the ribs. "You should definitely go after that."

Sam frowned. "Come on, James. He's just an old acquaintance from residency."

James looked back and forth between Alex and Sam. "Well, you two should definitely get reacquainted."

~

AFTER MIKE'S GRANDPARENTS LEFT, Sam joined Claire in the ICU. Claire was right, Mike did seem to be in good spirits despite the accident.

"Sorry, honey," Mike said with a lopsided grin. "When you wanted a po'boy for lunch, instead of going to that food truck you like, I thought we could make our own with fresh crawfish from the ditch." He chuckled, slapping his non-IV-tethered hand on his thigh.

Claire gave a small laugh, and when Mike saw Sam's expression, he asked, "You know, with my car? I crashed my car in the ditch to find some crawfish?"

"Did you spend the whole afternoon coming up with that one?" Claire sat next to him.

"I know, it's pretty bad, but I didn't have much material to work with."

A wistful smile bloomed on Claire's face. "Just means you'll be prepared to make bad dad jokes when we have kids."

Mike continued with a few more bad jokes in his attempt to cheer up Claire. Sam asked a couple of clinical questions—she couldn't get away from her nature—and Mike's responses reassured her he was going to be fine, other than some bumps and bruises.

As Claire preened over Mike, a calendar alert went off on Sam's phone. "Oh, I forgot I had plans for dinner." She pulled up the messaging app and started texting. "I'll just cancel."

"Dinner plans?" Claire cocked her head. "As in a date?"

"No, just a friend from college. We meet up about once a month for dinner."

Mike smiled and said, "You should go. I'm fine. But I really appreciate your stopping by." He patted Sam's hand. "And looking out for Claire."

"I'm so glad you're doing okay."

"Yeah, so am I," he said.

"I'll walk you out," Claire said.

As they approached the ICU exit doors, Claire stopped. "Thanks for being so supportive." She lowered her voice. "I'd appreciate it if you didn't mention my concerns in front of Mike. He thinks I'm being a little overly dramatic."

"Of course, I won't say anything." Why would she? She didn't know him that well, and she never saw him without Claire. Still, she wondered if there was another reason Claire didn't want Sam to talk to Mike about her ideas of foul play.

13

Even though the hospital was just a few blocks north of downtown, Sam was late meeting her friend, Lisa Saito, for dinner. Traffic was unusually busy for a weeknight, and as she circled around searching for a parking spot, the Paramount Theatre's brightly lit marquee announced a popular comedy duo's performance. Reluctantly, she parked in a nearby garage, then navigated through the crowds to the entrance of the Roaring Fork at the base of the Stephen F. Austin Hotel.

Patrons were clearing out of the restaurant to attend the show at the historic theater next door, and as Sam moved against the flow and down the short hallway separating the bar to the right from the dining room to the left, she came upon a stone hearth with an inviting fire, like one would find at a ski lodge—only it was June in Texas. Sam entered the dining room and found Lisa at a table near the open kitchen. She gave Lisa a quick hug and sat adjacent to her. They faced the windows, which gave a view of the lines of people outside waiting to enter the show.

"Thanks for waiting," Sam said.

"Are you kidding?" Lisa raised an eyebrow and smiled incredulously. "You were visiting someone in the hospital. I totally would have understood if you canceled." She cleared her throat. "Seriously, though, who's in the hospital?"

Sam recounted what had happened to Mike and how she knew him, with periodic interruptions by the waiter to collect orders and deliver food. She also told Lisa about Brad's death and the canceled wedding.

"Wow. That's a horrible series of events." Lisa took a sip of wine. "How is your friend holding up?"

"For now, she's doing okay." She lowered her voice. "But she thinks someone may have killed her brother, and now that her fiancé's been in an accident, she thinks the events are connected."

Lisa frowned. "Really?"

"Yeah, I know." Sam sat back and picked up her glass of wine. "But eventually, she'll have to deal with these events for what they are, just horrible coincidences. Brad had a drug problem. Unfortunately, many people never shake it and it overcomes them."

"And the car accident?"

"Mike had high carboxyhemoglobin levels, so there must have been a leak in his car."

"So these really are just a couple of unfortunate events."

Sam nodded. She didn't want to get into how Claire had asked her to look into Brad's death. The medical examiner would eventually get the toxicology report back from the lab, and it would explain everything, Sam was sure.

While they ate, Lisa talked about the various start-ups she worked with around town. Most were software companies creating apps that followed the craze to be the next

Tinder or DoorDash. As Lisa described them, Sam thought most of these companies were solving the problems of college-aged men, probably because their founders were ... college-aged men.

None of this really appealed to Sam, but she listened because Lisa seemed so eager about all of it. The chase for the next thing always excited her, and Lisa's law firm specialized in handling the legal requirements of these start-ups for a deeply discounted rate—along with a small stake in the companies, of course.

"Oh, listen to this," Lisa said after finishing a bite of her cedar-planked salmon. "Since the new medical school opened, there's a push for start-ups focusing on healthcare. Did you know we spend almost twenty percent of our GDP on healthcare every year?"

"No," Sam said. She could understand why Lisa thought she wanted to know these things, since it did relate to her line of work, even if it was a few orders removed from her daily practice in the clinic. But Sam liked the hard science of medicine because she didn't have to deal with money and financial issues, which she felt could arbitrarily change at any time.

"For entrepreneurs, that's a vast market with huge potential. Almost four trillion dollars! Many big name investors are paying attention now. It has massive untapped potential with an enormous upside."

Sam tried to appear attentive. She appreciated Lisa's enthusiasm, but what did this have to do with her?

"Anyway," Lisa said as she placed her hand on Sam's arm, "there's a professor who wants to commercialize his research, and he'll need people who understand medicine to help him. I'll keep an ear to the ground, and if an opportunity comes up, I can let you know—that is, if you're interested."

Now she had Sam's attention. This wasn't something Sam had ever considered before. Once she got into med school, she figured she was on her way to being a doctor, and that was it. She thought her life was kind of on autopilot.

And it was—until she had jumped off the moving train of medical education by leaving residency. Now it seemed like it would be almost impossible to get back on board. She'd reached out to her old residency program, but while apologetic, the program director had said there just weren't any available slots. Sam had also reached out to other programs, just to test the waters, and the response she'd received was less than supportive. One program director told her she was just too much of a risk for them to take a chance on her. What was that supposed to mean? It sounded like the program director was more worried about her own stats than the education of doctors.

Wasn't Sam allowed to take time off to grieve her mother's death?

But Sam was beginning to realize that the longer she stayed out of a residency program, the harder it would be for her to get back into one so she could complete her training and become board certified.

However, if Lisa knew of an opportunity for her, one where it didn't matter if she was board certified, maybe she should consider it.

Normally she wouldn't have given Lisa's suggestion a second thought and would have politely turned down Lisa's offer. Instead, she said, "I may be, especially since I might not have a job much longer."

"Really?"

Sam brushed her hand aside. "Perhaps I'm being overly paranoid, and the wine is talking, but I have a meeting with my boss tomorrow. I'm worried he might tell me they'll have to let me go."

Lisa raised her eyebrows. "Why's that?"

"He forwarded an email to me last week, announcing an ad campaign promoting how the doctors at our clinics are board certified."

"So that's not a problem, is it?"

"I'm not board certified."

"Couldn't you just get certified? I mean, if I wanted to get board certified, I'd have to study for a specialization and take a test. Of course, I have to show that I've been practicing in that specialization for a while before I could apply for board certification." Lisa shrugged. "Frankly, I'm not board certified, and all the other lawyers I work with aren't either."

"In medicine, it's the other way around—almost everyone is board certified. And in order to sit for the certification exam in a specialty, I need to finish residency in that specialty."

"Oh, I see. So the practice has to be supervised. What specialty are you practicing now?"

"It's urgent care and workers' comp. But there aren't really residencies for those—at least, I don't think so—and most of the other doctors I've worked with are these older guys who are semiretired. They practiced in a bunch of other areas before they joined ObraCare." In fact, one guy she'd worked with in Houston used to be an emergency medicine doctor and had told her the only reason he was still practicing was so he could pay his alimony. He would work a few weeks here and there then he would travel around the country, so he could go fishing for a month at a time.

Lisa pressed on with her line of questioning. "Did they ask you about board certification when you were hired?"

Sam picked at the tablecloth with her fingernail. "No, they just made sure I was licensed."

"They didn't care that you hadn't completed residency?"

Sam chuckled. "Are you kidding? I worked for them through a locum agency while I was still a resident."

"What's locum? That's Latin, right?"

"Oh, sorry. It's short for *locum tenens*. It's what they call the doctors who fill in for other doctors."

"Well, if they didn't care that you had not completed residency when they hired you, I'm sure you're fine. They just can't advertise that you, specifically, are board certified. And they just have to carefully word the ad copy so that they're not claiming *all* their doctors are board certified." She patted Sam's hand. "I think you're fine."

"I guess I'll find out from my boss tomorrow."

"And, hey, even if they let you go, there are opportunities for you. They just may not be practicing medicine." Lisa sipped from her wineglass, then said, "Just think of it. When you practice medicine, you see one patient at a time. But if you help bring a new technology to market, you can help thousands of people, maybe millions."

Sam had never really considered anything but practicing medicine before. Her entire life had been a push toward being a doctor. Perhaps this was a way for her to still make a difference in others' lives, while solving her own dilemma. She sat up. "Okay. Keep me posted if you learn more about that professor's plan."

14

The rest of the week was uneventful, and Sam didn't learn what was on Dr. Taylor's mind because he'd emailed Sam the next morning to let her know he had to cancel and would reach out soon to reschedule their meeting. Maybe she was just overthinking everything. If he was going to fire her, surely it would be more urgent, and he would handle it in a more expedient manner. The thought settled her somewhat.

Lisa texted her later that day to find out how the meeting went. Sam updated her.

I'm sure you're fine Lisa responded before adding *I'll still send info about that prof just in case.*

On Saturday morning, Sam's phone buzzed while she loaded the dryer in her apartment. It was Claire. "How are you? And how's Mike?" Sam asked.

Mike had been stepped down to a floor unit from the ICU the morning after his crash, and since he'd been doing well, the hospitalist had discharged him late Thursday evening.

"Mike's fine. He's sore and tired and spent most of

yesterday in bed. I'm letting him sleep in right now. But I need to talk to you. I was thinking about something, and it might explain a few things."

"I can come over. That way you can stay with Mike."

"No, that's okay. I'm dying to get out of the house. How about we meet at Mozart's?"

"Sounds good."

Sam zipped up MoPac to Lake Austin Boulevard, then drove past graduate student housing for the university on the left and the golf course on the right. This was one of the areas Sam loved most in Austin. By traveling just a couple of miles west of downtown, she could escape the bustle of the city to a nature-rich setting, even with a booming population. It was early enough that Sam found a parking spot next to Hula Hut, one of her favorite restaurants. The day was atypically cool for June in Austin, so Sam grabbed a cardigan from her car before she walked over to Mozart's Coffee Roasters.

The group of restaurants perched on the edge of the Colorado River. Dams—like the one next to Hula Hut—divided the river into a series of lakes, strung together like beads through Central Texas.

She found Claire waiting for her inside Mozart's, the smell of freshly roasted coffee hanging in the air.

After they got their steaming cups of java, they navigated the tiers of outdoor decks before claiming a picnic table on the edge of the lake, overlooking a marina. A fine mist hung over the water as a young family readied their boat for launch.

Claire smiled as she watched them. "That will be us someday."

The kids in their brightly colored life jackets chattered as the boat engine roared to life. After the parents untied the boat, the father idled the boat out to open water, throttling it once he was clear to the squealing delight of his children.

As the boat disappeared, Sam said, "What's going on, Claire? What did you want to talk about?"

"You know about Todd's gambling problem, right?"

"No, but I suspected. I remember that trip to Lake Charles way back when. He stayed at the craps table all weekend."

Claire nodded. "Emily hinted that Todd really needed the commission on the deal Brad had just landed." She leaned closer to Sam. "And frankly, I think it steamed Todd that Brad was taking all the credit. Emily said Todd was the one who spent the time to qualify the lead."

"Huh. Todd seemed pretty happy about Brad's work during the rehearsal dinner."

"Sure, in front of everyone else, but Emily said Todd was a bit annoyed by Brad's bragging."

"You don't think Todd killed Brad, do you?"

"I don't know. I have to admit, I know Brad was a big jerk in high school, even though he was always good to me. But the protective older brother role could get old, and I saw how he treated others. I have a feeling that even though Todd hung out with him, he didn't really like Brad."

"So what about Mike? How could that be related? Todd doesn't even know Mike that well, right?"

"Well, that's the thing. Last year Todd approached Mike to join a real estate investment with him, but Mike didn't like the terms, so he turned Todd down. From what I understand, Todd couldn't convince anyone else to invest. He could still be mad about it."

All this was news to Sam. She looked out over the lake. A cormorant glided inches above the water before diving to catch a fish. "So you're saying if Brad was murdered, and if Mike's accident wasn't really an accident, Todd might be behind it?"

"Well, it makes sense, doesn't it? If Todd went to Brad's room that night, Brad would have opened the door."

Sam frowned. "But if it was Todd, how did he kill Brad?"

"I don't know. The medical examiner thinks Brad died of a heart attack, right? They didn't outright say he died of a drug overdose, did they?"

"The toxicology isn't back, so it's not final." Sam cocked her head. "You and Emily are opening that soap shop together. You trust Emily, but you don't trust Todd?"

"Well, that's different. You, Emily, and I have been close for as long as I can remember. I would trust the two of you with my life. Plus, Emily is already selling her soaps on Etsy. She's got too much work to do, and that's why she asked me to help her." She shrugged. "Besides, I know she's profitable, because I've been doing her taxes."

Sam raised her eyebrows. "So does Emily trust Todd? What if he tries to take money away from the store you two are opening?"

"That is something to think about. But we've structured the entity so Todd shouldn't be able to touch it." They sat without speaking, listening to ducks below them vie for breadcrumbs two girls were tossing in the water from several tables away. After a moment, Claire brightened a touch. "You should stop by the store. The contractors started working on it this week." She looked down. "We had hoped things would be moving well along by the time Mike and I got back from our honeymoon."

"I'm sorry, Claire." Sam patted her hand.

She thought Claire was grasping at straws, but she wanted to be supportive. Even if Todd was behind Brad's death and Mike's accident, how did he do it? It seemed pretty far-fetched to Sam. She took a deep breath, then said, "How about this: I'm still planning on helping Emily tomorrow, to pack up some of her orders to ship, since we thought you would be away. Perhaps I could learn more about the situation with Todd."

"That would be great, Sam."

Sam scratched her head. Then something clicked. "I wonder about those headaches Brad was having. I would really like to talk to his doctor."

"Oh right." Claire dug through her purse. She handed Sam a business card. "I got this from my parents. Brad went to their doctor to get checked out."

Sam took the card. It was for Alan Black, internal medicine. "I know Dr. Black. I shadowed him while I was in college before I went to medical school."

"Shadowed?" Claire asked.

"I followed him around for a day, so I could see what it was like to be a doctor." A doctor that wasn't her father, Sam thought.

Claire's eyes flashed. "That's great, so he knows you then."

"Not really. I'm sure there were plenty of undergraduate students who followed him around. But I do remember he was very approachable and committed to his patients."

"Oh good. Well, my parents called Dr. Black to let him know Brad had passed away and that you might contact him to ask some questions."

"Thanks, Claire. Let's see what Dr. Black has to say about Brad's headaches."

15

After meeting with Claire, Sam ran a few errands while she was out before arriving back at her apartment complex. As she got out of her car, her phone buzzed. It was Dylan.

"Can we meet?" he said as a horn honked in the background. "There's something I need to talk to you about."

Sam took in a deep breath. Was she ready for this? She couldn't help wondering again if maybe Dylan was trying to squeeze his way back into her life even though he said he was dating someone else. He sounded concerned, though.

"Can't you just tell me over the phone?"

"I think it would be better if I showed you."

Sam checked the time. Since she had moved back to Austin and discovered James lived nearby, they had gotten into the routine of hiking nearly every Saturday morning on the greenbelt that ran behind their complex. They were supposed to leave in half an hour. And did she really want to see Dylan—not to mention letting him know where she lives?

Of course, he's a police officer, so he could look up where she lives if he wanted to, which would be creepy. She pinched her lips, chastising herself. She was over-thinking this. "Sure, you can come over."

She gave him directions to her apartment complex. He said he'd be there in ten minutes.

Sam ran up to her apartment. Maybe she could get a chart or two done before Dylan arrived.

Charts, charts, charts. Since they consumed her life when she wasn't in the clinic, she felt she had the job of a data entry clerk in addition to seeing patients. But she wanted to do a good job and make sure everything was documented so that someone else could take care of her patients if she wasn't around. Furthermore, she had to make sure her charts were complete so she could provide the necessary evidence to convince insurance companies she wasn't just ordering MRIs for no reason, as in Mrs. Rodriguez's case. Besides, she needed to remember what happened with each patient, since going from room to room and seeing as many as thirty patients a day caused some weeks to blend completely together. Honestly, if she didn't capture the details for each patient as soon as possi-ble, she hated to admit, she might confuse some facts with others. But the electronic medical record systems didn't make it easy.

Click this button, check that box. Some of her colleagues would just copy and paste the previous note, often making only a few modifications—or none—from visit to visit. That did no one any good. Even if a patient didn't have a change in their condition, a doctor should explicitly say that and come up with a plan to figure out why, or discharge the patient if they were better. The clinic could hire scribes to follow each doctor around—scribes were usually eager premed college students who were trying to learn medical terminology. But the executives at ObraCare didn't want to cut into their bottom line. Why would they need to hire two people when they could squeeze more work out of one? Instead of conforming to clicking this button and checking that box, Sam sometimes typed everything into the free text boxes. She didn't care if that screwed up their algorithms that tried to process how patients were treated. What mattered more was actually taking care of patients.

Sam typed away and was down to her last couple of charts when she heard a knock. As she opened the door, Sam said, "That was a little longer than ten—" She didn't finish her sentence when she saw it was James instead of Dylan on the other side of the door.

"Hey, Sam. I know we were planning on meeting at eleven, but I thought I'd come over a little early to talk. I'm concerned about Claire."

"So am I." Sam opened the door wider to let James in. They settled on her couch.

James let out a long exhale. "She's not letting go of this crazy idea that Brad's death and Mike's accident are connected. I know she's had a rough time and is looking for explanations."

"Yeah, I'm skeptical too. I had coffee with her this morning, and now she's focused on Todd. She thinks he has reasons to go after both Brad and Mike."

James raised his eyebrows. "Really?"

"I know. To placate her, I said I would talk to Emily tomorrow, since I was already planning on helping her package up some stuff to ship for her business while Claire was supposed to be on her honeymoon."

Sam's phone buzzed. It was a text from Dylan: *Took a little longer than expected. On my way now.*

James craned his neck to peer at her phone. "Oh, who's that?"

"It's Dylan. He's on his way over."

"So are you two ... you know?"

Sam wrinkled her nose. "Oh no. He just said he had something to tell me."

James squinted at her. "Uh, huh. Sure ..." He stood up and headed toward the door. "I'll get out of your hair then. I don't want to disrupt anything. Let me know when you're done." He smirked. "Or if I don't hear from you, that's fine too."

"It's no big deal. You can stay."

He opened the door. "No, I'll let you rekindle things with Dylan."

Sam rolled her eyes. "I told you, there's nothing going on."

"Sure there isn't. I'll catch you later."

"Okay, bye, James." Sam leaned back against the couch as he closed the door. That old familiar flutter in her stomach crept up. Was James right? Was Dylan trying to spend more time with her? No, Dylan has a girlfriend. And Sam definitely didn't want to get into a new relationship.

A knock interrupted Sam's thoughts. Okay, this time it had to be Dylan. Jeez, she hoped he wasn't just making an excuse to see her. Sam straightened her hair, then opened the door.

"Sorry I took so long. There was a fender bender I had to tend to."

"Oh, was anyone hurt?"

"No, it was pretty minor, but they wanted the police report for insurance, and I was the closest patrol."

She opened the door wider. "Please, come in. What did you need to tell me?"

Dylan sat at the dinette table. He placed a file down and opened it. "Here's what I wanted to show you."

Sam took a seat across from him. "What is it?"

Dylan pulled out some photos. They showed various angles of a car. "The insurance investigator looked at Mike's car." Dylan pointed to a dark area in one photo. "There was a hole in the exhaust pipe and in the floor of the passenger cabin right next to it."

"Really? That's unusual, isn't it?"

"Yes, especially since his car is only two years old. And it looks like something—or possibly someone—scraped and punctured these areas to create these holes."

Sam squinted at him. "You think someone did this on purpose?"

"Possibly."

"What did the investigator say?"

Dylan shrugged. "He said he couldn't rule out malicious intent."

Sam thought it sounded like a lot of radiology and pathology reports she'd seen. Suspicious mass, cannot rule out malignancy, recommend further studies … Still, she couldn't believe Dylan thought someone did this on purpose.

"So why are you here?"

"Well, considering Claire's concerns—that she thinks someone killed Brad, and now this happened with Mike— it's still too early to just say these are completely unrelated tragic accidents. It does seem too coincidental."

"Have you told Claire?"

"No."

"Then why are you telling me?"

He flattened his lips, then said, "I don't know, honestly. I haven't talked to Claire about it because this is an investigation into Mike's accident." He looked at her. "I just wanted to discuss this with someone who knows about the situation."

Sam furrowed her brow. "So the police are investigating Mike?"

"Oh, no, no." Dylan held up his hands as he tilted his head with a bit of a smirk. "The police don't have time to investigate every car accident. This is from the insurance company. It's standard procedure for them to inspect cars with significant damage that may be totaled."

"Then how did you get a copy?"

"The insurance investigator is an old buddy of mine. He used to work for the department, but with all the budget cuts, he went into the private sector. Says he should have made the move a while ago."

"Maybe there's another explanation."

"I know, but ..."

They sat in silence for a moment then Sam said, "What should we do about it?"

"What do you mean, 'we'? There's not anything to do about it right now."

Sam was confused. "You're the one who let me see the preliminary autopsy report, and you didn't have to. Now you're sharing this information about Mike's accident with me."

"No, Sam. You should stay out of it."

"Then why are you over here? Why did you tell me about this?"

"Well ..." He hesitated. "Because I'm concerned you may be in danger."

Sam wrinkled her forehead. "Why would I be in danger?"

"It seems like people around Claire, who care about Claire, are getting hurt."

"But there still may be another explanation."

"And I said I agree—that could be the case." Dylan stood up and collected the photos. "Look, I was just trying to help. But I shouldn't have come over. This was a mistake."

"Yeah, it was a mistake, because now I don't know what to think."

"Fine, I'm going. But be careful. And don't go snooping around."

Sam crossed her arms. "Don't worry about it. I've got too much else on my mind."

Dylan left without another word.

What was that all about? Dylan was sending all sorts of mixed messages, first sharing information but then telling her to stop looking into things.

She sighed. There was one thing Sam could do that wasn't directly related to any police investigation, potential or otherwise. And it was squarely in her domain.

She needed to find out more about Brad's condition before he died. Why was he having headaches? But she would have to wait until she could talk to Dr. Black on Monday.

16

S am hiked with James on the greenbelt behind their apartment complex after Dylan left, then they picked up lunch at Taco Deli and headed back to her apartment. While they ate, Sam told James about Dylan's visit, even though James had bugged Sam about it when they were on the trail. But she'd held out until lunch because she wanted to see James's reaction.

"I thought he might be drinking the same Kool-Aid as Claire," Sam said.

"Nah, sounds like he's just trying to come up with an excuse to see you."

"By saying that someone may have created a hole in Mike's car? That's not a very romantic way to go about it."

James shrugged. "I'm just sayin'. Men do weird things when they're in hot pursuit." Then he bit into his taco.

After James left, Sam checked her email. Dr. Taylor had sent her a message, apologizing for the cancellation with a new time proposed for the following Wednesday. So Sam still didn't know what was going on or why he had forwarded that announcement. She took a deep breath. She would just have to wait.

Only a few more charts, then she would be all caught up. Sam laughed. Maybe she should consider Lisa's idea about joining a start-up.

THE NEXT MORNING, Sam met Emily at the storefront for the shop she and Claire were opening in a few weeks. The shop was located in South Austin, on the edge of touristy South Congress Avenue, which had lately been shortened to SoCo by the hipsters. With Austin constantly hosting festivals and conventions, there was no shortage of people ready and willing to stay and spend their money in the funky shops and trendy restaurants along that stretch of road. Fortunately, the area was quiet since it was Sunday, so Sam found a spot to park right out front.

Brown paper covered the windows from the inside, and the logo and lettering on the door announced "SoCo Sweets" in a stylized script.

Sam rapped on the door. A couple walking their dog nodded at her as she waited.

After a few moments, the latch clanked, and Emily opened the door.

"Thanks again for offering to help. I can't believe how much this business is growing," Emily said with a smile.

"Wow, Emily! What a great location. How did you find it?" Sam asked as she stepped inside.

"Todd learned the previous tenants were filing for bankruptcy, but they had signed a five-year lease, so they were dying to get out of it. We're subletting it from them at the rates they negotiated three years ago. Needless to say, rent has gone way up, so the only thing on the market that we could afford would be way outside town. We hope to capitalize on the traffic from tourists visiting the area and staying at all these boutique hotels around here."

"That's wonderful," Sam said as she took in the clutter from construction. Several bistro tables and chairs were stacked in a corner, along with some lumber, and a counter with a display case ran along the back of the room.

"Thanks." Emily took a deep breath. "It will be a lot of work. Todd's got a line on someone at a boutique hotel that I can talk to about featuring our soaps in their guest rooms. I'm hoping that will give us a boost, so we can keep this thing going."

"You seem a bit doubtful."

"I'm just trying to be perfectly honest with myself. I know most small businesses fail, and everyone else is going the opposite direction—from physical store to digital." Emily shrugged. "If this doesn't work, I'll still have the online business. Anyway, let me show you around."

Emily explained her plans to add shelves displaying products in the front, and then she took Sam through an opening in the counter to a doorway leading to the back room. Stainless steel tables lined the walls, along with a cooktop and an oven. A large marble-topped table took up the center of the room, and a small desk was wedged between the back door and a refrigerator. Various boxes of soap-making supplies sat atop some tables, while neatly wrapped soaps lay on others. Hints of lavender, rose, and berries lingered in the air.

"We're keeping most of this equipment because I can use it to make my soaps. It's not much, but it's a start. And this is a lot better than using our kitchen at home."

Sam looked around the room, taking everything in. "I

think this is great. I wouldn't know what to do if I wanted to create a business."

"They don't teach you how to set up a practice in medical school?"

"Are you kidding? There's no business stuff at all in med school or residency. We have to figure it all out on our own. I guess that's why so many doctors just go work for an established practice or chain of clinics." Sam looked around. "So what do you want to start with?"

"Let's see how many orders we have."

Emily leaned over the desk and logged on to the laptop. She printed out several stacks of mailing labels and shipping slips, then showed Sam how to fulfill each order.

As they worked, Sam asked, "Have you talked to Claire?"

"I asked her if she was up to joining us today, but she said her parents wanted her to go to church with them."

"That's understandable."

Emily lowered her voice. "And I think they're meeting with the pastor one last time to go over Brad's funeral arrangements."

Sam pressed her lips together. The funeral was the next day. Fortunately, she'd been able to find someone to cover for her in the clinic. Then she inquired, "How's Todd taking this? He and Brad were pretty close."

"Pretty well, actually. I'm not really certain they were the best of friends. You remember how Brad was in high school. Todd ... let's just say Todd tolerated him."

"But Todd gave Brad a job, right?"

"He did. Kind of as a favor to Claire, because she's such a good friend of mine. And, surprisingly, Brad was doing pretty well. He had just closed that Volker deal, which was a relief to Todd too." She looked down. "Because, well, you know about his ... issues."

"You mean his gambling?"

Emily made a small nod as she tied a bit of twine around a stack of soaps.

"I had suspected," Sam said, "but I didn't know for sure. How has Todd been doing?"

"Todd got some help through a gambling addiction program." Emily paused a beat. "And as far as I know, he hasn't been to any casinos recently. He even let me put software on his devices to monitor access to online gambling sites." She sighed. "He had run up a lot of debt, but he was going to use some of the proceeds of the Volker deal to pay off the rest of his loans."

"And to pay for your trip?"

Emily smiled. "And to pay for our trip."

Sam spread her arms. "What about this place?"

"Believe it or not, I've made enough money from the online business to pay for the construction costs and rent for at least three months. So even if we don't have a lot of foot traffic for the business, I can keep this place going."

"I'm so impressed. I don't think I could ever do anything like this."

Emily put her hand on Sam's shoulder. "Don't sell yourself short."

They worked a while longer, and finally Sam garnered the courage to ask the question she hoped would put Claire's suspicions about Todd to rest.

"I don't mean to pry, but I was wondering ... what happens to Brad's commission, you know ... now that he's gone."

Emily looked up at the ceiling, tapping her finger to her lips. "That's a good question. I don't know. You'll have to ask Todd. He was the broker on this deal, and I think they were going to split the commission, but now ... well, I guess Todd would get his half of the commission too."

"Huh," Sam said. She really didn't want to dig too deeply into Emily and Todd's situation, but this could've provided a reason for Todd wanting Brad out of the way.

17

S am and James arrived at the church for Brad's funeral the following day. It was a megachurch, typical of those found in Texas, although this one was actually fairly modest as far as size was concerned, with a congregation of around five thousand. They navigated the maze of corridors to the church's auditorium. Along the way, Sam recognized many a forgotten face. The names were so distant that her mind cast multiple lines into the sea of her memory, hoping to catch them but only able to reel in one or two along with a class or activity they had once shared. Unlike Claire, she did not actively seek out connections with old schoolmates, and in fact, Claire and James were the only two she kept in touch with on a regular basis. She had just recently reconnected with Emily because of her duties as a bridesmaid, and she had to admit she enjoyed talking with Emily after being so intensely focused on medicine.

She followed James into the auditorium, and they chose seats in the back row. Far down below them, Claire sat between Mike and her parents, with Emily and Todd in the row behind them. Sam wondered what it was like now that Claire was focusing on Todd as a possible culprit for Brad's death and Mike's accident. Had she told anyone else of her suspicions?

Sam sighed. Given her feelings about Brad, she didn't really want to be there, but she wanted to support Claire. If nothing else, she figured this could be a way for her to observe Todd, now that she knew he had a possible motive. He draped his arm around Emily, who dabbed her eyes with a tissue.

As the lights dimmed, James said under this breath, "What a bunch of posers."

Sam blinked. "I'm sorry?"

"What a bunch of posers. How many of these people have seen Brad since high school?"

She shrugged. "I don't know. I do know that I haven't seen most of them since high school either."

"Exactly. But for some reason, when tragedy happens, people have to act like they were personally involved."

Sam couldn't completely disagree with that, although she thought it wasn't as nefarious as James made it out to be. She thought people just wanted a connection, and maybe those connections were a way to find meaning.

Like her, James didn't want to be there, but Claire had asked Sam to make sure he came.

"Are you kidding?" he had said when she asked him to go with her. "You want me to go to the funeral of the person who bullied me and made my life miserable for years?"

"But the funeral isn't really for Brad. I'm going, not for Brad, but for Claire." No, definitely not for Brad, she'd thought.

"You know," James had said, shaking his head, "I've often wondered if Claire and I would have been friends if circumstances were different. I have the feeling that if we hadn't been neighbors she wouldn't have given me the time of day."

"Oh, James. You could be hypothetical about everything to the point of being a nihilist." She had taken his hand. "What matters is she cares about you and loves you now. So could you come with me for Claire's sake—and for mine?"

So James relented, and Sam was grateful for his company, even though when she glanced over at him, he had a scowl on his face.

Remembrances and eulogies filled the service, with videos from all the major phases of Brad's life appearing on a massive center screen and still images cycling on two side screens. The production quality was quite impressive, but Sam wasn't surprised given the surroundings, which were more like a concert hall than a church. The speakers said such wonderful things about Brad—what a great friend he was, how much he cared for others. If you believed everything they said, you would have had the impression that Brad was a saint. And he certainly wasn't —certainly not after the way he'd treated James. And certainly not after he had destroyed Sam's view of life.

One of the side screens displayed a snapshot of Claire and Brad sitting on the couch in the game room at the home where they grew up, both wearing braces and beaming at the camera. Sam recalled that night when the first cracks had formed in her idealized perspective of the world—that night in the Johnson's game room.

Sam closed her eyes and steadied her breath. No. She didn't want to go there now. There was no point.

The service had ended, and everyone began to exit the auditorium. James took her hand. "Come on. Let's go."

As they made their way to the parking lot, Sam heard

her name. She turned to see Jessica Reynolds, someone she did remember immediately. Jessica gave Sam a big hug. "Isn't this just awful?"

Sam tentatively returned the hug. The last time Sam had seen Jessica was about a week into their freshman year of college. They had been in band together and were friendly enough in high school, but when Jessica had seen Sam at the university-wide orientation, she'd latched on to Sam, like she was a life-saving floatation device in the sea of unknown faces. They had hung out a few times, but when Jessica had met new friends, she'd ghosted Sam. There wasn't officially a term for that behavior back then, but that's exactly what it was—ghosting. Maybe James wasn't too far off in his assessment of these old high school acquaintances.

Jessica let go of Sam, then grabbed the hand of the man standing next to her. "This is my husband, Matt." She gave him an adoring look. "He's a cardiologist."

Matt extended his hand and said, "Good to meet you."

Sam shook his hand then stepped back to include James in the conversation, but he stayed put, giving her a surreptitious eye roll.

Jessica cocked her head and said, "Sam's father is a cardiologist too. And so is Sam, right?"

"Well, I'm not a cardiologist."

Matt raised his eyebrows. "Oh, what's your specialty?"

"I work at an urgent care clinic."

He gave a slight nod, wrinkling his nose as his gaze drifted above Sam's head.

James tugged at Sam's arm. "We need to go." He then gave Jessica a huge, fake smile. "Such a *pleasure* to see you again."

Sam drove the two of them to the cemetery, located a couple of miles away from the church. The group attending the graveside service had shrunken considerably in size, mainly with members of the would-be wedding party in attendance. This gave Sam a chance to observe Todd up close. He squeezed Emily's hand as his eyes glistened, and Sam thought at one point he tried to hold back a sob.

Claire buried her face in Mike's chest. He held her head with his hand, staring off at the distant hills. He didn't look as upset as Todd, but then again, he had only gotten to know Brad recently.

Sam's gaze drifted to Claire's parents, their posture closely resembling their daughter's and fiancé's, with one big difference. Tears streamed down Mr. Johnson's face, and he made no attempt to hide them or wipe them away. How awful it must be to bury your only son.

Then it struck Sam: Father's Day had been yesterday. How much more painful it must be for Mr. Johnson, being reminded the whole day, a day meant to celebrate his relationships with his children, now left with a void. Then Sam thought of her father, briefly. She had sent him a card and tried to have lunch with him, but he was out of town with his new girlfriend. How could he be dating again, so soon after her mother passed away?

AFTER THE FUNERAL, the group gathered at the Pearsons' house for lunch. They were friends of the Johnsons and lived just one street over in the same neighborhood. Sam trudged up the steep driveway, helping Emily carry the catered trays she had picked up from Whole Foods. Once in the kitchen, the two of them lined up the food on the island.

The Johnsons had moved to what used to be a retirement community west of Austin, in the hills with the river snaking around them. But as the city grew, so did the suburbs, with more and more young families displacing retirees.

Claire came over to Sam as Emily finished arranging everything. "Thanks so much for coming to the service and for dragging James along. It means so much to me."

Then she lowered her voice and put her hand on Sam's elbow to guide her toward the living room. "I'm so sorry about the other day. I may have been a little too hasty pointing the finger at Todd." Claire glanced over her shoulder into the dining room where Todd was talking to her parents. "Emily and Todd have been so supportive." She hung her head. "I'm just looking for answers."

Sam embraced Claire and rubbed her back. "It's only natural to look for answers." She paused a moment. "In fact, if it's still okay, I'm going to speak with Dr. Black this afternoon to learn more about the headaches Brad was having."

Claire shuddered as she took a breath, then looked up. "Thanks. You don't have to if you don't want to. I've asked too much of you."

"No, it's all right. And I do want to." Sam meant it. She wanted to know, to learn from another clinician how Brad was doing before he'd died—and from someone outside the family who could be objective.

18

D r. Alan Black's office was not far from Sam's apartment. Typical of this part of Austin, the medical complex was much larger than it looked from the road. It had several buildings nestled in the hill-side, with live oak trees providing shade and privacy.

Sam entered the office and stood in line to speak to the receptionist. There were several patients scattered about the waiting room, some reading magazines but most on their phones.

The man in front of Sam finished checking in and turned to find a seat.

"Can I help you?" a lady in turquoise scrubs asked from behind the desk.

"Yes, I'm here to see Dr. Black. I'm Dr. Jenkins. I spoke with him on the phone, and he should be expecting me."

"Oh yes, Dr. Jenkins. Come on back." She stood and let Sam in through a door beside the desk.

Sam followed her to an office at the end of a hallway. "Please have a seat," the receptionist said, indicating the chair in front of the desk. "Dr. Black should be just a few moments. Would you like coffee or water?"

"I'm fine, thanks."

"Okay, my name is Cindy. I'm just down the hall if you need me."

"Thank you, Cindy."

Sam took in her surroundings. A window looked out over the parking lot, nestled against an embankment covered with juniper. Bookshelves lined the walls, housing many of the same volumes Sam had at home, although most of Dr. Black's books were a couple of editions older. Framed pictures of a silver-haired man with his wife and two grown daughters sat on the credenza behind the desk. The last time Sam had seen Dr. Black, he was more salt-and-pepper than silver.

"Hello, Samantha. Or I guess I should say, Dr. Jenkins."

Sam stood and extended her hand. "Good afternoon, Dr. Black. And please, call me Sam. Thank you for seeing me."

"You're quite welcome." He shook Sam's hand, then motioned for her to sit back down as he settled behind his desk. "It's so good to see you again. When was the last time? You were still in college, right?"

"Yes, I believe so. You were a big influence in helping me to decide to go to medical school. Thanks so much for letting me shadow you."

"I'm flattered. I enjoy having young up-and-comers visit me. It feels good to pay it forward for the next generation of clinicians, and to help the daughter of a colleague. By the way, how's your father?"

When Sam had shadowed Dr. Black, he hadn't known Sam's father at that time. When he asked Sam why she was interested in medicine, she had told him about her father, who was part of a small cardiology practice. "Well, now I've got a reason to refer patients to him," Dr. Black had said.

Sam wasn't certain she really wanted to be a doctor until the day she'd shadowed Dr. Black. That was when she decided to apply to medical school, when she finally saw what a doctor could be, not the flashy doctors on TV and not the distant man who was her father. Seeing someone who seemed to care for both his patients and his family, and who had that affection fully returned, convinced her she could do it and not become like her father.

"He's doing fine," Sam answered, even though she wasn't exactly certain how her father was doing, except that he had been out of town with his girlfriend. In fact, she had only seen him a handful of times since her mother had passed away the year before. Images of her mother flooded her mind. She blinked. Not now.

She sat up. "So Brad came to see you a couple of weeks ago?"

"Yes. I was surprised to learn he passed away. He seemed to be a fit young man with a lot of promise."

"I was quite stunned too. Actually, I was there when he died." Her eyes misted up. She knew, however, she wasn't reacting to Brad's death, since he hadn't been one of her favorite people. But rather, the memory of her mother having recently passed away had stirred her emotions.

Dr. Black pulled a tissue from the box on his desk and handed it to her.

Sam dabbed her eyes. "I'm sorry. I didn't think it would affect me." Naturally, she wasn't going to let Dr. Black know what had really upset her. Heat filled her cheeks. She breathed in and blinked again. "I've known Brad a long time, and his sister is one of my best friends. I guess I just feel really bad for her and their parents."

"I'm so sorry, Sam," he said with a gentle tone. "We deal with life and death all the time, and we figure out ways to compartmentalize it. But when it's someone close to you ..." He paused, then looked up. "Well, how can I help?"

"I was wondering if you could tell me a little more about why Brad came to see you."

Dr. Black sat back in his chair. "I suppose it's okay to share this with you, being a friend of the family and a physician to boot. Back in the old days, we didn't have all these regulations to worry about." He half smiled and leaned toward his computer to peck at the keyboard. "Let's see ... He was a new patient to me, although his parents have been patients of mine for years. He said he was having headaches periodically. No unusual findings on the neuro exam. So from the history he gave, my differential included cluster headaches vs. migraines vs. plain old tension-type headaches. He complained of severe pain behind his right eye, some photophobia and nausea, but no aura."

"And did you send off any labs?"

"Just the usual, a comprehensive metabolic and CBC along with pituitary function tests, just to make sure there wasn't an underlying adenoma. You know how nonspecific headaches can be. Could be anything causing them. Anyway, the results came back a couple of days later, everything within normal limits. Why do you ask?"

"I was wondering if it might have anything to do with how he died."

Dr. Black leaned forward, furrowing his brow and placing his elbows on his desk. "The family isn't thinking about a lawsuit, are they? He was a healthy young man, and his exam was normal as were his labs."

Sam held up her hands with open palms. "No, please

don't get the wrong idea, Dr. Black. I'm sure you know about Brad's history of drug use."

He leaned back. "Yes, he did mention that he was a recovering addict. Said he'd been clean for over a year. So we discussed how there may be a link to cluster headaches and drug use. I read a recent study that there seems to be a higher prevalence of drug use in patients with cluster headaches. Although it's hard to tell cause and effect— whether the patients are using the illicit drugs to treat the headaches or whether the headaches are triggered by the drugs."

"Yes, I remember: Always treat the substance abuse first because it can imitate or mask an organic disorder."

"Exactly. But in Brad's case, I don't think the two were related. He seemed sincere when he said he was clean and sober. And the headaches had only started about two months ago."

"That's interesting. But when Brad died, my first thought was that maybe he overdosed, because of his history."

"It makes sense." Dr. Black steepled his fingers. "Unfortunately many people recovering from substance abuse struggle with cravings their whole lives. And relapses are common. I planned on discussing this more with him at his follow-up appointment."

"Yes, so you see why I thought it was a possibility he might have overdosed. But Claire, Brad's sister, was told that the preliminary results showed that Brad had died of a myocardial infarction."

Dr. Black raised his eyebrows. "Well, that isn't consistent with the substance he told me he used, which was prescription opiates. And I didn't see any indication of heart disease—his lipid panel looked fine." He scratched his chin. "Of course, I didn't do an EKG or any other cardiac workup since they weren't indicated. But still, there were no overt signs."

"Right. But maybe he used another drug instead."

"Yes, cocaine or methamphetamines could cause a myocardial infarction. And addicts do switch drugs at times. Has the family heard anything else from the medical examiner's office?"

"No. I think they're waiting for the toxicology results."

He nodded. "Toxicology tests do take a bit of time. I guess we'll just have to wait to know for sure."

"I agree. I just wanted to make sure there wasn't anything obvious we're missing. You see, I think Claire's in a bit of denial right now, and that's the real reason she asked me to look into this. I'll let her know there wasn't anything that can provide answers just yet." Sam stood up and grabbed her purse off the floor. "Anyway, thanks again for your time."

Sam extended her hand. Dr. Black stood and shook it. "Sure, I'm happy to help. Let me know if you need anything else," he said as he followed her out the door.

Sam stopped in the hallway. "Oh, I do have one more question. Where would Brad have gone for the lab tests?"

"There's a lab collection center on the first floor by the elevators. Why do you ask?"

Sam didn't want to let on that she had seen the autopsy report. "I just noticed he had a couple of venipuncture wounds on his arm when he died. Not too unusual, but just wondering why he was stuck twice, being that he was young and healthy."

"Hmm. I wouldn't know. But I'm sure you can talk to the tech who drew his blood."

"Okay. Thanks again, Dr. Black."

Sam took the elevator down to the first floor, found the lab collection office, and approached the front desk. "Hi, I was wondering if I could talk to someone about a patient that came here last week."

The lady sitting behind the desk looked up from her computer. "I'm sorry, but we cannot talk about any patients that come here. You know, for privacy reasons."

"Sure, but ..." Sam lowered her voice. "This patient passed away last week. I'm a friend of the family and a doctor. I was just wondering if I could speak to the tech who drew his blood."

"I'm sorry, but we can't discuss this with you." She looked over her shoulder. "You can talk to my manager, if you'd like."

Sam nodded. "That would be great."

"Wait just a second and I'll get her."

A few moments later, she returned with another woman in a tailored shirt. "Hi, ma'am. How can I help you?"

"I was wondering if I could talk to the tech who drew the blood on a patient last week."

"Well, we aren't allowed to give out any information on our patients. You know, HIPAA and all that."

"Yes, ma'am. I'm a doctor, so I'm well aware. But I'm not asking about any specific medical information on this patient." She leaned forward and lowered her voice again. "He passed away recently, and I'm a friend of the family. I already know what labs were ordered and the results, because I just came from Dr. Black's office upstairs."

The manager's expression softened a little. "Okay, so why do you need to speak with the tech?"

"Well, I noticed he had two venipuncture wounds in his left antecubital fossa, but he was a young man. His veins were in pretty good shape, so I was wondering why he was stuck twice."

"Hmm, that is puzzling. There must have been some

reason. We document everything, so if he was stuck twice, that would have been noted on the requisition form." The manager paused. "You know what? I'll just take a quick look and let you know. I don't see how it would cause any harm letting you know something like that. What was the patient's name and date of birth?"

Sam gave her the information. "Have a seat. I'll be back," the manager said as she turned toward her office.

A couple of minutes later, she appeared again at the front desk.

"He came in Thursday a week ago." She looked down at the req form. "No issues with venipuncture."

Sam's eyebrows raised. "You're sure?"

"Yes, one of our best phlebotomists performed the draw. And she definitely would have noted if she needed to stick him twice, you know, since a lot of older people have tricky veins. But you're right, he was young, and he was only stuck once."

"Hmm. That's strange." Could the autopsy report be wrong? No, not on something like that. "He definitely had two venipuncture wounds."

The manager shrugged. "Well, maybe he had to get another set of labs drawn somewhere else. We only show him coming here the one time. And if he needed a second stick, we would have noted it."

19

After leaving the lab, Sam sat in her car in the parking garage to gather her thoughts. If the phlebotomist didn't stick Brad twice, why did he have two venipuncture wounds on his arm? Sam was confused.

Plus, she hadn't expected her reaction when Dr. Black asked about her father, which then triggered memories of her mother.

Sam's father had pushed her to become a cardiologist like him, and until she had spent a day shadowing Dr. Black, she wasn't even certain she wanted to be a doctor. Her father was hardly ever home, and when he was, his foul mood usually engulfed him.

When Sam went to college, her mother told her she could do whatever she wanted. She just wanted Sam to be happy. When Sam said she wanted to help others, her mother replied, "Being a doctor isn't the only way."

But Sam joined the premedical society, as was expected of her, and eventually came to shadow Dr. Black one day. Seeing how much Dr. Black's patients appreciated him finally convinced her that being a doctor was right for her. And when she was accepted to medical school, she felt her father finally recognized her, and she finally had an actual relationship with him—a grown-up relationship.

That period was short-lived, lasting only through the first couple of years of medical school, before she started her clinical rotations. General surgery was her second rotation, known to have grueling hours and to be grueling on the body. While she fought her interest, not wanting to follow the path to surgery because she knew it would dominate her life, eventually she decided that's what she wanted to do. Her father, on the other hand, looked down at surgeons. "They're so unintellectual," he would say. "They just cut and then dump all the patient's problems on the internists." Their budding relationship became distant again.

By then she had met Jeff at a party thrown by one of her medical school classmates. He was the host's roommate and worked for a software company. They started dating, then became more serious. They got engaged after dating for a year and moved in together. Things were great during her fourth year of medical school. In the fall of that year, she finished up her electives and applied to residency programs. She traveled around to interview at the programs interested in her, and by the spring, with all her coursework essentially complete, she and her classmates just waited for match day. Jeff's schedule was fairly flexible, so they frequently took long weekends, traveling around the country, visiting friends.

Perhaps Jeff expected Sam to continue having free time, because once she started her general surgery residency, their relationship soured. The long hours strained their connection to each other, and one evening, right after she had called Jeff to tell him she would be home soon, a patient on her service took a turn for the worse. She had to transfer the patient to the ICU. She worked for several hours to stabilize her patient, and by the time she got home, she found Jeff drunk, looking at old photos. "Is this how it's always going to be?" he asked. "I need you here with me. I don't want a wife that doesn't put me first."

Then her mother developed endometrial cancer. Her mom came to Houston for treatment at MD Anderson Cancer Center, and that stressed Sam's relationship with Jeff even more. Every free minute she had while she wasn't taking care of patients, she spent visiting her mother.

Ultimately, the cancer was too advanced. Her father had the attitude that Sam just needed to suck it up, but she could tell he was just as devastated on the inside as she was.

When her mother died just a few months after diagnosis, Sam was allowed a couple of days off to mourn, but the residency program wouldn't let her have any more time. Finally, when she insisted that she just wasn't mentally ready to continue the demanding and emotionally draining schedule, the program swapped her coveted place in the clinical track with a resident who was stuck doing research.

Sam didn't feel too badly because her clinical spot went to Amelie Cote, a foreign medical graduate who was also a fully trained surgeon from France. Amelie wasn't allowed to practice as a surgeon in the United States until she repeated her surgery residency in America. She was glad Amelie was finally moving out of residency purgatory, but now Sam's future was uncertain.

The residency program assigned Sam to a research lab, and she was stuck in limbo, waiting for a clinical spot to open up so she could complete her residency training. Even though she had more time to spend with Jeff, their relationship continued to deteriorate.

At first, things seemed to be better between them, and they reprised their long weekends traveling for the first few months. But Sam didn't want to lose her clinical acumen, so she started working *locum tenens* jobs, and that's how she began working part time for ObraCare. As Sam took on more and more shifts, she again had less and less time for Jeff.

By the time ObraCare offered Sam a full-time job in Austin, which she had not known was a possibility without completing residency, she had decided to call it quits with Jeff. They broke off their engagement, and Sam didn't feel she had the strength to keep fighting for a clinical spot in the residency program, so she took the job, looking for a fresh start.

And even though Sam's father was also in Austin, she rarely saw him. Without her mom around, there wasn't a reason. Sam's mom had been the only thing tethering Sam to her father.

A HORN BEEPED. Someone wanted Sam's parking spot. Sam blinked to clear those unexpected memories, started up her car, and navigated her way onto the freeway. She had the rest of the day off and was planning to go back to her apartment, just to zone out and relax.

She had not taken any time for herself since Brad died. And for once, she was caught up on all of her charts. But an idea tickled the back of her mind: what if Brad's headaches were from carbon monoxide exposure? She hadn't thought to mention it to Dr. Black. Even though he had said Brad's lab results were all normal, they would not have included carboxyhemoglobin, the test for carbon monoxide exposure.

How could she find out? Then she remembered the night of the wedding rehearsal. Two identical shadows, parked side by side. Brad and Mike both had Mustangs. Could there be an issue with that car model?

Sam recalled a problem with the SUVs that the Austin Police Department had used a couple of years before. It had been a big enough story to make the national news. Several police officers had complained about headaches and nausea after sitting in their cruisers for long periods, and it turned out the vehicles had loose gaskets, allowing exhaust fumes to enter the passenger compartment. Was there a similar problem with Brad's and Mike's cars?

She passed up the exit for her apartment complex and kept going. Sam wanted to talk to Claire. Maybe there was a simple but unfortunate explanation.

After pulling up in front of Claire's house, Sam put the car in park and brought up the web browser on her phone, searching to see if there were carbon monoxide issues with the Mustang. The only results she could find were stories about the Ford SUVs involved with various police departments around the country that had reported the same problem after the Austin PD broke the story.

Sam put her phone down and sat back to think. There was also the fact that Dylan showed her pictures of the holes in the bottom of Mike's car. Those certainly weren't the result of a manufacturing problem. Maybe she should talk to Dylan about this. Things didn't go well with him the other day, but if she talked to him, she might be able to reach someone at the medical examiner's office so that they could add on a carboxyhemoglobin test to the labs for Brad's autopsy.

She got out of her car, ran up the sidewalk of Claire's bungalow, and rang the doorbell. After a few barks from Kerbey, Claire answered, rubbing her eyes. "Hey, Sam."

"Hey, Claire. Sorry to bother you. I have some questions."

"Sure, I was just napping. My body clock is all messed up right now."

"That's perfectly understandable." Sam squeezed Claire's shoulder. "You've been through so much." She paused. Maybe now wasn't a good time to do this. She should let Claire rest.

But then Claire asked, "Did you find out anything at Dr. Black's office?"

"Not much. Dr. Black thought Brad was having cluster headaches or migraines, and he ordered some labs just to rule out any other issues, but all the results were normal."

Claire nodded. "Is there something else on your mind, then?"

Sam followed Claire to the couch. "Well, there are a couple of things I was thinking about. Maybe it's just my imagination looking for connections, but since Mike had that accident and suffered from carbon monoxide poisoning, maybe Brad had been exposed to it too."

"But you said Brad's lab tests were normal."

"I did, but doctors don't test for carbon monoxide exposure unless they suspect it—most commonly when someone passes out in their car."

"Like Mike did."

"Exactly. Or if there's been a fire, or if someone was using camping equipment improperly—like a few years ago, when we had that winter storm and people lost power, so they tried to stay warm with camping stoves inside. Many of them ended up in the emergency room, so that's where the tests are performed, not in an outpatient setting, like a doctor's office." Sam shrugged. "It's just not the first thing you think of when someone comes in complaining of headaches, especially if they've been having them for a few months, like Brad."

"Do you think this has been going on for a while?"

"Maybe. Do you know where Brad's car is?"

"Sure. It's over at my parents' house. We moved it there that morning after ... you know ..." Claire sniffed.

"I'm so sorry. Maybe I should just go." Sam began to get up.

"No, that's okay." Claire placed her hand on Sam's arm. "I'm the one who told you I thought someone wanted to hurt him, and I asked you to look into it. That's exactly what you're doing." She paused before asking, "So you want to check out Brad's car?"

"Yeah. Do you think your parents will mind?"

"No. They're always happy to see you. And they want to know what happened to Brad too."

"Oh, and there's another thing. Do you know if Brad went to see anyone else? Another doctor besides Dr. Black?"

"Not that I know of, but maybe my parents would know."

"Okay. Let's head over to your parents. That is, if you're up for it." Sam looked around. "Do you want to tell Mike?"

"He's not here. His boss called and asked him to take care of something at work, you know, since we would have been back from our honeymoon by now." Claire paused. "And I guess it's his way of dealing with everything."

Sam made a sad smile. "That's one way to cope." The thought that maybe this wasn't the right time crept into her head again. After all, the funeral had been just a few hours before, and here she was, asking questions, picking at a scab that needed to heal.

Claire took a deep breath. "Anyway, I'm up for

checking out Brad's car. I want to find out what happened to him. And if it's connected to Mike, then we really need to know what's going on and who's behind it."

Sam pulled out her phone. "Okay. I need to call Dylan first."

Claire raised an eyebrow. "So how are things between you two?"

"It's nothing like that." Sam pursed her lips. "Besides, he has a girlfriend, and I am *so* not ready for another relationship right now." She hesitated. Claire didn't know about the insurance investigation—at least, Sam didn't think she knew. She thought of the horns beeping in the background when Dylan last called her. "I just thought maybe he would know what to look for. You know, since he's dealt with a lot of accidents before. Plus, the police department had that problem with carbon monoxide leaks a couple of years ago."

Claire looked at her skeptically. "Sure. That makes sense."

20

Sam drove the two of them to Claire's parents' neighborhood, where they had just been earlier in the day. Tall oak trees formed a canopy over the yard in front of the Johnsons' red brick home. Brad's Mustang was parked on the driveway so as not to block the garage. Sam pulled behind Dylan's cruiser on the street and then climbed up the steep driveway.

As they approached the top, Claire said, "Let me tell Mom and Dad what's going on and get the keys." She split off and followed the sidewalk to the front door. As she disappeared into the house, Sam approached Dylan, who was already standing next to Brad's car.

Dylan pointed to the concrete seam in front of Sam. "Watch out. I almost tripped on that root."

Sam carefully stepped over the bump. Wouldn't that have been embarrassing if she tripped in front of Dylan? She straightened up and said, "Thanks for meeting us. Claire wouldn't know about the insurance investigator's findings, would she?"

"Not yet." Dylan looked at her appreciatively. "Thanks for not telling her. How did you explain things to her?"

"I just said that you're used to dealing with car accidents and such, so you would know what to look for."

Dylan nodded. "So what are you thinking here?"

"Brad saw a doctor for his headaches right before he died, so I got to wondering, what if Brad was being poisoned with carbon monoxide, like Mike? There are some cases of chronic exposure causing headaches but it's not common. And since your friend found that Mike's car had been tampered with, we might find evidence of the same type of tampering with Brad's car."

"Let's not call it tampering just yet. That still remains to be seen." Dylan looked skeptical. "But would this explain how Brad died?"

"That's the thing. It could, but if someone were to die from carbon monoxide poisoning, they would have to be exposed to pretty high levels of it. From the report, it doesn't look like the medical examiner saw any evidence of it during the autopsy. Usually if someone's been exposed to high levels of carbon monoxide, you'll see a bright red tongue among other things, because it changes the chemistry in the tissues." She tugged on her purse strap. "Honestly, I don't know if he died of carbon monoxide poisoning. But he could have been exposed, which may have caused the headaches."

"Okay. Would the medical examiner be able to check?"

"I think so. If someone comes in the hospital with suspected carbon monoxide exposure, like if they were involved in a fire, we check carboxyhemoglobin levels. It's basically hemoglobin with carbon monoxide molecules bound to them instead of oxygen."

"What does that mean?" Dylan frowned. "I never understood chemistry."

"You know how hemoglobin carries oxygen in our blood, right?"

"I kind of remember from that biology class we had to take."

"It's how our muscles, our heart, and other organs get the oxygen they need. But when you're exposed to carbon monoxide, it displaces the oxygen off the hemoglobin. So your body doesn't get the oxygen it needs."

"Like when you work out too hard?"

"Not exactly." She hesitated. She was going to explain about the difference between aerobic and anaerobic respiration, oxygen demand during exercise, and what have you. But she thought about the times she would try to explain a medical issue to someone, and their eyes would glaze over. Sam searched her mind for a better way to explain it. "Think of hemoglobin like a car that travels through your blood to carry oxygen from your lungs to the rest of your body."

"Okay."

"With carbon monoxide poisoning, it's like the carbon monoxide molecule is hijacking that hemoglobin car, so the oxygen can't get a ride. The carbon monoxide shoves it out."

"That makes sense."

"And if the concentration is high enough, if there are too many carbon monoxide molecules pushing out oxygen from those hemoglobin cars, then even the heart doesn't get enough oxygen. And the heart is a different type of muscle from most of your muscles, like the skeletal muscles in your arms and legs. So it dies pretty quickly if it doesn't get the oxygen it needs."

"So that's how carbon monoxide could cause a heart attack."

"It's a possibility." She didn't want to get into the minutiae of how it also affects the brain, among other things, for risk of losing his attention or confusing him. That was enough of a physiology lesson for now, but she was glad Dylan showed some interest. "Where did your friend find the hole? If someone did tamper with Mike's car, wouldn't they do it in the same way on Brad's car?"

"Yeah, people usually stick to the same MO." Dylan looked skeptical again. "But we'll see. In Mike's car, there was a hole in the floorboard for the rear passenger area, along with another hole in the exhaust pipe next to it."

Just then Claire came out with the keys. She clicked the fob, flashing the lights on the car. "Here you go. So what are we looking for?"

"Let's check out the floorboard below the rear passenger seats." Dylan pulled the flashlight off his belt and opened the driver's door. He unlatched the seat to hinge it forward and got down on his knees. "I don't see anything on this side. Let's check the other side."

Sam opened the passenger door and unlatched the seat on that side. Dylan bent down and inspected the floorboard. As he poked around, beads of sweat formed on Sam's brow, with the relentless rattling of cicadas engulfing her.

After a few moments, Dylan's muffled voice drifted up to Sam and Claire. "Aha! I think I found something." He extracted himself and stood up. "There might be a hole in the floorboard. It looks like it goes through, but the carpet was covering it up. We'll need someone to inspect the undercarriage to be sure."

Sam asked, "So what do you think now?"

Dylan looked at Claire as he stood up. "This is a little suspicious."

Claire stoically looked ahead. "You think he was murdered?"

Dylan held up his hand. "Well, let's not go that far yet. Sure, someone may have tried to tamper with Brad's car, or there could be something that caused this."

Claire cocked her head. "Like what?"

Dylan shrugged. "I don't know. Mustangs ride pretty low." He looked around the neighborhood. "It's pretty hilly around here. Cars bottom out all the time. And since Brad and Mike have the same model, maybe the same thing happened to both cars."

Claire squinted at Dylan. "How do you know Mike had a Mustang?"

Sam jumped in before Dylan could answer. "I told him. That's why I wanted to check out Brad's car. I was thinking about how they had the same type of car and how they sometimes have the same problems."

Claire slowly nodded. "Okay. What do we do with this?"

"I know someone who could do a more thorough inspection of Brad's car, if you'd like." He looked at Sam, and she wondered if it was his same friend who was investigating Mike's accident for the insurance company.

"I'm so confused." Claire put her hands over her face and rubbed her eyelids. Then she said, "Sure. Let's have your friend look at the car."

They went inside the house so that Dylan could write down his friend's contact information. The crisp air conditioning cascaded over them, allowing them to breathe again after standing in the Texas heat. "Mom, this is Dylan. You probably don't remember, but he went to high school with us."

"Nice to meet you, Dylan," Mrs. Johnson said as she looked at his nameplate on his uniform. Her eyes were red, no doubt from the events of the day. "What did you find? Is this something for the police?"

Sam took Mrs. Johnson's hand and led her to the couch to sit down. "I'm afraid this is my doing. I talked to Dr. Black this afternoon about Brad's headaches, and then I got to thinking about Mike's accident."

She went on to explain her theory about how Brad may have been exposed to carbon monoxide just like Mike, and since they had the same type of car, there might be an issue that had affected both cars.

By then Claire had joined them on the couch. "Dylan thinks he might have found something in Brad's car. He knows someone who can look into it more."

Mrs. Johnson's eyes widened but she said nothing. Sam wanted to ask her if Brad had seen another doctor, but her flat affect made Sam hesitate.

Then Claire said, "Mom, Sam was wondering if Brad saw any other doctors last week."

Mrs. Johnson furrowed her eyebrows. "Why's that, Sam?"

"Dr. Black had ordered lab tests, but it looked like Brad may have had blood drawn twice. I talked to someone at the lab collection center, and she said he was only stuck once."

"No, I don't think he went to another doctor."

Sam tugged at her ear. Maybe the phlebotomist just forgot to note the second stick. It still didn't make sense to Sam that Brad would be stuck twice, but sometimes these things happen.

She thought of a time when she was a medical student. She had to draw blood on a patient with good veins, but she ended up sticking him twice. After Sam had filled up one tube of blood, she pulled the needle out of the patient's vein and disposed of it in the sharps container. But then the resident supervising her pointed out she needed to draw more than one tube. Flustered, she stuck the poor patient again to get the second tube of blood, apologizing profusely. She had been glad that this wasn't something doctors normally did, unless they chose to go into anesthesiology. So perhaps something similar had happened with Brad. The manager had said the phlebotomist who drew Brad's blood was one of their best, but even the best get distracted.

So she left it at that, not wanting to cause any more pain or concern. Mrs. Johnson needed to grieve, and Sam had already done enough to stir things up on the day of her son's funeral.

21

"Good afternoon, Mrs. Rodriguez," Sam said as she closed the exam room door. "Any change in your arm since I saw you last?"

A week had already passed since Mrs. Rodriguez's previous visit, and as far as Sam could tell, the only thing that had changed was the faxed message she held in her hand.

"No, Dr. Jenkins. It's the same. My work doesn't have light duty for me, so I'm just sitting at home. Sure, I'm getting workers' comp, but it's only seventy percent of my normal wages, and I was planning on working extra shifts over the summer to give Christina some extra money when she starts school in the fall. Now I can't."

"I'm so sorry, ma'am. I know it's frustrating. But haven't you gotten a phone call?"

Mrs. Rodriguez hung her head. "No. I haven't heard anything."

"Hmm. Well, I just got a fax from the insurance company—and I'm sorry they didn't call you—but since I knew you were coming in today, I had one of our MAs reach out to them. They finally approved your MRI."

"At last." Mrs. Rodriguez's shoulders relaxed. "What's next?"

"Let's make sure we get you scheduled today, so there are no other delays."

"And then what happens? Do you think this numbness I'm feeling is going to be permanent?"

"We'll have to see. I'm sorry it's taking so long, and I know it's distressing for you."

Mrs. Rodriguez smiled. "Oh, sweetie, it's not your fault. You're doing what you can."

"I appreciate it, Mrs. Rodriguez." Sam quickly examined her, so she could document there had been no change in her condition. They chatted a little more, then finished up the visit.

As they left the room and walked toward the check-out area, Sam glanced at the board. Fortunately, Mrs. Rodriguez was the last patient of the day, and the board was clear, with all rooms marked as empty. She filled out an order form for a local imaging company, then took the form to Cynthia, instructing her to make an appointment for Mrs. Rodriguez and give the information to her before she left.

As Sam sat down at her workstation, Jill walked up, a sly smile on her face as she leaned over and whispered, "Dr. Jenkins, that handsome police officer is back. Is there something going on between you two?"

Sam looked at Jill. "No. He's an old friend from high school, and one of our mutual friends ended up in the hospital the other day." She really didn't want to get into the details with her.

The smile slipped off Jill's face, and she straightened up. "Oh, okay. Do you want me to bring him back?"

Sam looked at the time. "I'm almost done here anyway. Let me finish this note, and then I'll come out to the lobby to meet him."

"I'll let him know, Dr. Jenkins," Jill said as she turned away.

Sam quickly typed up the note for Mrs. Rodriguez. Even though the MRI had been approved, she did not want any reason for the insurance company to delay things further. She looked at the outstanding notes in the EHR. She would just have to log in and finish the rest up tonight.

She headed out toward the lobby and found Dylan sitting in one of the chairs. Thankfully, the room was empty, and the ladies working reception had taken off as soon as the clock hit five.

"Hi, Dylan. To what do I owe this pleasure?" She plopped down in the chair next to him.

He smiled. "Oh, so now it's a pleasure to see me?"

Sam picked at a button on her coat. "It's just good to see you."

"The question is: How are you? You look rather stressed out. And I'm afraid what I'm about to tell you may stress you out further."

Sam raised her eyebrows. "What do you mean?"

"My buddy examined the floorboard of Brad's car, and it appears that the hole there is the same size and shape as the one they found in Mike's car. And there's a hole in the exhaust pipe as well, just like in Mike's car. He's going to analyze the markings around the holes."

Sam sat up. "So Brad's death and Mike's accident might be linked after all."

"It looks that way. That's why I'm here. I'm concerned about you. I'd like to have Eric check out your car to make sure nothing's been tampered with."

"Are they ruling Brad's death a murder?"

"No. And even if they find his car was tampered with, it's not a contributing factor to his death. I spoke with the ME about that, and he said there weren't any signs of carbon monoxide poisoning at autopsy."

"Are you sure?"

"Well, that's what he told me."

"Hmm." She thought for a moment, wondering if carboxyhemoglobin remained stable long enough to test in a blood specimen after a couple of weeks. "Is the ME going to add on any labs to check?"

She had muttered the question to herself, but Dylan shook his head. "I have no idea."

"Sorry, I just have a lot of questions about this. I'll do some research and see if I can find some answers on my own."

"Okay. I don't really understand much more than what you told me the other day. But isn't carbon monoxide poisoning more immediate? If it did kill him, how would he have died in his room?"

"Well, I need to figure out how long it would take for carbon monoxide to build up to levels that lead to death. And then how long it would take for those levels to drop without any treatment. I'm sure there are some studies I could find." Sam put her hand over her mouth. "What about Claire? Do you think she's in danger?"

"I am also worried about Claire. But Eric, my buddy who works with the insurance company, already checked her car, and he didn't find anything."

"And what about her parents? We should let them know."

"Eric checked their cars too. They were fine."

Sam stood up and grabbed her keys out of her purse. "I need to talk to Claire." She checked her watch.

"Wait. Eric is on his way here to check out your car. I

don't want to risk your driving right now if your car's been tampered with." Dylan checked his phone and grimaced. " He just texted and said he's tied up with a case right now, so we'll have to wait."

Sam took a deep breath. "Don't you think you're being paranoid? Why would someone want to hurt me?"

"You're worried about Claire."

"I am, but she's got a direct connection to two people who actually had their cars tampered with. I don't."

"That's true, but we don't know everything about the situation yet. The safest thing would be to take a look at your car, just in case."

"I don't want to sit around here waiting. I have plans tonight." Claire had asked Sam to meet her at the soap shop, but Sam was hoping Dylan might think she actually had a date. "How long is your friend going to be?"

"It might be awhile. Why don't I give you a ride?" Dylan checked his watch. "But I have to start my shift in an hour. Do you think you can get home afterward?"

Okay, so Dylan didn't bite on thinking she had a date. Sam crossed her arms. "I don't want to be stuck without a car."

"You could just Uber."

Sam felt like she was losing control. "I don't want to Uber. You're making too big of a deal about this." She stood up. "I'm leaving."

Dylan also stood. "Will you at least let me take a quick look at your car?"

Sam flared her nostrils. "Fine."

22

After Dylan checked out Sam's car at the clinic and didn't find any evidence of tampering, Sam drove to the storefront Emily and Claire had leased for their soap shop. She circled around the block, trying to avoid the pedestrians ambling about, finally finding a spot in front of a bungalow that was wedged between two construction sites on one of the side streets off South Congress. This neighborhood, like most of Austin, was undergoing a transformation, as techies relocated in droves from the Bay Area, attracted to the jobs and relatively low-cost housing. Someday Sam would need to think about finding a house, but by then would she be able to afford it? Probably not in an area like this, where she could walk to so many shops and restaurants. But then she thought, as she walked past the line of cars in the street, she wouldn't want to deal with a bunch of random strangers parking in front of her home.

When Sam got to the storefront, she rapped on the front door, and a moment later, Mike swung the door open, welcoming her into the shop.

"I'm just waiting for the boss to show up, so she can give me instructions," Mike said with a grin.

Sam chuckled. "So Claire's keeping you in line, huh?"

He motioned to a stack of boxes in the corner. "Yeah, she ordered me to bring a bunch of stuff over. She should be here soon."

"I guess you've fully recovered if she's got you lifting boxes. Are you still sore?" Sam looked him over with a clinical eye. Mike didn't seem like he was favoring anything as he moved about.

"Not too bad. I don't notice it much unless I reach for something with my left arm. Then I feel just a twinge right here." He rubbed his left collarbone.

"Yeah, that's probably from the shoulder belt locking when you crashed."

"That makes sense." He leaned on the counter that ran across the back of the room. "Thanks again for being such a good friend through all of this. Claire really trusts you."

"Of course. We've been through a lot together, and she was always there for me when everything happened last year. She seems to be doing okay, though. What do you think?"

"Sure, I suppose she's managing. I'm glad this shop is giving her something to focus on, to give her a creative outlet—"he frowned—"especially since she seems to be getting all riled up about someone being behind Brad's death."

"I have to agree." Sam rolled her eyes. "I'm afraid her imaginative ideas have spread to one of my old boyfriends."

Mike squinted. "Do you mean that police officer?"

"Yeah, Dylan." Sam huffed. "He insisted on checking out my car just before I got here."

He raised his eyebrows. "Why?"

"I'm afraid some of it is my doing. After your accident —you know, since you were exposed to carbon monoxide …" Sam's words trailed off as she paused for a moment, not sure if Mike knew about the insurance investigation. "Well, after we found out you had been exposed to carbon monoxide, I got to thinking that maybe Brad had been too. You know, since he was having headaches and …"

"And?"

"Since you both have—or had—the same model car, and they ride pretty low."

"Yeah, I was bottoming out all the time in that Mustang, especially in the hilly areas." He turned around to face the counter, flicking the corners of a notepad next to the cash register. "So that police officer—what was his name again?"

"Dylan."

"So Dylan wanted to check out your car?"

"Yeah, he checked out my car, and of course he didn't find anything." She sighed. "Honestly, I think he just wanted an excuse to see me. We dated in high school for a little bit. And since Claire called him to see if he could connect me with someone at the medical examiner's office —because she won't believe Brad died of an overdose— he's been finding every excuse to stop by and talk to me."

Mike turned toward her, smirking, and said, "Well, who wouldn't want to find an excuse to see you? An eligible, young, beautiful doctor?"

Sam blushed. "Oh stop."

He stood up a little straighter, more serious. "So that's your clinical decision, then? That Brad died of an overdose?"

"I think so." She lowered her voice, even though they were alone. "Dylan let me see the preliminary autopsy report, and while it doesn't directly point to an overdose, it still seems likely."

The smirk returned to Mike's face. "So those visits from Dylan have helped, at least to satisfy that clinical curiosity."

"Yeah, I suppose it's hard to turn that part of my brain off."

Mike nodded. "I see it all the time in the doctors I work with." Sam knew Mike worked as a rep for a medical supply distribution company, so he spent his days in hospitals and clinics calling on doctors and making sales, but she didn't know much else about him.

"Anyway," Sam continued, "I think Claire's in denial. She really wanted to believe Brad had turned his life around, but sometimes … sometimes you can't completely exorcise those demons."

"She'll get through this." He spread his arms. "And now she's got this to keep her busy."

"So you're good with her taking on this risky venture?"

"It makes her happy, and that's all that matters."

Sam felt a pang of jealousy over Claire finding a man who let her follow her passion.

They stood in silence, the conversation having run its course. Then Sam remembered something from the rehearsal dinner. "I didn't know your cousin went to high school with us."

Mike smiled. "Yeah, Michelle. Did you know her?"

"I had an art class with her. I remember she was quite talented."

"Yes, she's gifted. She got an art degree and found a job doing graphic design in LA."

"Wow! That's great. I'm sure she's in her element out there."

"She certainly is, but I miss her." A hint of wistfulness crossed his face.

"Sounds like you were close."

"She was like a sister to me, always there for me after my mom died."

"I'm sorry about your mom."

Mike waved his hand. "Oh, it was a long time ago. I was eight, and my mom was always leaving me at my grandparents' while she … while she went off and did her own thing." He took a deep breath, then said, "So when she died, it wasn't very different from what I was used to. And Michelle was always there for me. She and my aunt and uncle lived next door to my grandparents, and we'd play in a woody area behind their house. There was this brushy spot, where the plants created … almost like a cave, and we would pretend it was our Rebel base, fighting off the evil Empire. You know, like in Star Wars." He paused with a wistful look on his face. "And then she moved down here, while I stayed with Gram and Gramps in Grand Prairie."

Sam tilted her head. "That's up near Dallas, right?"

"Yep. So we still got to see each other a lot. Probably about once a month."

"Did you know Michelle and Claire had gone to high school together when you met Claire?"

Mike shook his head. "No, it wasn't until after Claire and I had been dating a while that I found out she went to the same high school as Michelle. And you know how big your high school was, like mine was, like so many around Texas. They're all so big. Just because you went to the same high school doesn't mean you knew each other."

Sam agreed with that. There were tons of people she didn't know who went to her high school. The conversation lulled again, then Sam said, "Even though Michelle moved away, I'm sure it's easier to keep in touch these days, you know, with all the technology we have—social media and what not?"

"Yeah," he said, his look a bit distant. "Keeping in touch is easier these days."

"I guess it's too bad she came all the way here, and the wedding didn't happen. Will she be able to make it when you guys reschedule?"

Mike didn't get a chance to answer because the door rattled open and Claire entered, her hands filled with white plastic bags from Office Depot. Mike rushed over. "Here, let me help you with that."

Once they set everything down, Claire pecked him on the cheek. Beaming, she said, "Thanks, hon."

"Should I unload the rest?" he asked.

Claire walked to the end of the counter and lifted the section up to open a path to the back. "That'd be great. I parked in the alley and knocked on the door, but I guess you didn't hear me."

"Right, I have the keys." Mike reached in his pocket, pulled them out, and handed them to Claire. "Sorry about that."

"Not a problem. Walking around the block gave me a chance to check out the foot traffic around the store. Looks pretty good, even for a weeknight."

"That's great, hon." Mike passed through the opening in the counter. He paused before he went into the back room. "What did you want me to unload? I assume you put everything in the back?"

"Yeah, all the stuff behind the back bench needs to come inside."

"I'm on it!" Mike disappeared.

Claire turned to Sam. "Thanks so much for meeting me tonight."

"No problem." It wasn't like she had anything exciting going on, although she could have waited for Dylan's friend, but it would have been for nothing. Sam squeezed Claire's shoulder. "Mike's such a great guy. I'm so happy for you."

"Oh, thanks, Sam. I was a little nervous when I told him about opening this shop, but he's been behind me—and Emily—one hundred percent."

"And what about Todd? Is he all in too?"

"Absolutely. And Emily told you he found this place for us, right? We're getting it for a steal!"

Rustling sounds came from the back room. Mike called out, "Where do you want these?"

"Just set them down next to the desk," Claire responded, grabbing the bags she'd brought in earlier as she headed to the back.

Sam followed Claire. "So what do you need help with?"

"Same thing you helped Emily with the other day. Emily's got more orders to ship, but she and Todd are taking his mom out to celebrate her birthday, otherwise she'd also be here. Seems like her soaps are super-popular for bridesmaids' gift baskets." Claire unpacked office supplies from her bags on the desk next to the back door. Then she looked at Sam and smiled, raising an eyebrow. "But that's not what I got you—it's still a secret."

Sam smiled back, glad that Claire seemed to be feeling better. "Have you and Mike come up with alternate plans, then?"

"Since it's summer, all the popular venues are booked up, so we're going to do something small. But Todd said he's got a line on a place we could use."

Mike came through the alley door, his arms loaded. "This is the last of it. Where should I put these?"

Claire pointed. "Just set them down by the shelves over there, and we'll take care of it."

"Anything else you need me to do?"

"No, hon. Thanks."

"Then I'll see you back at the ranch." Mike gave her a quick smooch.

After he left, Claire leaned over the desk, logged into the computer, and pulled up customer orders for shipments. The printer next to the computer whirred and churned, producing the packing slips they needed.

Sam said, "Dylan stopped by the clinic. He wanted to have his friend Eric check out my car."

Claire straightened up. "Did he find anything?"

"Well, I didn't want to wait for Eric, so Dylan checked, and no, he didn't find anything wrong with my car."

"Eric didn't find anything wrong with my car or my parents' cars either." Claire turned back toward the computer.

"But honestly, Claire, don't you think this may be …"

Claire glared at Sam. "What? That I'm making this up? I know what I heard. Someone was threatening Brad on that phone call. He sounded worried. Why else would he talk to someone that way?"

"I don't know. Tell me what happened again."

"It was on a Sunday afternoon last month, and we had gone over to my parents' house for dinner. I was helping Mom cook, and the guys were watching golf. At one point, as I was coming out of the bathroom—you know, that half bath just off the living room?"

Sam nodded.

"So I came out of that bathroom, and I could hear Brad talking to someone down the hallway in the guest room. But his tone of voice—he sounded angry. Dad was by himself on the couch, so I was worried that Brad and

Mike were arguing about something. I went down the hallway to see what was going on. It turns out Brad was on the phone with someone, and that's when I heard him say, 'I will not let you scare me!'"

"Did he say anything else?"

"No, he saw me at that point and just hung up. I asked him what it was about, but he told me it was something related to his job. I told him it didn't sound like work, and he said it was another real estate agent threatening to discourage a client from making an offer on one of the properties he represented." She paused and breathed in deeply, her body shuddering before continuing. "But he sounded really angry, and—despite saying he wasn't—he did sound scared. I believed him at the time, but now after what happened …"

Claire flopped into the chair at the desk, staring at the computer screen. Sam was at a loss for words. She worried if she told Claire her opinion—that it was still likely Brad died from an overdose—Claire could become more withdrawn.

Since Sam remembered how Emily liked to package everything the last time she'd helped out, she picked up the list of orders Claire had printed. She went over to the stainless steel table and arranged the varieties of soaps customers had requested. Handling the soaps released the soothing scents of lavender and rose, calming her. She hoped they also had the same effect on Claire.

As Sam moved around a table, she stepped in a puddle of water, making a small splashing sound. She traced its origin. "Looks like there's a leak under the sink."

Claire looked over and said, "Great. We'll need to find someone to take care of that." She grabbed a roll of paper towels and squatted down near the puddle, sopping up the water. "This should do for now."

Sam joined her, gathering up the soaked towels and tossing them in the large trash can in the corner.

Claire laughed. "Such are the joys of starting a business, right? We already need an electrician to rewire some of the circuits in this old building, and now we'll need a plumber."

Sam smiled, glad that her friend was coming around. "You and Emily are going to do well. And you've got great guys supporting you."

"Yeah, I don't know why I ever thought Todd could have hurt Brad or Mike." She ran her finger along the edge of the marble table. "And can you imagine? How awful it would be for Emily if Todd had turned out to be this ... this killer?"

"You were just looking for answers. The mind sometimes goes to pretty dark places when someone you love dies." Sam knew this from her own experience after her mom passed away.

They continued to work in tandem for a few moments, both relishing in the distraction of the task before them—wrapping, folding, tying, stacking, and focusing on the bits of delight others would have when they received the scented soaps.

Then Claire stopped and looked at Sam. "But I know what you think."

"We should wait for the toxicology report."

"You're right." Claire sighed. "But what if it doesn't show Brad OD'd? Then what?"

Sam shrugged. "Well, who would want to kill Brad?"

"I shouldn't say this, because he is one of my oldest friends," Claire said, "but if I had to make a list, at the very top would be James."

❧

CLAIRE AND SAM worked for the next hour, chatting about Claire's plans for the rescheduled wedding as they bundled up soaps, packed them in boxes, and applied shipping labels. They loaded up the back of Claire's SUV with the fruits of their labor, so Claire could take them to UPS in the morning.

"Thanks so much for helping me out," Claire said after she locked up the store. "It would have taken me much longer and been a lot less fun."

Sam was glad to have had the distraction, and she had enjoyed spending time with Claire and the lovely scents lingering in the air as they worked.

Claire drove off down the alley, and Sam headed toward her car on the adjacent street. As she turned to walk toward her car, she could see couples and conference-goers meandering along Congress Avenue, some of them with lanyards still around their necks.

She walked down the neighborhood street, the chatter of the pedestrians fading behind her, as did the brightness of the busy street. Tall oaks lined the street, towering over Sam, and when the breeze caught their branches, the shadows they cast danced around her, creating the effect as if she were on a turbulent stream.

Sam's meeting with Dr. Taylor was set for the next day, and other than an email to confirm the meeting, she had not heard from him. So she supposed everything was okay. Objectively, she had performed well during her six months at Obracare. The company had given her a report card, showing that she was hitting most of the metrics they considered important. And the net promoter scores for her clinic were fairly strong, with only the occasional comment complaining about wait times and no sugar for coffee in the lobby.

But still, the original thought she had when Dr. Taylor

forwarded the email about the ad campaign lingered in her mind—that she wasn't board certified, and they could let her go. And even if Lisa and Jerry were right—that it didn't matter because she was already working at Obracare and they'd already hired her knowing she hadn't finished residency and wasn't eligible to become board certified— they could still let her go with a simple change of policy.

Sam stopped at her car and put her hand in her purse for her keys. "Always make sure you already have your keys in hand before you walk to your car alone," her father had said when she'd first learned to drive. Sam hadn't done that this time, and her keys weren't in the top pocket of her purse where she usually kept them. They must have slipped into the bottom of the bag, so she dug some more, cursing herself for carrying too much stuff in her purse.

Something snapped behind her. She stopped and looked around. It sounded like it had come from the construction site she had just walked past. She waited a second, but all she could hear was the rustling of the breeze in the trees surrounding her. She put her purse on the trunk of her car, keeping an eye on the place where the sound had come from, even though she was standing slightly in the street. She felt around the bottom of her purse, not feeling the familiar cold bits of metal with the jagged edges.

Sam glanced around. She was alone. Congress Avenue was two blocks behind her—not too far away, but far enough. She rattled her purse and heard the reassuring clink of her key chain. They were in there but they were hiding. Damn those keys!

As she reached into her purse, spreading her fingers to maximize their detection ability, she saw a movement out of the corner of her eye. Adrenaline surged as her heart thumped, and her eyes went wide.

The movement had been next to the dumpster in front of the framed skeleton of a house. She moved her hand more frantically through her purse, staring at the dumpster, not wanting to take her eyes off the construction site. And just as she saw another flicker of movement, her fingers closed on them—those elusive keys. She quickly pushed the fob button, unlocking her car. She scrambled in, slamming the door as she shoved the ignition key into the steering column. The engine came roaring to life. As she drove down the street, she looked in the rearview mirror, and a hooded figure emerged with a white skull on his back, then turned toward the bustling anonymity on Congress Avenue.

Sam let out a long breath, her pulse still palpable. She hadn't imagined it. She had to be more careful.

23

T hank goodness for chamomile tea. Sam made a steaming cup to calm her nerves as soon as she got to her apartment. The man she saw was probably homeless and harmless, but she was startled nonetheless, her nerves frazzled.

Sam slept fitfully, and the next morning when she saw Ed Mason on the schedule, she braced herself for the visit, expecting resistance from the abrasive man. She had reviewed the notes from his ER visit, confirming that he did have a DVT. As she read through everything again, she realized she should have sent him to the ER to begin with, since he needed the D-dimer test first, the blood test that indicated if the body was forming a lot of clots.

She could have ordered that test as an outpatient, sending Mr. Mason to a lab first, but then she'd have to follow up on the results, call him back, then convince him to get the ultrasound. She would have had to manage everything from afar, since the lab and the imaging centers were located in different places. Plus, she knew that outpatient labs didn't routinely perform stat orders—those that should be carried out immediately—so she would have had to constantly stay on top of it all. Not only would she have to make sure Mr. Mason went to the lab in the first place and that the lab ran the test quickly so she could get the result, but then she would have to convince Mr. Mason he needed to go to a different place to get the ultrasound if the test came back positive.

She rubbed the back of her neck. Who knows how long that would have taken and if she would've been able to get Mr. Mason to comply. Such is the life of a doctor.

In the end, having Mr. Mason go to the ER was the best thing. The ER had a stat lab on site, separate from the hospital lab, and the notes showed that the ER docs had received the results within an hour, then sent Mr. Mason for an ultrasound immediately. As a result of everything being in one place, Mr. Mason spent about two hours total at the hospital.

The ER docs had started him on a newer anticoagulant, Xarelto. When Sam was in med school, Xarelto had just been released on the market, and because there was no way to reverse it—no antidote—her surgery attendings had said to stay away from it.

Sam had expected the ER docs to start Mr. Mason on Coumadin, which was the mainstay treatment for DVTs the last time she had a patient with one in residency. But the problem with Coumadin—which was first developed as a rat poison—was that doctors had to monitor blood tests to make sure the amount patients took was just right. Too low, and the clot could get bigger. Too high, and the patient could bleed to death.

But at least with Coumadin, if a patient was in an accident and needed emergency surgery, doctors could reverse its anticoagulant effects with vitamin K.

Things change quickly in medicine, though. Sam

searched online to see if a reversal agent for Xarelto was now available. The results showed the FDA had approved an antidote called Andexxa just the year before, and because of that, all the guidelines had changed for DVT management.

She sighed, relieved that she wouldn't have to twist Mr. Mason's arm and explain the need for frequent labs. All he would need to do was take Xarelto for three months and then repeat the ultrasound to make sure the DVT was gone. She printed out a sheaf of papers and took them into the exam room, armed with information to answer his questions.

And Mr. Mason certainly had questions, but based on his reaction, he seemed satisfied with her answers. She checked his leg, both for the swelling and the infection that had brought him in originally. His right leg was still slightly swollen, but nowhere near the amount it had been the week before, and the cellulitis had decreased significantly.

Then he said, "Now I have to pay an arm and a leg for all of this."

"I think it will be covered through your company's workers' comp insurance," Sam said.

"Even this DVT?"

"The cellulitis and the DVT resulted from a business trip, right?"

"That's right."

"Then I recommend you talk to your HR rep or whoever sent you here for your initial visit. It should all be covered."

"God, I hope so. I have a high-deductible plan, and they estimated it would cost me three grand when I checked in at the ER. And that medicine—nearly another grand for that."

Sam checked the prescription he had received from the ER. "They gave you the starter pack, right?"

Mr. Mason grimaced. "The pack looks like the one my wife's birth control comes in. But it tells me exactly when I need to take each pill. Two a day for three weeks, then one a day after that. It even says when I need to see you, so I can get a refill from you."

"Let's see …" She looked at the date of his ER visit. "That works out well. Assuming you don't have any issues, we'll schedule you in two weeks so that I can check on you and send in the prescription to continue your treatment."

He stood, holding the stack of papers she had given him, then shook his head. "Never knew how complicated all this could be. Thanks for answering all my questions."

Sam smiled. "That's what I'm here for."

AFTER SAM HAD A BRIEF LUNCH, Dr. Taylor arrived for his meeting with Sam. He worked in Houston, three hours away by car, and had driven to Austin for the afternoon to meet with Sam and Jerry individually, along with the doctors and physician assistants at the other two clinics in town. He booted Owen, the sales guy, out of his office, so they would have a place to meet.

When Sam first started working at the clinic in Austin, she was just happy to have a job. But she noticed that the clinic had only two offices: one in the front by the lobby for Jill, the clinic operations manager who often dealt with patient complaints, and one in the back by the exam rooms —not for the doctor, but for sales. Sam soon learned the way ObraCare found patients to treat for workers' comp was by selling employee drug testing packages to companies at cost, or even at a little loss, so the companies would send their employees to ObraCare when they were injured. She understood why Owen was important, but he was hardly ever at the clinic, since he spent most of his days driving around town and pitching to companies.

So instead of an office, Sam and Jerry had workstations behind the medical assistants' counter. Sam thought this could be an issue for patient privacy, since people could see their computer screens, but she didn't feel she was in a position to say anything.

After the usual introductory pleasantries, Dr. Taylor— who had insisted she call him Pete—said, "Sam, I've been really happy with your performance since we brought you on full time." He sifted through the papers in front of him, including the report card ObraCare had generated on her treatment patterns, quantifying things such as how many times she'd ordered physical therapy and how many patients she'd referred to specialists, then comparing her to the other ObraCare doctors around the country. "These look very good, indeed. I do want to remind you that these are just informational, to use as feedback so you can make better decisions about how you treat patients and so you know how you compare to your peers. You do understand that ObraCare cannot dictate how you treat patients and that all clinical decisions are entirely yours to make."

"I think so," Sam said. Technically, she did not work for ObraCare—that was the company that managed and operated the clinic where she practiced. Her contract was with Texas Occupational Physicians—the legal entity comprised only of doctors and other healthcare providers. And even though no one at ObraCare ever told her how to treat patients, she certainly had some employers try to do exactly that.

Then he looked directly at her. "But I need to talk to you about something."

Sam's stomach clinched. Oh no. Here it comes.

"I understand you took off Monday?"

"Yes, sir," Sam said, frowning. "I had to go to a funeral, so I got Bill to fill in for me." Bill was Dr. Cunningham, a semiretired physician who floated around the ObraCare clinics to help out if a clinic was busy with a high-patient volume, or to cover a shift when a doctor was sick or needed to take time off. She couldn't see how this was related to the email he'd forwarded to her.

"I understand," Pete said, "but you called him directly, and that doesn't follow our procedures for requesting time off. In the future, I need you to contact my admin or text me if it's short notice."

"Okay. I'm sorry, sir." Sam let out her breath. She should have known better, but she hadn't been in that situation before. "I'll make sure I do that next time."

"Good. Now the other thing I need to talk to you about is that email I sent you. I was hoping we could have discussed it last week but something came up. Do you remember that message?"

Sam nodded. At least he didn't say there wouldn't be a next time, so maybe she was worrying about nothing.

"You may have noticed at the bottom of the email that the marketing department was seeking employee 'models' to use for the ads. I think you would be an ideal person for the campaign."

She raised her eyebrows, not expecting this. "Why would they want me?"

"Well, you may have noticed most of your colleagues are, how shall I say this … a bit long in the tooth."

Sam had noticed that most of the other doctors and PAs she worked with were not exactly young.

"We'd like to expand into more urgent care markets, and our target demographic includes families, particularly those with young children. The marketing team believes ads featuring doctors that patients can identify with will be more effective. And women make the majority of health-care decisions for their families."

"Okay." So they wanted her picture in the ads because mothers would see themselves in someone like her.

"Would you be willing to be part of the ad campaign?"

She didn't see much of a downside to this. And if her picture was integral to the company's image, then maybe that would give her more job security. "Sure, I can do that."

"Great. I'll let them know."

"But …" Sam hesitated. Maybe she shouldn't bring up her concerns—about her lack of board certification.

"Yes?"

She waved her hand. "Oh, it's nothing. I was just wondering about the part about board-certified doctors."

Pete wrinkled his brow. "I'm sorry? I don't understand."

She had to ask about it now that she had mentioned it. She swallowed, then said, "Well, the email mentioned part of the campaign would promote how ObraCare has board-certified doctors."

"That's right," he said, but the frown didn't fade. "All the big hospital systems, the other urgent care chains, and all of our competitors are using that in their advertising. We're trying to differentiate ourselves from the retail clinics who mainly use nurse practitioners."

"Oh, okay," Sam said, hoping he didn't press her on what she meant and that he would let things be.

"So what's your concern about—oh, I see." He dipped his chin. "Are you concerned you aren't board certified?"

She bobbed her head.

"That's not an issue."

"But what about the ad campaign?"

He shrugged. "The ad copy will just say something along the lines of 'come see our board-certified doctors.' It won't specifically say all of our doctors are board certified, or that you'll even see a doctor, since we do have physician assistants and nurse practitioners as well."

Sam sat back in her chair. It was just as Lisa had told her.

Pete leaned forward on the desk. "Now, I will say, even though our hiring practices currently do not require you to have board certification—just that you have an unrestricted license and can maintain your DEA registration—you might want to consider becoming board certified, because even I can't guarantee our policies won't change."

"But I'd need to get back into a residency program to do that, right?"

"There is a complementary pathway for achieving board certification in preventive medicine. I'm not certain of all the requirements for those programs, but this may be a way for you to become board eligible."

Sam had never considered this before, mainly because she didn't know this was a possibility. "Would I be able to continue working here?"

"I believe so. We've sponsored other doctors in a similar situation as yours." He tapped his chin. "In fact, I believe a doctor at one of our clinics in San Antonio just passed her boards." He scribbled on his notepad. "I'll have to look her up and put her in touch with you. It's something to consider."

"Thanks, Pete. I'll look into it."

On Saturday afternoon, Sam joined Emily and James as they cleaned out Brad's apartment. Claire said she wasn't up to it yet, and neither were her parents. So Sam and the others agreed to do the first pass and sort through everything—"Cleanse and redact to make it suitable for parental units," James had said—before Claire's parents decided what to keep and what to donate.

Brad's apartment was modest, a single bedroom with a living area and small kitchen. It did have a nice balcony that looked out over a wooded area next to the apartment complex property.

Despite Brad's improved attitude over the last couple of years, his place was a complete mess. Dishes stacked in the sink, papers strewn about on his desk next to his dinette table, clothes piled on the floor of his closet. After the trio surveyed the apartment, they divvied up the tasks.

While Emily sorted through Brad's clothes for donation items, James went through the papers on Brad's desk, and

Sam took care of the kitchen. She rinsed off all the dirty dishes and loaded up the dishwasher to run. Then she cleaned out the food from the refrigerator. There wasn't much in it, just a few beers and some leftovers in takeout containers, which were starting to spoil. When she peeked inside one of the containers, the odor from the hairy mold covering the top of the food filled the room, causing her to gag.

Sam quickly put the leftovers and the beer bottles in the trash bag, then she ran down to the dumpster behind the apartment building to toss them. As she climbed the stairs to return to the apartment, she wondered what Brad's counselors in his recovery program would have thought about his alcohol use. Brad wasn't drinking wine with everyone else during the rehearsal dinner, but maybe that was just for show. Some addiction medicine specialists believed it was best to completely abstain from all potentially habit-forming substances, since some patients can transfer their addiction behavior from one substance to another. Regardless of whatever his doctors thought, Brad must have thought he could handle it.

The pantry was fairly empty as well. Just a couple of shelves with stacks of protein bars and large jars of protein shake mix. After she filled up the trash bags with the pantry items, she turned her attention to Brad's bathroom, figuring she'd return to the kitchen to pack up the dishes for donation once the dishwasher finished its cycle.

Sam wondered what she would find in the bathroom, since the medical examiner's investigator found an unlabeled prescription bottle among Brad's things in his room at the bed-and-breakfast. She felt like an intruder going through Brad's personal effects, like she was violating him, even though he was dead. In the small bathroom, she found no medicine cabinet behind the mirror—those had gone out of favor a few years ago—but there were a couple of drawers next to the sink.

Before she tackled the drawers, she cleared off the counter, cluttered with a razor, shaving cream, an electric toothbrush, and a tube of toothpaste, which was lumpy and misshapen, the cap askew and caked with bright blue paste. She opened the top drawer and found the usual stuff. A comb, a tube of hair gel. And in the other drawer, she found a prescription bottle of verapamil from Dr. Black. So Dr. Black must have been leaning toward cluster headaches, which are more common in men, as opposed to migraines, which are more common in women. Even though it was mainly used as a blood pressure medication, verapamil could be used to prevent cluster headaches. Along with the prescription bottle, Sam found a bottle of ibuprofen and a box of antihistamine pills—nothing too unusual, certainly no narcotics or other drug paraphernalia.

As Sam straightened up, she jumped. James stood in the doorway. "You startled me!"

"Sorry. I just wanted you to see something," he whispered. He looked over his shoulder toward the bedroom, then walked down the hallway to the dinette area with Sam following.

Brad had a particle board cabinet against the wall with mail and other papers piled on top. James picked up what looked like a contract. He looked over his shoulder again, then pointed to the paper.

"I don't want to bring this up in front of Emily, but this is the agreement between Todd and Brad for how they would split up the commission on any sales that Brad made while working for Todd's brokerage." He flipped a page. "Look at this. It says normally, the commission would be split fifty-fifty between the two of them." He glanced toward the hallway, then angled his body so it would block Emily's view should she come into the room. He lowered his voice further. "But in the event of either party's termination before the close of the deal, the other would receive the full commission."

"That doesn't seem to be too unusual, but—" Sam began.

"But what exactly does the contract mean by 'termination?'" James interrupted. "I think whatever was originally intended when they signed the contract doesn't matter now, so Todd gets all the money Brad would have received."

Sam nodded. "So this could be a motive."

"And we know Todd has been dealing with his gambling debts."

"But does that mean Todd would've killed Brad?" Sam thought back to the rehearsal dinner. Todd was in a good mood until Brad started to bring up how relieved Todd would be, then Todd had cut him off and changed the subject.

"Even though Todd and Brad were teammates in high school, and Todd had decided to give Brad a chance with a job at his real estate brokerage, I don't think there was much love lost between the two." James checked the hallway again before saying, "I think Todd mainly did it as a favor to Emily and her friendship with Claire. And now we have proof he had a reason to kill him."

Sam took a deep breath, not sure what to think. Claire no longer suspected Todd. In fact, Claire had hinted that she wasn't so sure about James, although she had made it seem like she was joking. But it had planted the seed in Sam's mind that James was not beyond culpability.

"You seem like you're paranoid," Sam said.

Or was she becoming paranoid? Could James be trying

to draw suspicion away from himself? She never thought James would hurt anyone. Sure, he had a sharp tongue at times, but he used it as a defense mechanism to get under people's skin. She certainly understood his anger, and at least he had a way to express it, but she didn't. Women weren't allowed to show their anger, so she usually swallowed it and replaced it with guilt.

"But it's possible, isn't it?"

Sam blinked. "What, that Todd would've killed Brad?"

"Yes."

They stood silently for a moment, then Emily swooshed in, carrying a graduation gown wrapped in dry cleaning plastic. "Hey, guys, what do you think I should do with this?"

Sam's heart thumped in her chest as James quickly slid the contract under the mail on the desk and turned around.

Emily looked up from the gown. "Do you think his parents would want this instead of giving it away?"

Sam steadied her breath to slow her heart. "I think they may want it. Better keep it separate from everything else."

Then Emily narrowed her eyes. "What are you two doing?"

"We're just sorting through Brad's bills and things," Sam said.

"But you looked like you were trying to hide something from me."

James laughed. "Yeah, you wouldn't believe how much he spent on strip clubs and porn!"

Emily gasped, almost dropping the gown. A blush bloomed on her neck and cheeks, then she turned and left without a word.

Sam glared at James, but she couldn't keep a smirk from creeping onto her face.

"What?" he whispered. "I got her out of the room, right?" He pulled the contract back out from its hiding place. "So what should we do with this?"

Sam snapped images of the document. "I have a friend I can ask about it."

25

After the trio finished sorting and clearing out most of Brad's belongings, making several trips to the dumpster to discard things that couldn't be kept (including Brad's stash of adult magazines), they left the rest for Claire and her parents to decide what to keep and what to donate.

When Sam got back to her apartment, she texted Lisa to see if they could get together for coffee the next day. Since Lisa said she dealt with the contracts for all kinds of small businesses, Sam hoped she could shed some light on the one between Todd and Brad. Sam didn't know what a typical split was between an agent and a broker for a deal like this. For all she knew, the contract was pretty standard, but she wanted to check.

A few minutes later, Lisa texted back, saying she was on her way to a conference in Las Vegas and would be gone the whole week. They agreed to find a time to meet when she got back.

Sam spent most of the following day researching how she could become board certified in preventive medicine, based on the information her boss had given her. She discovered that if she got her Master of Public Health degree, then she could apply to some residency programs, and she might only need one more year of residency training to sit for the board exam. That year could include doing what she was already doing at ObraCare.

After learning all of this, Sam had a pretty positive outlook when she went to work Monday morning. As she bustled around the busy clinic, everything seemed to flow smoothly. Patients were progressing, healing as expected from their injuries, and she was able to release quite a few patients back to work.

And then she saw Mrs. Rodriguez. Even though Sam was hoping Mrs. Rodriguez would get her MRI right after her visit the week before, she wasn't able to have it until that Friday, then the radiologist had to read it, so here it was, Tuesday again. Another week's delay in her care.

"Let's see what the radiology report says." Sam rolled her stool over next to Mrs. Rodriguez so they could read it together. "As we suspected, you do have a herniated disc in your neck."

Mrs. Rodriguez's eyes widened. "Do I need surgery?"

"Maybe not. It looks like the disc is irritating the nerve, but it isn't actually impinging it."

"I don't understand."

"It means you could be a candidate for an epidural steroid injection."

"Epidural, like that thing they do when you have a baby?"

"Kind of. The epidural space is the layer right around your spinal cord and nerve roots. And just like an anesthesiologist does to relieve pain during labor, a pain specialist can insert a needle into that space. But instead of injecting an anesthetic, the pain specialist will inject a steroid."

"Will that help make my arm work better again?"

"It should decrease the inflammation around the nerve, so the swelling goes down and lets the nerve heal. Then you'll keep doing physical therapy to build up your strength again."

"So I need to see another doctor, then?"

"Yes, because I can't do those types of injections. They need to be done using special X-ray machines during the procedure to make sure the needle is in the right place. But I know an excellent pain management specialist who has taken very good care of some of my other patients. His name is Dr. Popescu."

"Is the insurance company going to give us a hard time about this?"

"I hope not, since they let us get the MRI, and they should have received the results as well. So they should have no problem approving the injection. After all, the injection is a lot less expensive than surgery."

Mrs. Rodriguez slumped her shoulders. "Then it's still going to be awhile before I get back to work."

"Unfortunately, yes." Sam patted Mrs. Rodriguez's knee. "But at least we are a step closer. I'll put in the referral for you to see Dr. Popescu, and hopefully he'll be able to get you on the schedule very soon." She closed the chart and stood. "Then we'll get you going with PT again."

"Thank you, Dr. Jenkins. But really, when do you think I'll be back at work?"

"Assuming everything goes well, it could be within a couple of weeks."

"And what if things don't go well?"

"Dr. Popescu can talk to you more about this, but sometimes people do need to have more than one injection." Sam tapped the chart. "But the radiologist says the disc has just prolapsed, which is not the most severe type of herniation. So I'm optimistic that you'll do well."

"Okay. I hope you're right."

"I hope so too." She stood and opened the door. "I'll tell you what. I'll call Dr. Popescu's office right now to see if he can get you in this afternoon."

"Oh, that would be great, Dr. Jenkins. Thank you!"

"You're quite welcome." Sam pulled out her phone as she followed Mrs. Rodriguez out of the room.

She had felt her watch tap her wrist during the visit, but she'd ignored it, not wanting to be rude. Maybe this watch wasn't such a good idea if she constantly got notifications. She just didn't want to miss anything big—like when Claire had tried to call her after Mike's accident.

The notification she received was a text message from Alex Crawford. He wanted to know if she would like to meet. Was she ready for that? Or maybe he wasn't interested in her in that way. Maybe this would be completely platonic. She had had plenty of male friends over the years, but it seemed like these friendships were becoming fewer and fewer. One time while she was still in college, a guy at a party told her that it was impossible for men and women to have completely platonic relationships. He claimed one side always wanted more from the relationship than the other. She didn't think that was entirely true, at least not from her perspective. Although ...

There was one time when she'd gone out to a movie with a male classmate in college. She thought they were just friends, usually getting together to study and to work on homework together. But halfway through the movie, he'd reached over and grabbed her hand. Surprised, she'd pulled away. After that, she'd had to find another study partner.

Whatever. It was all too confusing. She was sure Alex

just wanted to reconnect, since she was a familiar face in Austin. It didn't have to mean anything. But maybe she could learn more about his intentions first.

She texted Alex back, asking what he had in mind.

When she looked up, Jill was standing before her, smiling. "Dr. Jenkins, that handsome cop is back."

DYLAN SHUT the door after he followed Sam into an empty exam room.

Sam crossed her arms. "Why do you keep showing up here?"

"Good to see you too. I just thought you'd want to see this." He handed her some papers.

"What's this?"

"It's the preliminary toxicology report for Brad."

Sam flipped through the pages, then looked at Dylan in disbelief. No opiates, no cocaine, no methamphetamines. Just a low level of alcohol and the metabolite for clonazepam. Analysis of the stomach contents also showed trace amounts of the active form of clonazepam. She double-checked that they had run tests for fentanyl analogs. They had, but there was no evidence of it. "He was pretty much clean. Clonazepam alone is not enough to kill him, especially in the amounts they found."

"Yeah. Surprising, huh?"

"And it must have been the drug in the bottle they found in Brad's room. I remember from the preliminary report you let me see that the pills had been marked with a "C" and a "2." I thought it might be a form of fentanyl, but the other possibility was clonazepam."

"That's right, you mentioned those two drugs." Dylan

looked at her appraisingly. "You know, you'd make a pretty good detective."

Sam leaned back on the edge of the exam table. "Do you have any idea what the medical examiner is thinking about doing next?"

"Since Mike's and Brad's cars both had similar damage to the undercarriage, they're checking for carbon monoxide poisoning now."

"Is the police department going to investigate?"

Dylan shook his head. "There's not much to go on, and the ME still hasn't made a decision on the final cause of death."

"Are you saying the ME needs to rule Brad's death a homicide before they'll investigate?"

"Unfortunately, there's just not a clear picture yet that someone killed Brad."

"But?"

Dylan stepped closer to Sam. "But I'm concerned. I'm worried about you."

"And Claire?"

"Well, yes, and Claire too."

"So why don't you check on Claire? Make sure she's safe? You don't need to keep tabs on me."

Dylan let out a long breath. "Sam, don't be like this."

"Like what? Like an independent woman? Like someone who can take care of herself? What reason do you really have that I'm in danger?" Sam's watch tapped her wrist. "Based on what we know, you should be worried about Claire. I think you're just using this as an excuse to spend time with me." She peeked at her watch. Alex wanted to meet at Hula Hut Saturday night. "But guess what? I have a date this weekend."

"I don't know why you're acting this way. What did I ever

do to you?" Dylan stepped back, frowning. "And you've got it all wrong. As I told you before, I'm seeing someone. I'm just concerned about you—as a friend." His eyes narrowed. "You're too self-centered. You think this is all about you. Well, you're wrong. I'm sorry I ever cared about you, that I ever wanted to help you." He opened the door and stormed out.

26

S am took her time leaving the exam room, knowing the office staff would be lingering again. And she was right.

Cynthia stood just outside the door. "Dr. Jenkins, are you okay?"

"I'm fine, Cynthia," Sam said as she tried to maintain her composure. "Has Mrs. Rodriguez checked out yet?"

"No, she's still waiting. She said that you were going to call Dr. Popescu."

Sam looked at the board. All the rooms except the one she'd just left were full. "Could you do me a favor, Cynthia? Could you call his office for me and see if they have a slot to squeeze in Mrs. Rodriguez this afternoon?"

"Of course, Dr. Jenkins." Cynthia walked away to carry out Sam's orders.

Instead of rushing into the next patient visit, Sam sat down at her workstation. She was stunned. She didn't mean to lash out at Dylan. He was right—he hadn't really done anything to warrant her anger. All he had done was help her find the truth. And was he right about everything else? Was she really self-centered? Why would he say that to her?

To Sam, being a doctor meant putting herself last. She supposed Jeff had thought the same thing as Dylan, that by putting others first, she was really being self-centered. She looked at the text message from Alex. Maybe that was the only way to find love, to find a satisfying relationship. Maybe dating another physician was the only way she could have a life partner who fully understood the sacrifices she had to make to be a good doctor.

She texted Alex back: *Saturday at Hula Hut sounds great. What time?*

Then she took a deep breath, cleared her mind, and moved on to the next patient.

"So it wasn't an overdose? What does that mean?" James asked when Sam filled him in on the events of the day.

They sat on his balcony overlooking the greenbelt. Sam needed to talk to someone, to process everything, so she went over to James's apartment after she got home. She loved this time of year, when the days seemed to last forever. She could get home late, like she did this evening, and still have a couple of hours before the sun sank completely, with the air cooling as the breezes picked up.

"Dylan said the ME would now check for carbon monoxide poisoning," Sam said.

James smirked. "Any chance of that old romance rekindling?"

Sam rolled her eyes. "You just won't let up on my love life, will you? Maybe I should dig around in yours too."

"Fine with me. I'm perfectly happy with my main beau. I'm not shy about sharing."

"How is Kyle, by the way? I haven't seen him around lately."

Kyle was a software engineer at Facebook, which had followed other big tech companies in opening satellite offices in Austin.

"Busy at work. Apparently there's some big deadline coming up, but he says he'll have a lot more free time once his team hits their milestones. So what will it mean if it turns out Brad died of carbon monoxide poisoning?"

"Well, maybe the police will start to take this all seriously and try to find out who wanted to hurt both Brad and Mike." Sam paused, taking a sip of iced tea. "And I still don't know what it means that Brad had two venipuncture wounds. It's going to gnaw at me until I figure it out."

James wrinkled his brow. "What's veni—whatever you said?"

"Venipuncture. It's just the fancy word we use that means the vein was, well, punctured by a hypodermic needle, usually to draw blood. Brad had two venipuncture wounds on his left arm." She tapped her arm in front of her elbow. "So I talked to Brad's doctor, and he was having headaches and dizziness. His doctor just thought it was migraines or cluster headaches, but he ordered routine lab work just to make sure nothing else was going on. But for some reason, Brad was stuck twice."

"So? What does that mean?"

"Since Brad was healthy, there's not really a reason to stick him twice, and I talked to the manager at the lab collection site in the same office building as Brad's doctor, and she said Brad was only stuck once. So either, they didn't document the second stick, or someone else stuck Brad."

James cocked his head. "You mean to inject something?"

"Maybe. Or it could be he went somewhere else to get blood drawn. But why?" She watched the sky darken to burnt orange, furthering its journey to twilight. "If someone injected something into Brad," she said, "it didn't show up on the toxicology report. The only thing he had in his bloodstream, besides a moderate level of alcohol, was a metabolite for clonazepam, an anti-anxiety medication. So those are probably the pills they found in Brad's room."

"They found pills in Brad's room? Wait, didn't you say he met Chris the night before he died?"

"Yeah, after he tried to make nice with you, he told us he was going to see Chris's band. So maybe that's how Brad got those pills." She then remembered how Dylan warned her not to go snooping around. But he couldn't tell her what to do. "We should talk to Chris."

James stood up and headed inside. Sam watch him through the sliding glass door as he moved a one of his hoodies off a stack of newspapers on the coffee table. He rummaged through the stack, then came back outside a few moments later, holding a copy of the *Austin Chronicle*. As he flipped through the pages of the weekly newspaper, he asked, "What was the name of his band, again?"

Sam shrugged.

"Right, I remember now," he said. "It's called No Joystick." He tapped an ad on the open page. "And they're playing at the Continental Club Saturday night." He looked up. "We should go talk to him. The set starts at nine, and I don't have a gig that night, so I'm free anytime."

"Oh," Sam said.

"What's wrong?"

"Uh … I'll have to meet you there. I'm meeting someone for dinner."

James raised his eyebrows. "Oh really? Who?"

"Nobody, really. Just that doctor I knew in residency."

"You mean Dr. Gorgeous from the hospital?"

Sam punched James on the shoulder. "Stop it. Yes, I'm going to have dinner with Alex. I wasn't sure I wanted to, but when he texted me, I was arguing with Dylan."

"Ah, so Dylan's involved with this too."

"No, he's not." Sam twisted her lips. "He's got a girl-friend, anyway. She works in the ME's office and has been giving him the info on Brad's autopsy."

"But Dylan keeps showing up at your clinic." James cocked an eyebrow as he nodded. "Right."

"Come on, James. It's not like that."

"Then what were you arguing about? And why did you accept a date with Dr. Dreamy?"

"Fine, you're right. I thought Dylan kept coming to see me because he wanted to restart things." She paused. "But I guess I was wrong. I guess he just wanted to help out."

"Sure. So then why are you having dinner with what's-his-name?"

"Alex. You know, it's hard to meet people when you're working all the time. And you know what a turnoff it is to most men when they find out you're not willing to play the ditz."

"Good point. But you said you didn't really want it to be a date."

"Yeah, I don't. So you'll be my excuse to leave if things aren't going well."

"Gee, thanks. I'm glad I can be an excuse."

"Come on, James, I didn't mean it that way."

James grinned. "I know. I just like giving you a hard time, honey."

27

Sam arrived at the Continental Club on South Congress Saturday evening after she met Alex for ... well, she wasn't really certain it was a date. She knew parking would be difficult on the busiest night of the week, so she Ubered. The driver dropped her off out front and she entered through the iconic red doors. Since it was still early as far as these venues went, there was only a smattering of groups around the bar and the rest of the room, making it easy for her to find James.

"Why didn't you bring Dr. McDreamy with you?" James asked as Sam approached.

"You really are a card." Sam smiled. "He's on call tonight, and he got paged to see a patient."

James tilted his head. "Doctors still use pagers? What century is this?"

Sam rolled her eyes. "I know. And we still use a fax machine in our clinic."

"Really?"

Sam nodded. "They're actually more secure than

email, even if it's encrypted. You'd have to directly intercept the call to read the fax. And as far as pagers are concerned, they don't interfere with equipment, and they work everywhere in the hospital."

He stared at her for a second. "That's what I love about you—your ability to regurgitate random trivia like Cliff Clavin. So dinosaur tech is why you didn't bring that handsome thing with you after your date."

"It wasn't really a date."

"That's too bad. He sure is something to look at." James motioned to the back hallway. "Chris's band goes on at nine, but I know Trent, one of the managers here. I told him we're old high school friends of Chris, and he said we can go back to see him before the set."

"You sure seem to know everyone."

"Comes from working all these gigs."

"Well, it certainly helps that you know your way around."

James held up his longneck and nodded. "Indeed, it does. Do you want to order something? Or should we head on back?"

Sam looked around. In just the few minutes since she had arrived, the tables around the room had filled up. She looked at her watch. Thirty minutes to showtime. "Let's talk to him now before it gets too crazy around here. If we wait until the set is over, we could be here a while."

"What? You don't want to be out all night like the good old days?"

Sam shook her head as she fiddled with her watch. "I'm not really into the club scene. Never was, even in college."

James gulped down the rest of his beer and set his bottle down on the table with a clunk. "Let's go then."

They weaved their way through the growing crowd to the back of the room. Sam turned to James. "Do you think Chris will remember us?"

He gave her a questioning look as a group of girls from a bachelorette party started cackling. He cupped his hand to his ear. "What?"

Sam leaned closer to him and repeated her question, a little louder this time. "Do you think Chris will remember us?"

James made a sour face. "Maybe. He was there when Brad tried to stuff me in my locker and a few other times when Brad picked on me." His nostrils flared. "I'm not really looking forward to seeing him again, but he was so stoned all the time, he probably doesn't remember me very well. Do you think he'll remember you?"

"Maybe. Even though Chris was a stoner, he was rather bright. We had quite a few classes together, but we never really talked to each other much."

"I guess we'll just have to see."

They had to step aside as a guy carrying an amp needed to get to the stage. They passed the stage and started down the hallway. A man with a scraggly beard who sat on a stool near the entrance looked at them. "Hey, James. You here to see Chris?"

"Yup."

The guy tilted his head toward the back. "Go on. He should be getting ready."

"Thanks, man," James said.

Sam put her hand on James's arm as he led her down the narrow hallway, since several more band members were coming in the opposite direction. They found what passed for a dressing room.

James rapped on the open door. A man with a shaved

head and goatee looked up. "Hi, Chris. It's James Lewis and Samantha Jenkins. We went to high school together."

A faint flash of recognition crossed Chris's face. "Oh yeah. Man, it's been a while." He extended his hand.

James didn't take it. "You don't really remember me, do you?"

Chris looked thoughtful for a moment, then squinted. "You look familiar, but you're right, I don't remember you." He dropped his hand, turned to Sam, and said, "But I do remember you. We had trig together and some other classes, I think."

"Yeah, we actually had quite a few classes together."

"So are you guys here to catch some tunes?"

"Actually," Sam said, "we're here to talk to you about Brad Johnson."

"Oh yeah, Brad. Just saw him a few weeks ago. We catch up every now and then. So what's going on with him?"

James furrowed his brow. "You haven't heard, have you?"

"Heard what, man?"

Sam put her hand on Chris's shoulder. "Maybe you should sit down for this."

"Why? What's going on?"

"Trust me," she said as she directed him toward a couch against the back wall next to a lighted mirror.

James continued to stand near the door and crossed his arms, while Sam sat down next to Chris on the couch.

Sam took a deep breath. "I'm sorry to tell you this, but Brad died the morning after he saw you."

Chris sat up and widened his eyes. "Whoa. What? No way!"

Sam felt her stomach sink. What were they doing?

Chris was about to play a show, and they just told him an old friend died. Good going. "I'm sorry. We shouldn't have told you this right now."

"Yeah, I have to get ready for this gig, but … but now I need to process this." Chris scratched his jaw. "What happened to Brad? And why are you here?"

"Well, Brad's sister Claire asked me to look into what happened to him. You remember her, right?"

Chris nodded.

"And"—Sam splayed out her hands—"I thought he probably OD'd since he, you know, had a problem." Chris started to say something but Sam pushed on. "It turns out, though, that the preliminary tox report shows he was clean, except for some benzos."

Chris frowned. "When I saw him, I asked if he wanted a hit and he said no. If he had something in his system, I don't know where he got it." He looked down. "And I know what you're thinking, but I got this under control."

Sam held up her hands. "Look, I'm not here to judge you." She glanced at James, but he continued to cross his arms, scowling at the floor. "We just want to know what happened to him." She paused for a second. "Would you be okay if we asked a couple of questions?"

"Well, if he only had benzos in him, how did he die, then? Benzos don't kill, do they?"

"You're right. They usually don't. The autopsy showed Brad had cardiac ischemia, a heart attack. It could be from natural causes, but Claire thinks something else was going on, which is why she asked me to look into it."

"Why you?"

"Well, I'm her friend, and I guess she thought because I'm a doctor, I would know a little more about these things."

"Yeah, you always were acing everything. Figures you became a doctor." Chris looked at her appraisingly. "So what do you want to know?"

"Just what you guys did that night. And what did you talk about?"

"Well, Brad showed up sometime during my set, I guess. The place was packed, so I don't really know when he got there. But afterward, he found me backstage, and I was starving, so we decided to go to Torchy's, then catch up on things."

"And you mentioned that you tried to get him to do a hit? Of what?"

Chris crossed his arms. "I didn't try to get him to take a hit. I just offered."

"Okay, so you just offered. What did you offer him?"

Chris looked down sheepishly. "Well, sometimes after a set, I need something to wind down, so I asked if he wanted to do some handlebars."

"You mean Xanax?" Sam asked.

James raised his eyebrows and looked at Sam as if she'd just said she was into bondage.

Chris nodded. "I'm usually too amped up, and then I need to get some sleep because I work at the Goliad during the day."

"So what did Brad say?"

"He said he was clean—been sober for the last year and a half—so I didn't pressure him at all."

"And you didn't offer him anything else?"

"Like what?"

"Like cocaine or amphetamines?"

"Na, man. I don't do that hard shit."

Sam pressed on. "So you got your tacos, you took a hit of Xanax, then what?"

"We drove around a bit, you know, for old time's sake. Drove around UT, West Campus. Brad's old frat house. Man, it's changed a lot." Chris looked at Sam and then James. "Even though I'm here in Austin, I don't usually go around campus. But it sure was eye-opening. All these high rises everywhere. It's crazy."

James chimed in. "Yeah, if there weren't the handful of landmarks still there, I would think it was another university."

Sam focused on Chris again. "So how long did you guys hang out?"

"Not too long. Brad said he needed to get back to the B&B for Claire's wedding. And like I said, I had work the next morning."

"Okay. So after cruising around, you guys went back to Maggie Mae's?"

"Yeah, but we got caught up in traffic after a concert at the Erwin Center. Took us half an hour to go one block along Red River." Chris smiled. "Guess we picked a bad time to cruise around."

Sam returned the smile. "It just added to the experience, right? Did you talk about anything in particular?"

"Brad said I should consider one of those rehab programs with the twelve steps. He said it was really helping him work through all of his issues. He was going through the step where you apologize to everyone." He sighed. "He admitted there were a lot of people he hurt and was a real ass around. He couldn't reach out to all of them but he was trying."

Sam started thinking: could he have reached out to someone who didn't want to forgive him? "Did he talk about anyone he reached out to specifically?"

"Nah. But he did say he just learned about someone he had hurt and was going to try to reach out to her."

"Did he say who?"

"Yeah, but I can't remember her name. He asked if I remembered her, said we all knew each other." Chris shrugged. "But I think he knew her better than me. He tried to jog my memory by saying I had sold her stuff, but … I sold lots of people stuff back then."

Sam glanced at James, raising her eyebrows to see if he had any questions. When he shook his head, she turned back toward Chris and asked, "Was there anything else you talked about?"

He looked at his watch. "How many more questions do you have? My set starts in ten minutes. And if I don't do this gig, I'll be short on rent this month."

"That's not all you'll be short on," James muttered.

Chris snapped, "What's that supposed to mean?"

Sam held up her hands. "I just have one more question. Was there anything unusual that happened that night?"

"Well, now that you mentioned it, right when Brad dropped me off at Maggie Mae's, I had a pounding headache. It was kinda weird, you know? I mentioned it to Brad, and he said his head was hurting too. We just chalked it up to sitting in traffic. There were a lot of those pick 'em up trucks around, and even though the night was nice, we had to roll up the windows in his car to avoid the fumes."

James said, "Huh."

He must have been thinking the same thing Sam was: that Chris also had some mild carbon monoxide exposure that night.

She then said, "Well, I'm glad you guys got to catch up."

Chris bowed his head, shaking it. "Yeah, I can't believe he's gone."

"Sorry we had to be the ones to tell you." She put her hand on his shoulder. "You gonna be okay?"

He blew out through pursed lips, then nodded. "Yeah, I will."

"Thanks for answering our questions." Sam lowered her voice. "Listen, Chris, have you really thought about trying to kick the drug habit? Like Brad said?"

"Yeah, but I don't have insurance. Brad said the program he went through was great, but his parents paid a pretty penny for it."

She dug into her purse and pulled out a card with her clinic's info on it. She found a pen and scratched her cell number on the back. "Here. You can call or text me. There are resources available, even if you don't have insurance, but you have to know where to look. If you want, I can help you find one that will work for you."

Chris took the card and rubbed it in his fingers. "You don't have to do that."

"It's what I do. I help people and you need help. I'm happy to do it." She looked at him eye to eye. "Promise you'll give me a call next week?"

"I promise."

SINCE SAM HAD UBERED to the club, she asked James if she could have a ride back to their apartment complex. He shrugged, seeming a bit indifferent to her.

Once they were in the car, she said, "You were a little standoffish when we were talking to Chris. I thought you wanted to find out what happened."

"It just brought back some bad memories. That's all." His knuckles blanched as he gripped the steering wheel.

Sam turned in her seat to face him. "What do you mean?"

James kept looking straight ahead as he spoke. "Well, you know Brad was always picking on me."

Sam nodded. Brad picked on everyone, actually, but James did seem to garner more of Brad's ire, probably because of James's friendship with Claire. When Sam had pointed this out to Claire, she'd brushed it off, saying Brad was just being a protective older brother. Sam didn't agree, but she didn't want to push the point too hard because she didn't want to ruin her own friendship with Claire. In Claire's eyes, Brad was a great older brother, but she often overlooked his flaws and bad behavior—perhaps a little too much.

James took a deep breath. "One time Mr. Arnott, the photography teacher, asked me to take some boxes and empty chemical containers out to the dumpsters behind the school. Brad was there with Chris, skipping class. And they were both pretty high. So Brad comes over and shoves me, knocking everything out of my hands. He said, 'I guess you're the janitor now, huh?'"

Sam put her hand on his shoulder. "I'm so sorry."

"I tried to ignore him, but when I leaned over to pick stuff up, he pushed me onto the ground, then started laughing."

"And what did Chris do?"

"Nothing. He just sat against the wall and laughed too. I thought I had gotten over all this stuff, but seeing Chris again tonight brought it all back." They sat in silence while James continued to drive. After a few moments, he asked, "You wanted to help him. Why?"

"It's just what I do. I wanted to become a doctor to help people, and when I was in med school and residency, you learn to take care of people, even those who do horrible things. I feel obligated. In my view, no one is below receiving help—no matter how reprehensible their behavior may be."

"So you'd help a drug dealer? Someone who destroyed other's lives?"

"Yes, I've helped drug dealers and others even more awful."

She thought back to her time at Ben Taub, one of the Level One Trauma Centers in Houston. Some nights the emergency department could seem like a war zone, and she often would have to treat members of rival gangs who had attacked each other. Police officers would accompany them, and after their wounds were treated, some of them would be handcuffed to their beds with police stationed outside their rooms. Others were discharged and taken to jail.

She didn't know what they had done or how they'd gotten there, but she took care of them, nonetheless. Everyone deserved to be healed. And then the judicial system could take over.

"So that's why I gave Chris my number. It's up to him to get help for his drug problem. He still has to decide to call me, and if he does, I'll point him in the direction of the resources available to him. That's all I can do."

"Well, I guess that makes sense. So do you believe Chris? Do you think Brad refused to do any drugs that night?"

"Maybe. But the toxicology report showed Brad had taken clonazepam, not Xanax. So maybe Chris was telling the truth. If he was, then where did Brad get clonazepam?"

James shrugged. "So another dead end?"

"I suppose so. It does seem like Brad and Chris did get a dose of carbon monoxide that night, since they both had headaches. If Brad sat in his car longer after he dropped off Chris, then maybe he did get a big enough dose to cause a heart attack. Maybe this is just a bad accident."

"So what are you saying? Do you think there isn't anything nefarious going on?"

"Perhaps." Sam rubbed her eyes. "Honestly, I don't know."

28

T he next day was Sunday, so Sam slept in. When she woke up, she decided to treat herself to coffee and a pastry by riding her bike to Mozart's. She loved that she could ride along the greenbelt for half the journey, and then it was a straight shot down Lake Austin Boulevard to the coffee shop. The wind carried banter from golfers playing at the old Lions Municipal course as she rode along. She was thankful for the mesh strung up on high poles that prevented errant balls from flying into the street and the bike lane.

After the golf course, she continued riding to the entrance of the parking lot for the row of restaurants upstream of Tom Miller Dam. She dismounted and waited for a red Camaro to pull onto the street from the lot. As the driver hit the accelerator, his car scraped the ridge where the concrete from the steep drive met the sidewalk next to the street. Once it was clear, Sam walked her bike down the drive and locked it up next to the coffeehouse.

The smell of roasted coffee permeated the old stone building, and she ordered her usual latte and danish. She wanted a table on the deck overlooking Lake Austin, but the place was bustling, so she settled for a spot under the massive oak tree near the parking lot.

When she first sat down, Sam pulled her laptop out of her backpack and opened up a web browser. She wanted to continue looking into what her boss had told her—that there may be a way for her to become board certified while working at Obracare—but the conversation with Chris from the night before kept entering her mind, making it hard for her to focus. After a few minutes, she relented to her preoccupation and took out her Moleskin notebook.

She wrote down all the facts she knew about Brad's case. It did not appear that he died of an overdose, but this issue with the carbon monoxide poisoning was worrisome. What was the likelihood of two people getting carbon monoxide exposure from two different cars, one of whom received a dose high enough to cause death? Brad had been having headaches for a few months before the wedding was supposed to take place. Then he dies the morning of the wedding, but from myocardial ischemia, not an overdose.

Four days later, Mike has a car accident after he passed out while he was driving. Thank goodness he didn't hurt anyone and only had minor injuries himself.

And apparently, the night before Brad died, he and Chris both had headaches after sitting in traffic. Maybe Brad did die of carbon monoxide poisoning. It would probably depend on how long he'd sat in his car right before he died, though.

So how common would it be if two people she knew, and actually three now that she talked to Chris, all had exposure and possible poisoning from carbon monoxide? Even though it appeared there may have been tampering with both Mike's and Brad's cars, she felt there must be something else linking the two, since they had the same type of car.

Sam suddenly had a thought. She remembered the root she had almost tripped over—the root that had pushed up the concrete on the steep driveway at the Johnsons' house. Just then, she heard a loud scrape as another car, this time an electric blue Toyota Supra, pulled into the parking lot, bottoming out on the ridge from the sidewalk.

She needed to get over to the Johnsons' house.

Sam quickly finished her latte, gathered up her things, and tossed the rest of her danish in the trash. Once she unlocked her bike, she sprinted up the steep drive and pedaled as fast as she could to get back home. Twenty minutes later, she was in her car, heading west into the hills.

She thought about calling Claire or her parents, but they were probably at church. And if this ended up being a harebrained idea, no one would have to know.

When she pulled up to the Johnsons' home, the street was quiet, the stillness palpable. She parked as she had before on the street, then climbed the driveway to the point where the root of the towering oak tree shading the driveway jutted out, right at the seam between the mostly flat slab of concrete leading to the garage and the angled slab on the hillside.

Sam squatted next to the protrusion, inspecting the area, which was about four feet from the edge of the driveway—exactly where Brad or Mike would have pulled up to avoid blocking the garage where Claire's parents parked. She spread her arms, imagining the width of a car, glancing around to make sure there wasn't anyone staring at her strange gesture. She nodded to herself. Yes, this would be about where the damage was located on the Mustangs.

It appeared the root had caused the seam to spread apart, cracking the concrete on the sloping slab. She didn't think the wood from the root would be strong enough to damage the bottom of a car. And the concrete around the root appeared smoothed out. Then she noticed what she thought had been part of the root before were actually two pieces of rebar sticking out, ever so slightly. The rust of the rebar blended in with the root. Could this have punctured the bottom of the Mustangs?

She took a few pictures to document what she found, then she got in her car and started the engine to get the air conditioning going. She did a few searches on the web to see if her theory was even plausible.

The footwells of a car are also called floor pans, and they were usually made of 18-gauge steel sheet metal. How thick was that? Another search told Sam 18-gauge steel was 0.05 inches thick—so just over a millimeter. That didn't seem like much. How thick are exhaust pipes? More searching. Only slightly thicker at 0.065 inches. Okay. Seemed like a piece of rebar might be able to puncture that.

So how much force would something need to punch through steel? A website with a nice table showed it would take about 0.9 tons of pressure to punch a quarter-inch hole in 18-gauge steel. Right, it's pressure—force over area —not just force. And a ton of pressure would be about two thousand pounds per square inch, or psi. Rebar has a tensile strength of forty thousand psi. And the cross-sectional area of the exposed rebar was certainly less than a square inch, maybe about the size of one of her fingers. Then Sam remembered tensile strength had to do with stretch, not compression. But she found a page that told her for most metals, tensile and compressive strength were about the same.

So yes, it was at least plausible that the rebar poking out through the crack in the driveway punctured the bottom of Brad's and Mike's cars.

Sam pulled away from the curb and drove back to her apartment, rethinking through her logic on the way. She was still processing what she had discovered and trying to decide what she should do next when the clack of the door knocker interrupted her thoughts.

Sam looked through the peephole. It was James. She opened the door, and he rushed in with a wild look on his face.

"Have you heard?"

"Heard what?"

"Chris is dead!"

29

"What happened?" Sam asked.

James sat on Sam's couch opposite her. "I got a text from Trent this morning, you know, the manager we saw last night at the Continental Club?"

Sam nodded.

"Apparently he's buddies with one of Chris's band-mates, and after the set last night, they went to his buddy's house on the east side. They partied, some shot up, including Chris, and after a while, everyone passed out. When they woke up this morning, Chris was dead."

"Really? Maybe talking to him about Brad's death upset him more than I thought." Sam felt a pit in her stomach. Did they push him toward this end last night?

"Yeah, or it could have just been a bad batch of heroine."

Sam thought back to the previous night when they talked with Chris. "Do you remember what kind of shirt Chris had on?"

"If I remember correctly," James said, looking up at

the ceiling, "he had on a T-shirt, with an unbuttoned tailored shirt over it, like a jacket. The sleeves were rolled up."

"But not above his elbow. Yeah, I was just trying to remember if I noticed track marks last night. But if he had on that long-sleeved shirt, we wouldn't have been able to see them."

"He probably wore the long-sleeved shirt on purpose to hide the track marks."

"If that's the case, I wonder how long he was using heroin."

"Yeah, I didn't think he was shooting up in high school. But it's been a while."

"And many drug users escalate the dosages or start using stronger drugs as their bodies build up a tolerance. Someone could start off abusing prescription drugs and then eventually move to heroin to get a stronger effect. Plus injecting straight into the bloodstream brings on a faster onset."

"Okay, now you're sounding very medical."

"Sorry, I can't help it sometimes."

"Hey, you don't have to apologize for being smart and working hard. You've accomplished some amazing things. You take care of people and you've saved lives. Don't ever apologize for that."

"Tell that to everyone else. Seems people only appreciate YouTubers and TikTokers these days."

"Well, you're here with me and I appreciate you."

Sam smiled. "Thanks, James." She thought a moment, then said, "So Chris died of an overdose, and even though Brad didn't die of an overdose, still, I think his death was an accident."

"You don't think Brad was murdered?"

"No, I don't." She went on to explain her findings at

the Johnsons' house and how she thought the exposed rebar in their driveway punctured the bottom of Mike's and Brad's Mustangs.

"What about that contract Brad had with Todd?"

Sam shrugged. "Even if Todd may have been trying to take advantage of Brad—and we don't know that, because it could just be a standard contract—it doesn't mean he murdered Brad." She leaned forward, resting her elbows on her thighs, her head in her hands. "I don't know, James. I'm just tired of all this. I don't know why I ever agreed to look into this for Claire."

James rubbed Sam's back. "You just wanted to help."

She sat up, glaring at him. "But look what good that did. We were the ones that told Chris his old high school friend died right after they last saw each other, that Chris may have been the last person to see him alive." She grimaced. "He seemed pretty shaken up. What if Chris OD'd on purpose because of it?"

"Hey, don't blame yourself. Chris had a problem. And you were actually trying to help him, remember? You wanted to help him get into a rehab program."

Sam hung her head, letting out an exasperated huff. "Yeah, well … I just need to stick to what I know, and that's taking care of patients—patients whom I have an obligation to take care of and who depend on me. I should stop doing favors for friends." She looked at James. "Let the professionals deal with Brad's death. I'm not a detective."

30

L ater that day, as Sam focused on chores around her apartment, putting off her decision about what to do with her findings that morning in the Johnsons' driveway, Claire texted. Sam hadn't spoken to her since the previous weekend after the first-pass cleanup of Brad's apartment, and then it had just been briefly. Claire and Emily were working furiously to get the soap shop ready for their grand opening in a few weeks, and Sam hoped it would provide Claire with the salve she needed to heal.

Sam knew she had to meet with Claire, to tell her she couldn't keep digging into Brad's death, especially after Chris's overdose. Claire invited Sam to stop by, so Sam picked up some chips and queso on the way, hoping the Tex-Mex comfort food would soften the expected disappointment.

Mike was mowing the front yard when Sam arrived, and he waved as she walked up to the front door. Sam rang the doorbell, and she was quickly greeted with Kerbey's yips.

As Claire opened the door, Sam held out the bag that contained the gooey goodness and said, "I bear gifts from Kerbey's namesake."

Claire's eyes widened. "Kerbey Queso! Thank you!"

They sat down at the small kitchen table and snacked while Claire filled Sam in on all the progress she and Emily had made during the week at the shop. Sam was glad Claire was consumed with her new venture, hoping maybe she had finally moved on from her brother's death, but then Claire said, "I heard the toxicology report for Brad's autopsy is back, but I don't know what it says. Have you heard anything from Dylan?"

Sam turned her chair to face Claire head-on. "Yes, he came by the clinic this week."

"Why didn't you tell me?"

"Because I knew you were bu—"

"What did it show?" Claire interrupted, leaning closer to Sam. "Did he overdose?"

Sam shook her head. "No. He didn't have any opiates in his system. The only thing the test results showed was clonazepam and—"

"Then he must have been murdered," Claire interrupted again, sitting up straight.

"I don't think so."

Claire knitted her eyebrows. "Why not?"

"I found something this morning at your parents' house." Sam pulled out her phone to show Claire the pictures. "This is from their driveway. A root from the oak tree separated the seam between the concrete slabs and exposed these pieces of rebar," she said as she pointed to the structures in the image.

Claire sat back in her chair. "So what are you saying?"

"This may have caused the damage to those cars,

leading to Mike's accident and Brad's headaches, possibly his death."

"But you aren't completely certain, right?"

"No, not completely, but …" Sam hesitated, uncertain how Claire would react. She took a deep breath, then said, "I'm done looking into this."

"Why?" Claire leaned forward, putting her forearms on the table, her hands balled into fists. "There's something going on. I know what I heard."

Sam closed her eyes for a moment. What should she do? How would this end? When she opened her eyes, Claire was scowling at her.

"Why don't you believe me?"

"Brad also had alcohol and a benzodiazepine in his system."

"But Brad wasn't drinking anymore." Claire crossed her arms. "He wasn't drinking the night before he died at the rehearsal dinner."

"I know. I remember, but he may have had something to drink afterward."

"And what was that other thing you claim was in his system?"

"A benzodiazepine. It's a sedative, used for a lot of different reasons, like treating epilepsy or anxiety—"

"You know who has anxiety? Emily does. She takes something for it. Maybe that's how Brad got it. Why don't you ask her? Or …" Claire's words trailed off as she paused. "Or what about Chris? Brad saw him the night before he died. That's who you should ask."

Sam hung her head. "I did. He said he offered some to Brad that night, but Brad refused."

"See, I bet he's lying, or maybe he snuck some into Brad's drink. Why don't you tell Dylan about that?" Claire stood up and grabbed her phone off the kitchen counter.

"Did you tell Dylan he should talk to Chris? I'm going to call Dylan right—"

"Chris is dead."

Claire stopped. "What?"

Sam looked down. "Chris is dead."

Claire blinked and dropped back down into her chair. "What do you mean, Chris is dead?"

"James and I talked to him last night. He didn't know Brad had died."

"Oh. We tried to let everyone know about the funeral, but he must not have …" Claire looked up. "How did you find out?"

"The manager at the club where Chris's band played last night called James this morning. Chris overdosed after we talked to him."

"I … I don't know what to say."

Sam sat up. "Well, I do. I'm done asking questions and looking into this. If I hadn't talked to Chris last night, he might still be alive."

Claire stitched her eyebrows together. "You don't know that."

"I'm going to send these pictures to Dylan and let him decide what to do with them." Sam looked at Claire and took her hand. "I'm sorry, Claire, but you need to let this go."

"No. You're giving up on me?" Claire pulled her hand away. "You never believed me, did you?"

"Claire, please don't be like this. I know you're hurting. I know you're looking for answers." Sam's mouth felt dry. She was tiptoeing around Claire's emotions, as if she might step on a landmine if she weren't careful. She needed this to end. She wasn't helping anyone, and in Chris's case, she made things worse. Much worse. She clumsily pushed forward. "But the answers just aren't there. I'm sorry, but I think you're in denial, and you're trying to cope with a horrible thing—the death of your beloved brother, someone who was so young and full of promise, who seemed to be turning his life around. And for his death to happen on what was supposed to be your wedding day ..."

Claire glared at her, tears streaming down her face and grief dancing in her eyes with something else, but Sam pressed on.

"I wanted to help you, but I only made things worse." Sam sighed. "I think this was all a terrible, tragic accident. Brad was chronically exposed to carbon monoxide from the damage to his car, and—"she shrugged—"I don't know. I suppose he was already in a hypoxic state, and the benzos and alcohol suppressed his respiratory drive enough to kill him."

Anger flashed in Claire's eyes—what Sam had missed earlier—overpowering her grief. She said, "That's the problem with you. You use all this jargon, make everyone feel inferior. No wonder Dylan and Jeff broke up with you."

Sam inhaled sharply, surprised by Claire's reaction, realizing too late how much she had hurt her. "I'm sorry." She stood, picking up her purse.

When she turned toward the front door, Mike was standing there. He had heard everything. As she approached, he opened the door for her, then he followed her outside, pulling the door shut behind him.

"I'm sorry. I ... I know I hurt her by being so blunt. She wasn't ready to hear that."

"It's okay," Mike said. "I'll talk to her, and she'll come around."

31

After her encounter with Claire, Sam was shaken and kept replaying the conversation in her mind. She felt hurt, just like Claire had. She tried not to blame Claire, who was lashing out from her own pain, but she sure knew how to make it sting.

Yet Sam still believed her theory was plausible, and after she got back to her apartment, she sent Dylan the images of the driveway. He called her shortly afterward, asking her to explain her thinking, so she did. He thanked her and said he would pass the information along to the medical examiner's office. She was a little concerned after their last exchange, but the call had been completely professional. In fact, she felt like she had just spoken to one of her colleagues.

She had to force herself to breathe deeply, to gain perspective. Was Claire right? The anger she had seen in Claire's eyes was the same anger she had seen before, in the coworker who had smashed Mr. Campbell's thumb— in Frank's eyes. Sam wasn't using medical jargon to make anyone feel inferior, it was just the best way to efficiently communicate her ideas—or so she thought. Was she wielding her knowledge like a weapon?

That certainly was not her intent. She had used a bunch of jargon with Dylan on the phone just now, and if he didn't understand something, he just asked. No big deal. He hadn't seemed defensive.

And Claire had it wrong. Sam was the one who had broken up with Dylan, not the other way around. At least that was the narrative she had formed in her mind. It had been so long ago that she'd forgotten the specific circumstances. But then she remembered the real reason things fell apart … that night.

One weekend in the spring of their sophomore year, Sam had gone over to Claire's house to spend the night, as she had done dozens of times before. Claire's mom had ordered pizza, and as everyone sat around the dinner table eating, Claire announced, "Sam won second place in the science fair."

Mrs. Johnson smiled warmly. "That's wonderful, Sam. You always were so smart."

Mr. Johnson joined in, saying, "Good job, kid." It was one of the rare interactions Sam had with him, so he must have been impressed.

Sam beamed. When she told her own parents, her mother said she was proud of her and promised to take Sam shopping as a reward, but her father had seemed distracted. He nodded, saying, "Not bad. Not bad. Next year you might consider doing the experiment we talked about. That would give you the chance to win first place."

The experiment he had wanted her to do involved testing various substances on earthworms to see how they would affect the worms' circulatory systems. Sam hadn't wanted to experiment on live animals, even if they were just worms, and she didn't think the science fair committee would have allowed it, anyway. Instead, she performed the experiment her science teacher had recommended, testing which essential oils could be used as disinfectants.

Sam was proud of her second place finish in the fair, especially since she was just a sophomore, but apparently her father thought otherwise.

So when Claire's parents praised her, she thought, *This is how a normal family should be.* Then Brad, her first crush, gazed at her, his eyes narrowing. Even though she was dating Dylan, her stomach fluttered and she looked away.

He stood up and said, "Gotta go meet Billy," and left.

Sam thought that would be the last she'd see of him that evening, but later while she and Claire sat on the couch upstairs in the family game room, watching a silly romantic comedy and giggling at all the predictable misunderstandings, Brad came up the stairs.

"Mom needs you to help her with something."

Claire sat up. "What? Right now?"

Brad shrugged. "I don't know. Go ask her."

So Claire got up and disappeared down the stairs.

Brad came to the couch and flopped down next to Sam. "Well, hello there."

Sam looked at him, her heart thumping. She could smell alcohol on his breath.

He leaned closer to her, running his fingers along her shoulder. "Pretty impressive what you did with the science fair."

Was this really happening? In her schoolgirl crush, when she had imagined being with Brad, it was always vague and innocent.

Suddenly he was on top of her, grabbing her breasts, pressing his body on hers, his lips smashing hers—not passionately but angrily. When she tried to make a sound —some kind of sound, any kind of sound—he clamped his hand over her mouth. He laughed. "You know you want it. Girls always do."

His free hand snaked down to her crotch and she froze. In her mind, she screamed at her body to push, fight, thrash, do something. She tried to yell, but he clamped his hand down harder over her mouth. She could barely breathe, with tears on her face, her nose stuffy. Her heart hammered, and her only focus was on escaping. But she couldn't. She was paralyzed. She didn't know what to do. And she certainly did not want this.

Then Claire's voice came from the stairwell. "Brad! You dork. Mom doesn't know what you're talking about."

And just as suddenly, he was off her. He stood, straightening his clothes.

Sam sat up, straightening her clothes, too, and feeling guilty, even though she had done nothing wrong.

Claire appeared at the top of the stairs. "She said she wanted me to help her clean out and rearrange her sewing room, but it can wait until tomorrow, since Sam's over."

Brad cocked his head. "My bad. Thought she said she needed you now." He went into his bedroom and shut the door.

Sam slowed her breath, hoping Claire didn't notice anything amiss. Claire sat down, picked up the remote, and started the movie again. She finally looked over at Sam. "Are you okay? You don't look so good."

"Yeah, I'm not feeling very well." Sam stood, her legs a bit wobbly. "Must have been something I ate. I'm gonna go home."

After that night, Sam did not go to Claire's house again until Brad had graduated and left for college. The next week in school, when Dylan asked her out, she made up an excuse. The cycle continued a few more times until Dylan stopped asking. In all, they had only been dating a couple of months before Brad attacked her, but for a high school sophomore, it had felt like an eternity.

Sam hadn't thought about why exactly she'd stopped dating Dylan until now. The axis of her world perspective had shifted that night. Sam had suppressed the memory fully. And she now realized, when Brad had attacked her, he'd sowed the idea in her that maybe all boys saw girls the same way—as a threat. A threat that must be neutralized through domination.

32

S am started off the following week in clinic a bit more somberly. Even though the "investigation" had ended badly, she was glad she didn't have Claire and her conspiracy ideas around Brad's death hanging over her head.

Members of Chris Baker's band had set up a GoFundMe page to help pay for the cost of his funeral, and Sam had made a contribution, a small penance. Rationally, she knew his death wasn't her fault, but she couldn't shake the guilt that crept into her mind when she thought about him.

As the week progressed, she continued to look into preventive medicine residency programs, shooting off emails to learn more about the requirements, trying to form a plan and a course correction for her career path. Even though some programs included a Master of Public Health degree as part of their curriculum, it seemed if she finished her MPH before she applied, she could increase her chances of acceptance. So then she started looking into various MPH programs and found some that could be completed part time while taking courses remotely. Learning about her options and realizing she had choices greatly improved her mood.

With all the patients to see, Sam hardly had a chance to talk to Jerry, but at one point the wave of patients slowed enough for them to have a brief conversation.

"Hey, Doc, I forgot to ask how your meeting with Dr. Taylor went last week. You're still here, so I'm assuming everything is good."

Sam smiled. "Yes, I was worrying about nothing. And he told me about some options I might have to get board certified."

"Oh, is that so?"

Sam spelled out what she had found in her research and how she was considering getting an MPH.

"So you're going back to school, then."

"Just part time."

He nodded. "That's medicine, always learning." Then he frowned as he looked at her wrist. "What's wrong with your watch? Is it broken?"

Sam glanced down and tapped it, waking up the screen. "No, I just left it in theater mode. I was out last weekend, and it seemed too bright in the dark room, so I turned on this mode. Now the screen stays off unless you tap it." She shrugged. "I decided to keep it that way. Seems less distracting when I'm seeing patients."

He smiled ironically. "These newfangled gadgets. Now you've got a watch that looks like it's broken and doesn't show you the time."

～

BY THE TIME Thursday rolled around, the shock of the past weekend's events had faded. Sam hardly had time to think about them, anyway, as summer brought more activity, more construction projects, and more injuries. Mrs. Rodriguez was back for another visit. Sam was glad to see that even though she didn't know how things had gone with the specialist, Mrs. Rodriguez was already doing physical therapy again, having completed a session just now.

"How are you doing today?" Sam said as she walked into the exam room. "The last time I saw you, we set you up to see Dr. Popescu. How did that appointment go?"

"Oh, Dr. Jenkins! I feel so much better. I'm able to move my arm a bit more. I feel a little weak still, but I've already made progress, even after just three PT sessions." She flapped her arm with her elbow bent, like she was doing the chicken dance. "That Bob—he really works me out!"

Sam smiled. "That's wonderful, Mrs. Rodriguez." She unlocked the PC in the room and scrolled through Mrs. Rodriguez's chart. "I don't have anything back yet from Dr. Popescu. Could you tell me what he decided to do?"

"He did one of those injections." Mrs. Rodriguez pointed to her neck. "He told me to wait a day, and then I started PT. So that's what I did. It's good to feel normal again."

"I'm so glad. Let's take a look at you."

Sam tested Mrs. Rodriguez's strength and range of motion, and they had, indeed, improved. In fact, they were almost completely back to normal.

"Do you feel like you're ready to go back to work, Mrs. Rodriguez?"

"Oh yes. I would love to go back to work."

"Okay. Let me check with Bob." Bob was one of the physical therapists who worked in Sam's clinic. She knew he would be a better judge of Mrs. Rodriguez's capabili-

ties, and he'd also know her employer's exact job requirements. "Do you mind waiting here for just a second?"

Mrs. Rodriguez nodded. "Of course, Doctora."

When Sam stepped out into the hallway, she was
surprised to see Dylan sitting in one of the chairs, tapping
away on his phone. She glowered at him. "Why are you
here?"

Dylan looked up at her. "Nice to see you too."

"Why are you here?" Sam repeated.

"I'm here to take my Aunt Becky home."

"Your Aunt Becky?"

"Yes, the lady in the exam room you just came out of."

Sam was speechless for a second.

Dylan smirked. "You know, not everything is about
you."

Sam humphed, but she could feel her cheeks burning.
"I'm almost done with her visit. I just need to check on
something."

"By the way," Dylan said, "the department is closing
Brad's case. The medical examiner is ruling his death an
accident due to the carbon monoxide exposure from his
car."

Sam nodded.

Dylan continued, "Thanks again for sending those
pictures of the ridge and the exposed rebar in the driveway. It looks like the rebar matches the markings on the
cars." He shook his head. "Good thing it didn't affect
anybody else's cars. From what Claire's parents said, it
sounds like Brad and Mike were the only ones who parked
on that side and had low-riding vehicles."

"That settles it then." She thought about letting Dylan
know about Chris's death, but then she didn't want to have
to explain to him how she knew and why she was even
talking to him to begin with. Plus, it wasn't really related.

"I'll be right back." She turned down the hallway to the physical therapy room.

After she got the information she needed from Bob, she returned to the exam room where she had left Mrs. Rodriguez. Dylan was now in the room with her.

"Oh, Doctora! Dylan just told me you two knew each other in high school," Mrs. Rodriguez said. "I didn't realize he knew you, but I kept seeing him here at the clinic. He said he was working on a case. I asked him if he could bring me today so that my daughter could use my car to go to work right after school."

Sam looked at Dylan and he blushed.

"Yes, ma'am. We were in the same grade," she said, wondering what else he had told his aunt.

"That is so nice, you two seeing each other again." Mrs. Rodriguez glanced at Sam's left hand. Sam assumed she was looking for a wedding ring. "Do you have a special someone?"

Now it was Sam's turn to blush. "No, ma'am."

Mrs. Rodriguez patted Dylan's hand. "My nephew is a good man."

Sam shot Dylan a look.

"Aunt Becky, please. I'm in a relationship right now," Dylan said.

"But is she a doctora?" Mrs. Rodriguez said, arching an eyebrow.

"No, but she works with doctors." Then Dylan looked at Sam. "And Dr. Jenkins and I are just friends who help each other out." He gave a slight nod.

Sam sighed. "Honestly, Mrs. Rodriguez, I'm fine." Then she thought about Alex Crawford. She felt a bit uncomfortable discussing her dating life with one of her patients and her old high school sweetheart, but she said, "And I do have a date tomorrow night."

Mrs. Rodriguez squeezed her hand. "Of course you do. How could a beautiful doctora not be taken?"

As they left the room, Sam couldn't help noticing Dylan glancing back at her with a strange look, maybe tinged with regret.

33

After a busy week seeing nearly thirty patients a day and spending a couple of hours each evening finishing up charts at home, Sam was exhausted. But she was looking forward to having dinner with Alex Crawford.

That Friday evening, as she waited for him at Perla's— a fabulous seafood restaurant in a land-locked city—she thought about how they came to know each other. She didn't remember exactly when they'd first met, because much of her residency was a blur, but she remembered there had been a hint of attraction.

In some ways, residency had been like perpetual summer camp with other smart kids. You felt like an insider, knowing all these secrets for how the body worked, how complex hospitals functioned, and how to save lives. Of course there were plenty of days when tragedy struck, and patients did die, but for the most part, even on the services with the sickest patients and in the most dire conditions, those tragedies were not too common. The majority of days were spent healing people. Performing complex procedures—things most normal people never heard of—and potentially curing patients of cancer, or alleviating their pain from appendicitis or gallbladder disease, were the most rewarding days. But being a doctor often didn't allow for much else in the way of a personal life.

And even the surgeons Sam worked with, who seemed to have a good life, had to deal with disappointment. She remembered one Friday evening in particular. She had been on call, so it didn't matter to her if a patient had to go back to the operating room, and in fact, it made her time on call in the hospital pass much more quickly. But her attending, Dr. Rogers, was supposed to take his son to a baseball game.

Late that afternoon, Mr. Griffin, one of the patients Dr. Rogers had operated on the day before, started to develop a fever and abdominal pain. Dr. Rogers had performed a left hemicolectomy, which is an operation to remove the left side of the colon, in this case for a sessile polyp—a sign of early stage colon cancer. The lymph nodes from the surgical specimen came back negative, so Mr. Griffin would essentially be cured of his colon cancer.

But it was late on a Friday afternoon, and Mr. Griffin's fever and abdominal pain indicated he needed a CT scan. The results showed that the anastomosis—where the ends of the remaining colon had been reconnected—had broken down and started to leak. And intestinal contents leaking into the abdomen led to infection, which if left untreated, could turn into sepsis, then death.

Unfortunately that meant everything was inflamed in poor Mr. Griffin's belly. So not only would he need to go back to the operating room to flush out the contamination, but he would also need a colostomy. Then he would need another surgery a couple of weeks later to put everything back together again once the infection cleared.

So there was Dr. Rogers on the phone right outside the operating room. Sam stood there, witnessing his anguish.

"I know I said I would take you to the Astros game tonight, son. I'm sorry I can't do that now," Dr. Rogers said.

Sam fidgeted with the drawstrings on her scrubs, trying to act like she wasn't listening.

"I know I missed your game last month too. I'm sorry about that as well," Dr. Rogers said as he hung his head. "But you know I have to take care of my patients."

Sam pulled her list of patients out of her back pocket and ran her finger down the census. Fortunately, she'd already checked on almost all of them. Just two more to see, but she could do that after this case. She would be there all night, anyway.

"Of course I love you, Brian," Dr. Rogers said.

Sam glanced over at Dr. Rogers. He was leaning against the wall, twisting the phone cord around his fingers and staring at the floor.

Dr. Rogers lowered his voice. "I love you and your sister and Mom very much." There was a crack in his voice. "You all mean the world to me."

Sam paced down the hallway a bit to give Dr. Rogers more space.

He then cleared his throat. "Okay. This case shouldn't take more than a couple of hours." He looked in Sam's direction. "And I have a very good resident who will take care of my patient tonight." He nodded at her. "So if everything goes well, I'll come home and take you to the game. We should be there by the fifth inning."

At that moment, Sam felt pride but also sorrow. She

suddenly could see her own future—a future with heart-break, for children she did not yet have.

"I know, I know." Dr. Rogers sighed. "But it's the best I can do. I'll see you in a few hours. Love you." And he hung up.

Fortunately, the surgery went as smoothly as a take-back could, and Sam told Dr. Rogers he should leave as soon as the skin was closed. He said he would talk to Mr. Griffin's family if she would take care of the post-op orders and make sure he got to his room after the PACU, the post-anesthesia care unit.

But after seeing Dr. Rogers nearly break down from disappointing his son, Sam knew she couldn't see herself living this life, where she would have to make sacrifices for her patients at the expense of her family.

These thoughts were running through Sam's mind as she waited for Alex to arrive. She checked her watch, tapping it to see the time. Fifteen minutes late. She figured he must have had something come up. Perhaps that's why she was thinking of Dr. Rogers and his son. Such is the life of a doctor, especially a surgeon. And Alex had gone on to do a specialty in critical care, so he was taking care of some pretty sick patients in the ICU.

Her phone buzzed. It was a text from Alex: *Sorry. Running late. Be there in 5.*

Sam shook her head as she smiled. Yep, that's how things are. She texted back: *No problem.*

She sipped her wine and cleared her mind. At least she didn't have to deal with call now—just patients during regular business hours and then a bunch of charts to finish in the evenings so that the clinic could bill for all her work. She thought about checking Facebook, but then she didn't want to see anything about Brad. She should have never gotten involved, so she resorted to working on some cross-word puzzles while she waited.

A few minutes later, Alex arrived, a little flushed. "Sorry I'm late, Sam."

She stood up to give him a brief hug, and he pecked her cheek. She wasn't certain where this was going, but she supposed this was considered a date. Last weekend they had just met for drinks, or rather, she had a drink while Alex drank a club soda, since he was on call.

He looked quite handsome, having changed into a button-down, with the sleeves rolled up, and khakis with loafers. His sandy blond hair had that intentional slightly disheveled look. He gave her a warm smile.

"It's okay," Sam said. "I've been in your position before."

Alex nodded.

A waiter walked up and they ordered dinner. They engaged in chitchat while the waiter shuttled back and forth to drop off Alex's cocktail and some warm cornbread with honey butter.

"So whatever happened to your friend that you always hung out with? She was in plastics, right?" Alex asked.

"Oh, you mean Nicole?"

"Yeah, you were the two hotties with the sweet cars."

Sam rolled her eyes. Nicole was married, and her husband had bought her a BMW roadster. Sam's fiancé had bought her a Mercedes roadster, which she gave back to him when they broke off their engagement.

Nicole was one of her best friends from residency. She'd been in the plastic surgery residency program, but she left shortly after Sam had left the general surgery program. Nicole realized that she wanted to have a family and a life outside the hospital, which plastic surgery could provide—that is, if Nicole wanted to cater to the wealthy by focusing on cosmetic surgery. But her whole reason for going into plastic surgery was to focus on reconstructive surgery for burn patients. It was a grueling and taxing career. Nicole had told Sam she'd looked at the areas where she could do shift work while still doing procedures. The two areas she narrowed things down to were emergency medicine and anesthesiology. But she was afraid that she would always be looking over the curtain at what the surgeons were doing if she went into anesthesiology. So she chose emergency medicine, which meant applying to a new residency program in a different state.

"Nicole's almost done with her emergency medicine program in New York," Sam said. "Fortunately, they counted her first year of plastics as an intern year, so she only lost one year in the transfer."

"Oh, so that's what she decided to do." Alex looked a little bashful. "And sorry about the hottie remark."

Sam smiled. It was flattering and somehow demeaning at the same time.

"So how was your day?" she asked. "Anything exciting happen?"

In medicine, when doctors talked about something exciting happening, it usually wasn't a good situation for the patient—not that the doctors weren't doing what they needed to do, but that they were performing obscure procedures or taking care of the sickest patients, which made them feel like they were pushing the limits of medicine and really saving someone's life.

"It was pretty slow until right before I had to leave, of course. One of the patients on the floor crumped, and the hospitalist had to transfer him to the ICU. They asked me to float a Swan, which is why I was late."

Sam nodded. When a patient crumped, it meant their condition went downhill quickly and they needed immediate critical care or they would die. The fact that this patient required a Swan, short for Swan-Ganz catheter, meant that the doctors needed to measure the blood pressure directly inside the heart and the pulmonary arteries.

"Did the patient already have a central line?"

"No, he had a PICC on the right, so we had to pull that first, then I had to put in a subclavian."

He meant he had to put a central line catheter into the subclavian vein, just below the collarbone, like the one Mrs. Rodriguez had during childbirth.

Alex continued, "But the bed they used to bring him into the ICU was broken, and it couldn't put him in Trendelenburg."

"Ugh. That's a pain." Trendelenburg was just the medical way of saying the bed needed to be tilted with the head down.

"We had to scramble to move him onto another bed before I could do anything. Plus I had to wait to pull the PICC until after they moved him, to make sure we maintained access."

PICC lines were peripherally inserted central catheters, usually pronounced as "pick," like picking fruit. They became popular while Sam was in residency because a nurse could do the procedure instead of a doctor, and the hospital could bill for it. The nurse, of course, was just paid her usual wage, while the hospital could make a few hundred dollars for thirty minutes of her time. The PICC line would be inserted just above the antecubital fossa, using ultrasound to guide its placement. The lines were a couple of feet long because the catheter had to travel all the way from the arm to the entrance of the patient's heart. Of course, another advantage of the PICC line was that, unlike a subclavian central line, there was no risk of collapsing the patient's lung.

If Alex had to insert a Swan-Ganz to measure pressure in the patient's heart, he could not do that through a PICC line, which is why he needed to put in the subclavian central line. However, the PICC line would get in the way of the central line, since they traveled in the same veins, and that's why he had to pull it out first. But if he had pulled the PICC line out before they moved the patient and he didn't have a new central line in, they could lose access to the patient's veins if they needed to give him medications quickly.

"But it all worked out?" Sam asked.

"Yep. Once we got everything set up, it was no problem. It just figures we would have all these little hiccups when a patient is crashing."

"He's okay now?"

Alex nodded. "He's stable." He smiled. "Remember when we were on Osborne's service at the VA? And we had to put that subclavian in, and he happened to stop by the room right as I was about to puncture the poor guy? He kept yelling, 'Trendelenburg! You need him in Trendelenburg!'"

Sam laughed, "Yeah, I thought you were going to jump out of your clogs!"

SAM WAS ENJOYING her date with Alex, and yes, she now considered it a date. After dinner they walked along South Congress, the evening air with just the right touch of coolness, bright lights flashing, and music from various venues swelling out onto the sidewalk as they passed.

As they reached the end of the shops, even though the road continued, they crossed the opposite side of the street, and started walking north with the Texas State Capitol visible in the distance where the road ended. Sam pointed out the soap shop to Alex, the windows dark and still covered with paper.

"What a great location," he said. "How's your friend's fiancé doing?"

Sam swallowed the pang of remorse she had for how she had handled her last conversation with Claire. "He's doing fine. Like the accident never happened."

They continued to talk about their days in residency, people they knew, and where they had ended up. At one point Alex asked about Sam's job. "I always wondered what happened to people who left residency. How do you like where you are?"

"It's fine, actually. Nice that it's just regular work hours during the week, no call. But of course on busy days, I end up spending a bit of time charting. Sometimes I come home and spend my whole evening finishing notes in the EHR."

Alex laughed. "Yeah, those damn EHRs. I have the same problem."

"Nicole says she spends hours on her days off catching up after a busy shift in the ER."

"Sounds like even if you don't take call, it still creeps into the rest of your life."

"Yeah, but at least I don't have to go in, in the middle of the night."

"I could do without it, but—"he shrugged—"it's just how it is."

"Don't you get jealous of the hospitalists?"

"Well, we may rework things here soon. The hospital is looking to hire another critical care specialist, so maybe we'll switch to a more shift-like schedule. This way none of us will have to take call."

"That would be nice."

"So do you think you'll stay where you are, or are you thinking about going back to residency?"

Sam tugged at her earlobe. "Honestly, I don't know. I don't think I want to deal with the conditions of residency again. The pay is not bad where I am, and I just found out I can become board certified in preventive medicine if I get my MPH. I could do that remotely while I work. Not a bad option."

"Do you keep up with many people from residency?"

"Not really. I feel like a pariah. They seem to be treating me like an outcast—as if they might quit medicine, too, by talking to me too much."

Alex laughed. "That might not be far from the truth. I can't count the number of times I thought about quitting. I just don't know what I would do otherwise. Plus, I have a ton of debt I need to pay off. And how would I do that if I didn't work as a doctor?"

"I'm sorry, Alex. I don't know what to say." Sam felt fortunate in that respect. She didn't have any college loans because she had earned scholarships that paid for the inexpensive tuition at UT. And even though she'd gone to a private medical school, all the medical schools in Texas offered the same low tuition. When she was engaged and living with Jeff, he had helped to pay for their housing expenses. She took a deep breath. Yes, she was rather fortunate she didn't have to worry about the financial implications of leaving residency. And this clinic job wasn't so bad.

After they made a loop around the shops, restaurants, and bars, Alex said, "Well, I guess we should head back. I'm on tomorrow, so I need to round pretty early."

He walked Sam to her car, and before she got in, he said, "I really enjoyed having dinner with you this evening." He gazed at her as he caressed her hand, stepping closer. Sam's heart fluttered. "And I'd like to see you again."

Sam took his hand. "I'd like to see you again too."

He leaned in and kissed her. Maybe it was time to move on. She hadn't felt this way for some time. But she still wanted to be careful. Rebounds could be fun, but she didn't want to hurt Alex, either, especially if he was serious. Even though she wanted this kiss, and wanted it to last, she put her hand on his chest. Leaving it there for just a second, she felt the warmth and taut muscles underneath, before she gently pushed him away.

"But let's take this slowly."

Alex stepped back and smiled—a smile with a slight tinge of disappointment. "I understand."

She hugged him. "Thank you." Then she got in her car and drove away.

34

S aturday morning after her date, Sam woke up earlier than she had intended, her mind racing. She had nervous energy she needed to get out, but James had canceled their weekly hike. He had appointments with potential wedding clients and needed to stop by Claire's house to go over an agreement to do some work for her and Emily.

Sam rode her bike to the lake instead so she could rent a kayak to paddle on Lady Bird Lake. The air was dry with a touch of coolness that would give way to oppressive heat by the afternoon. But it was still morning, so Sam only had to share the lake with a handful of paddlers, and at times she felt like she was alone. By afternoon, the lake would be filled with colorful kayaks, canoes, and paddle boards. But for now, she could pretend she was alone, enjoying the rhythmic motion propelling her craft through the water, allowing her body to synchronize with nature and with the occasional egret gliding above the surface alongside her. While she paddled, her mind ran through her date with Alex.

She felt like a teenager who was going on her first date. Did she really want to advance things further with Alex? He'd been known as a player during residency, always going to clubs and staying out late, even when he had to get up early and round in the morning. But now he seemed more serious.

Since Sam had been engaged and living with her fiancé, she hadn't participated in these activities, except for one time when Jeff was out of town on a business trip. She'd mainly stayed with her friend Nicole and her husband Seth, who, unlike Jeff, did like to go clubbing. Alex was there, along with many of the other surgery residents who were mainly men. All of them were on the prowl, hitting on girls, looking for interludes from the grueling hours in the hospital.

Sam wasn't really into the club scene, but she did enjoy going out every once in a while, even if Jeff had no interest. Of course, Sam did not understand how her fellow residents could party so hard after working thirty-six-hour shifts. She supposed they were following the old adage—work hard, play harder. Sam thought back to some of the very juvenile behavior she had witnessed during medical school. She'd learned that it was a phenomenon called delayed adolescence. It was the notion that people who spent most of their lives in school tended to behave immaturely well into adulthood, whereas, supposedly, those who started working and were responsible for providing a living for themselves and families were forced to mature more quickly and at a younger age.

So Sam still wondered if she should keep her focus on Alex—or put too much hope into it being something more. Maybe she should just treat this as a fun fling. He could just be someone she found attractive and wouldn't mind spending time with. They had things in common—their days in residency, which was a shared trauma in some respects.

A splash drew her attention as a turtle flipped into the water, leaving his companions behind to continue sunning themselves on a nearby log. Sam smiled, marveling that moments before, when she had launched her kayak, the skyscrapers rapidly rising in downtown Austin were looming over her. But with a few strokes, she was on a stretch of the lake where the jogging path on the banks ensured that the trees and brush remained. Even though she could hear the cars and traffic surrounding her, she could savor nature for a few minutes, as if the city were gone. She paddled on.

Sam thought back to her conversation with Alex. They had certainly engaged in a lot of shop talk. And reminiscing about when they were on Dr. Osborne's service brought back a lot of memories, along with some of the insecurities she'd had when she was starting out as an intern. Some attendings were great, but others would yell at them about every little thing, or worse, throw instruments at them in the OR. In hindsight, she understood they were just stressed, and in medicine, small mistakes could sometimes result in big complications or lives lost. And Dr. Osborne did have a point about Trendelenburg, the name of the position the bed should be put in so that the patient's head was lower than his or her feet.

One of the weird things about medicine was the strange terminology. So if you needed to have a patient's head up, instead of just saying "head up," you'd say "put them in reverse Trendelenburg." And the regular Trendelenburg position, with the patient's feet up, increased the blood pressure in the head and neck so that when you did procedures where you punctured the large, low pressure veins in the neck and chest, you decreased the risk of …

Suddenly Sam realized this all made sense. Mrs. Rodriguez had mentioned this, too, that her head had to be put lower than her feet when she'd had complications after giving birth to her daughter. All to prevent an air embolism.

This might explain why Brad had two puncture wounds in his arm. Wow. This could have been a perfect murder, because the method of death left behind no evidence—unless it happened to a patient in the hospital, with doctors considering it was a possibility, so they could rush the patient to a CT scanner to catch the evidence before it disappeared.

Sam stuck one end of her paddle upright in the water, using it as a brake, then spun her kayak around to turn back toward the dock. She needed to talk to Claire right away—and apologize.

35

Sam rode her bike straight from the lake to Claire's house and rapped on the door. After a few muffled barks from Kerbey, Mike answered in pajama bottoms and a T-shirt.

"Hey, Sam." Mike yawned as Kerbey jumped on her legs to greet her. Sam bent over to pet the happy dog. "I guess you want to see Claire. I'll go get her."

"No, wait." Sam stopped petting Kerbey and stood. "How is she? I haven't talked to her since last week, and … and I feel bad about—"

He held up a hand. "No need to continue. You said what needed to be said, and Claire's okay with it. In fact, she feels bad about how she treated you." He motioned with his head. "Come on in. I'll get Claire."

As Mike turned around, Claire entered the room, stretching. She had just showered, her hair still damp. "Hey, Sam. How was your date last night?"

Sam raised her eyebrows. "How did you know?"

"James told me. In fact, he's supposed to stop by soon."

Sam smiled. It figured James would gossip about her.

And no grudge from Claire. Sam felt like she'd failed her, but Claire seemed to have moved on and was more interested in Sam's love life than anything else.

"I'll go make some coffee while you ladies talk." Mike retreated into the kitchen.

They moved to the couch and Claire said, "So? How was it?"

"It was good. I'm not sure if I want this to go anywhere, though. Alex is great and all, but he had a bit of a reputation when I knew him in residency."

"Men change. And whatever his intentions, you can still enjoy going out with him. Even if it doesn't turn out to be a long-term thing, you can just have fun. And it will help you get over Jeff." Claire put her hand on Sam's. "Because it has been almost a year."

Sam thought for a moment. Had it really been that long? She had been focusing on getting by, mainly on the clinic, learning the ins and outs of workers' comp, figuring out the system so she could take care of her patients.

"I've never really dated anyone casually before," Sam said. "But I guess now is as good a time as any."

"Sure, why not? I mean, you're beautiful and single."

Mike came in with two steaming cups of coffee for them. Sam was glad for the interruption after Claire's compliment.

Claire looked up at him, smiling. "Such great service here. I think I'll stay."

He bent down and kissed her on the head. "You're welcome to stay as long as you like." As he straightened up, he said, "I'm gonna change. I'll be working on some stuff out in the garage if you need me."

Before he could leave, the doorbell rang and Kerbey yipped. It was James. Kerbey greeted him with licks. "Come on in," Mike said. "The ladies are just getting into the juicy details of Sam's big date. You won't want to miss it."

After Mike disappeared down the hallway, James settled into the stuffed chair next to the couch so he and Claire flanked Sam on either side. "So? Where'd you go? What'd you do?" He leaned closer to Sam. "More importantly, where did you spend the night?"

Sam flushed and punched him on the shoulder. She recounted the events of the night before with James and Claire hanging on every word. When Sam ended with her decision to not rush the relationship, James looked slightly disappointed.

"As I told Claire, Alex was a bit of a player in residency, but he does seem a little more mature now." Sam shrugged. "If I keep seeing him, I guess it'll be nice to have someone to talk to, who understands the medical stuff."

Claire said, "Just have fun with Alex. I guess I never realized how all-consuming medicine could be."

"That was always an issue with Jeff." Sam sighed. "When we'd go out with my friends from residency, invariably the talk would veer toward various cases and interesting things that happened—or at least interesting things to us. Jeff would just sulk and act resentful."

"Sounds like it's good you left him," James said. "He didn't really appreciate you, did he?"

"No," Sam looked down at her lap. "No, he didn't." She turned toward Claire. "So of course, when Alex and I were at dinner last night, we talked about something that had happened during residency. And that's why I'm here."

Claire scrunched her brows. "I don't understand."

"Well, we talked about one of the first times we worked together, when we were putting a central line in a patient."

"What's that?" James asked.

"It's a large catheter that we put into one of the large

veins in the body"—Sam pointed to her collarbone—"and right here is one of the spots it can go. Doctors use these big catheters to give high dose antibiotics or really strong medications to increase a patient's blood pressure if they're in shock."

"So what does that have to do with me?" Claire asked.

Sam took Claire's hands in hers. "First, I wanted to apologize to you for doubting you about Brad. My thinking has been all over the place since he died. And last week, after finding that exposed rebar in your parents' driveway, I was certain that was what caused his death, since he had been having headaches for a while."

"Plus, when we talked to Chris," James said, "he mentioned he'd had a bad headache, too, after riding around with Brad."

Claire nodded, but her face darkened a bit as they talked.

"I thought that maybe you were too close to this, that you were just trying to find some reason why Brad didn't overdose." Sam looked directly at her. "So I was wrong, and I'm sorry."

"Okay, go on." Claire didn't seem quite ready to accept Sam's apology.

Sam glanced at James, who had cocked his head, a confused look on his face.

"So after my date with Alex last night, it hit me." Sam leaned back into the cushion so she could see both Claire's and James's faces. "We had been talking about putting in a central line in a patient, and our attending yelled at us because we had forgotten to put the patient in Trendelenburg."

Claire knitted her brow. "Come again?"

"Oh sorry. See, that's the issue when you get medical people together. It's like we're talking a different language.

Anyway, Trendelenburg is a position where you tilt the patient's bed so their head is down."

"Why would you do that?" James asked.

"Well, it increases the blood pressure in the veins near the head." Sam rubbed her finger under her collarbone. "Like this one that runs right here, the subclavian vein. The blood pressure in this vein is fairly low, and if it is lower than atmospheric pressure when you puncture it, there's the possibility of an air embolism." She saw confusion on both their faces, so she added, "It's a bubble of air that clogs up the blood vessel."

"So what does that have to do with Brad?" Claire asked.

"Usually if you have an air embolism in one of these large veins, it would go through the heart and into the lungs, causing a pulmonary embolism."

"Like that reporter had a while ago," James said.

"Exactly. He had a pulmonary embolism from a blood clot that formed in his leg, a deep vein thrombosis. The clot dislodged and traveled up through his heart and into his lungs, blocking the blood flow. It was so big that it blocked both pulmonary arteries, like a saddle, so he died. But the same thing can happen with a big bubble of air."

Claire narrowed her eyes. "I think I get it, but I still don't understand how this relates to Brad."

"Well, his autopsy report said he had a PFO, a patent foramen ovale, which is a hole in the septum of his heart."

"Septum. Like in the nose?" James asked.

"That's right. In the heart, the septum divides the left and right halves from each other. If there is a hole, then an embolism—from a blood clot or air—entering the heart on the right side can cross to the left side of the heart. Then it could block the coronary arteries, and cause a heart attack."

"So have you changed your mind?" Claire narrowed her eyes. "Do you really think he was murdered now?"

"I think it's a possibility—or at least I think this could be an explanation—because the thing that kept bugging me, that I couldn't get a good answer for, was why did he have two venipuncture wounds on his arm? I talked to the manager at the blood collection site, and she said the phlebotomist documented only one needle stick when she took Brad's blood. If she had to do it twice, she would have made a note on his paperwork."

"And there was no note?" James asked.

Sam shook her head. "There was no note."

"So who would've killed Brad?" Claire said.

"I'm not sure, but there were plenty of people who didn't like Brad."

"I know." Claire closed her eyes for a moment. "But how would someone stick a needle in Brad's arm? He surely wouldn't have just let them do it?"

"He did have alcohol and a sedative in his system, plus carbon monoxide exposure, so maybe he was unconscious. Do you know of anyone who has experience using syringes?"

Claire's eyes widened. "I suspected him before and changed my mind, but Todd worked as a paramedic for a while in college."

James sat up. "And while we were cleaning out Brad's apartment, I found a contract that looked like Todd would benefit if Brad was out of the way."

Claire flopped back on the couch, crossing her arms. She grimaced. "I can't do this anymore. I was so mad at you last week, but then Mike brought me around to your thinking, Sam. And I actually started to feel like I could move with my life." She looked at Sam and James with pleading eyes. "Maybe you were right last week. Maybe we should just let this go. The rebar did damage both cars, and fortunately Mike wasn't hurt too badly."

"But—"

Claire put her hand on Sam's. "No. You were right all along." A weak smile crossed her face. "It seems my over-active imagination has infected you now. Just let it go."

JAMES CHANGED the subject at that point, asking Claire about the agreement she had drafted for him. As they discussed the details, Sam felt confused, as if she were suddenly in Bizarro World.

Had she completely switched roles with Claire? Or did Sam suspect something all along? There were little details gnawing at her, like the two venipuncture wounds. And how did Brad get benzodiazepines? A drug addict getting drugs was probably not a surprising thing. But the venipuncture wounds still bothered her.

Claire and James finished their conversation after a few minutes, and James offered Sam a ride back to their apartment complex, since she'd ridden her bike to Claire's house.

After they loaded her bike into his Honda Civic hatchback, they had a chance to talk.

"Do you really think Brad was murdered?" James asked. "I thought you proved once and for all it was the damage to his car that did it."

"I did, but I still don't have a good explanation for why Brad had that second venipuncture wound. Maybe it really was just a documentation error, since I didn't actually talk to the tech who performed the phlebotomy. Claire's not bugging me about this anymore, and she's told me to leave it alone, so that's exactly what I should do."

"Are you sure? It seems like your mind is continuing to pick at it."

"You're right. My mind does keep picking at details, especially if there's not a satisfactory explanation. I constantly do that with my patients—worry that I missed something and they're going to suffer as a result." She turned in the seat to face James. "Okay, let's think through this. Who would want to kill Brad?"

"You already know I wanted to kill Brad many times when we were younger, since he constantly tormented me," James said.

"I know." She squinted at him. Could he really have done it? She remembered the hatred in his eyes, right after Brad died, when they had discussed this before. "But you didn't, did you?"

"No, but are you sure you can trust me?"

Sam stared at James. Why was he asking her this? Did she trust him?

They were now on MoPac, zipping between cars at seventy miles per hour, so her life was literally in his hands at that moment. Plus, she had often hiked with him alone, and she had to admit, sometimes she asked him to come along with her when she went out, not just for the company, but to have a man with her, because as independent as she wanted to be, she knew that women would always be seen as vulnerable.

But then again … Perhaps he was admitting he wanted to kill Brad just to throw Sam off, so she wouldn't suspect him. Was he using reverse psychology on her?

"You're sure taking a long time to answer. I'm just messing with you." James cracked a smile as he glanced at her. "Of course you can trust me."

She exhaled. James's weapon was his wit, his stinging

barbs often inflaming his tormentors to inflict more pain. He was not one to use force, as far as she knew.

James went on, "But my point is, it sounded like Brad was on that 'making amends' step, so maybe he reminded someone how much he pissed them off."

"Do you know who he might have spoken to recently? Who he reminded about his bad deeds?"

They thought for a moment. Then James said, "No. He picked on people he knew wouldn't attack back. That's how bullies work."

"So who would have wanted to kill him now? Who would have benefited?"

"Well, we found that contract, so possibly Todd," James said. "And Claire, actually. Now that Brad is dead, Claire will be the sole heir to her grandmother's inheritance."

Sam jerked her head to look at him. "What? Claire's grandmother is still alive. She was at the funeral. And Claire's got a ton of cousins. Are you sure she's the sole heir?"

He smirked. "I know, but if you're looking for suspects, why not Claire?"

Sam rolled her eyes. "You're impossible sometimes, James."

"I know. That's how I like it. So now what?"

She sighed. "I don't know. I guess I should drop it all. But I never had my lawyer friend look at that contract you found. I guess I'll do that first."

"And if it does look like Todd had a motive to kill Brad?"

"We need to come up with a plan to find out exactly where Todd was that night."

36

L isa was up for meeting the next morning at Houndstooth Coffee in the base of the Frost Bank Building downtown. Sam found a parking spot on the street nearby, and she passed a few pedestrians on her way to the building. Even though it was Sunday, there were quite a few early risers, like Lisa, who were going into work, just at a slower pace than during the week. While Mozart's had a rustic stone building and a lake view, Houndstooth had a modern mixture of wood and iron and, through a wall of windows, views of the lobby and the up-and-coming power brokers of Austin.

"What was so important we needed to meet?" Lisa asked.

Sam had printed the images she took of the contract, so she pulled these pages out of her bag and placed it on the table in front of Lisa. "I was wondering if you could help me understand this contract a little better."

"Where did you find this?" Lisa asked.

"Remember the friend I told you about? The one

whose fiancé had wrecked his car, causing me to be late for dinner that time?"

"Yeah, and her brother had just died, too, right?"

"That's the one. Well, I was helping her clean out her brother's apartment and found this contract."

Lisa peered at the pages. "Who is he in this document?"

"His name was Brad Johnson."

"And why didn't you talk to this Todd Daniels fellow?"

"Well, it seems like he might owe Brad, or at least his estate, some money, because Brad set up this deal with the Volker Company. The contract states they would split the proceeds fifty-fifty." Sam splayed out her hands on the table. "But Claire and I didn't want to cause any trouble by asking Todd about the money without fully understanding the contract. It looks like Todd gets the full commission because Brad died." She grimaced, feeling a little guilty for stretching the truth, but she didn't want to explain all the theories about a possible murder. "We weren't sure how to approach Todd because of the language in the contract. It says if either party is 'terminated' before the deal is closed. Anyway, I thought I could do a curbside consult with you."

"Curbside consult?"

"Sorry, that's what doctors call an informal consult, where a doctor asks another doctor, like a specialist, for an opinion about a patient's condition without formally bringing that specialist on board to treat the patient."

"Got it. That makes sense. We do that all the time in the legal world too. Let me take a closer look." Lisa scanned the document. After a few moments she said, "It does seem that this wording implies that Todd will get the full amount of the commission now that Brad is dead, even though I think the intent of the wording is based on employment status."

"That makes sense. But what about the split? Is fifty-fifty typical?"

"I think so. I think these arrangements can also be set up in any way the parties agree to. In some cases, the agent can make one hundred percent of the commission and just pay a monthly desk fee to the broker. But I suppose it depends on the relationship between the parties. However, I don't specialize in real estate law, so don't hold me to it."

"Sounds like a true law professional." Sam smiled. "Thanks for humoring me."

"So what are you going to do with this?"

"I'll let Claire and her parents know what you said. I guess this contract doesn't mean anything to them now." Sam felt a little squeamish as she put the contract back in her bag. She didn't like lying to her friend. But she didn't want to bring Lisa into what was going on, since it felt a little like a conspiracy theory she was trying to prove.

"They should also show this to their own lawyer. I'm assuming they have one handling his estate?"

"I don't know, but I'll mention it to them." Sam frowned. "Do they even need one? He wasn't very old, and I don't think he had very much."

"It's best if they do. Probate can be tricky, so a lawyer can help handle the process."

"That's good to know. Thanks for the advice." Sam decided to change the subject. "How was your conference in Vegas?"

Lisa filled Sam in on her trip. The conference focused on start-ups, of course, and Lisa looked energized as she talked about it.

"So much has changed," she said. "A few years ago, I went to that conference, and when someone asked me where I was from and I answered 'Texas,' they would ask me 'why?'"

"Really?" Sam asked between sips of her latte.

"Yeah, as if the coasts were the only place to be. But this year, when this guy who works with angels—"

"What's an angel?"

"An angel investor—a high-net-worth individual who invests their money in an early-stage start-up."

Sam didn't fully understand what that meant, but she didn't want to keep interrupting.

"So when this guy found out I lived in Austin, he said he was moving here as soon as he could. I asked him why, and he said he was looking for unicorns."

"Looking for unicorns?" Sam thought this talk of angels and unicorns sounded more like a fairy tale than business.

"Yeah, that's a start-up valued at $1 billion or more. There have been more and more of them lately, and if you get in early with a start-up that has potential, you could make a fortune."

Lisa continued talking about all the people she'd met at the conference and how they related to some of the start-ups she worked with in Austin. Eventually, the conversation came around to Lisa probing Sam again, seeing if Sam was interested in something outside of the traditional clinical career, like helping that college professor develop his research for a commercial medical application.

"I guess I never filled you in on my meeting with my boss," Sam said. "I still have a job—so I was worrying about nothing—but he did suggest that I consider getting board certified, since he can't guarantee their policies won't change."

"No, you weren't worrying about nothing. It could be an issue in the future," Lisa said. "But it's good things are stable for now. Are you considering going back to residency?"

"Not exactly." Sam laid out how she would need to get her MPH then apply for a program that partnered with companies to complete one more year of training. After that, she could sit for the board exam in preventive medicine with a specialty of occupational medicine. "So I'm looking at part-time MPH programs now."

Lisa cocked her head. "Sounds like a good option. Then I suppose you aren't really interested in talking to that professor now, are you?"

Sam shrugged. "It sounds intriguing, but honestly, I really don't know how I would help them. I know nothing of the business world."

Lisa laughed. "Neither do a lot of the entrepreneurs I work with, but that doesn't stop them."

37

Within minutes of getting back to her apartment, James knocked on Sam's door.

"So tell me, how did it go?" he said as soon as she let him in.

"How did what go?" Sam said as she sat on her couch, tucking her legs under her.

"Your meeting, silly." He joined her on the couch. "Weren't you meeting with your lawyer friend this morning?"

"Yes, I did, but I didn't realize you were going to accost me as soon as I got home."

"And? What did she say?"

"It's what we thought—although Lisa said Claire's parents should talk to their own lawyer to be sure. But it looks like Todd will get the full commission on that deal now that Brad is dead."

"That's motive right there, isn't it?" James asked.

"Yeah, that would be a pretty big motive, especially since Todd had a gambling problem. Emily swears he's had help, and it isn't an issue anymore." She shrugged.

"But you never know. She did say they are still paying down his debt, and she said Todd promised her a trip to the Caribbean. I wonder how much money we're talking about."

"You mean for that Volker deal? There was a profile of him in one of those Austin magazines recently. He's got a pretty big portfolio of office buildings. It said he usually doesn't deal in properties valued less than $4 million."

Sam pulled out her phone and brought up the web browser. "Let's see. Residential real estate commissions are usually six percent, right? What are commissions on commercial real estate?"

"Wouldn't it be the same?"

"No, here's a website that says there's a range from four to eight percent, and it depends on the value of the property. The higher the value, the lower the percentage. Let's say the commission is five percent, to make the math easier, and the value of the property Brad sold is $4 million, so we can come up with a conservative estimate. That would be $200,000."

James whistled. "That's some serious cash for one deal."

"Yes, and that's assuming there isn't another agent or broker involved. If there was another broker, then the amount going to Todd's firm is half that—$100,000. Based on that contract, it sounds like Brad would make $50,000."

"Still, that's nothing to sneeze at. Many people have committed murder for much less."

"That's true."

James tapped his chin. "If we assume Todd wanted to kill Brad, and that Brad died of a … what did you call it?"

"An air embolism."

"Okay, an air embolism. Todd would have to inject Brad with air, right?"

"Right."

"How would he get a syringe?"

"Honestly, it's really easy to get one these days. Needles are a little harder to find, but frankly, I'm surprised how many medical products you can find online. A lot are things you should only be able to get with a prescription or a medical license, but it doesn't look like anyone is checking anything anymore." She let out a huff. "It's like the Wild West out there."

"Okay, so if he wanted to, he could find a way to get what he needed." James scrunched his face. "But how would Todd have committed the act?"

"Remember, Claire said Todd worked as a paramedic in college, so he may have learned about air embolisms and how to give injections." Then Sam sat up. "She also told me Emily takes medication for anxiety. That could be how Todd did it."

James squinted at her. "What do you mean?"

"Well, Brad wouldn't just let someone inject him, would he? He would have to be unconscious, and if Emily takes a benzodiazepine, maybe Todd used it to knock Brad out."

"What's a benzo—?"

"It's a sedative, and the tox report from Brad's autopsy showed one type—clonazepam—in his system. So perhaps Todd sedated Brad, then injected him with a bolus of air."

They sat in silence for a moment as the ceiling fan above them stirred the air.

"What do you want to do now?"

"I need to talk to Emily and Todd. I've been helping Emily and Claire with their soap business, so I'll text Emily and see if she still needs help." She tapped out a text message to Emily.

James smirked. "So they've been getting free labor out of you. At least Claire put together an agreement for me."

Sam shrugged. "It's what friends do. They're planning on hiring someone once the store opens. But, honestly, I like helping them. It gives me a change of pace after working in the clinic."

"You're a good friend. And as it turns out, I'm supposed to go over to Emily's this afternoon to shoot her making soap in her kitchen. We figured customers would identify better with images in a home setting."

"That makes sense." Sam's phone buzzed. "Emily says she would love help this afternoon. She wants me to go to her house because there's too much dust at the store from the construction, and she mentioned you'd be there too. That will make it easy to ask Todd a few questions." She thought for a moment. "We should be mindful of what we say, though. If Todd isn't involved with Brad's death, they would be pretty upset if we accused him."

"And if Todd did do it?"

Sam let out a long breath. "We should be careful. Once someone thinks it's okay to kill, they may do it again."

38

That afternoon James texted Sam that he got a call to meet with a potential client for a wedding, so he couldn't go with her to Emily and Todd's house. Her plan to gather information was to let the conversation flow, hoping she could find out what she wanted to know without raising suspicion.

"I'm so glad you texted! These orders keep stacking up." Emily flipped through the sheaf of papers she had printed. "Of course, Claire's been working with me on these, but I don't think it's her favorite thing to do."

"I'm happy to help. And honestly, it's kind of soothing, smelling all these great scents, and just working with my hands instead of my brain."

As they worked, Emily filled Sam in on the progress of the improvements being made to the store. Sam was waiting for her chance to ask the questions she came to ask, but part of her was reluctant. What if she was completely off-base in her theory?

But then Emily said, "Claire told me that the medical

examiner's office doesn't think Brad died of an overdose. Is that right?"

"Yeah, they're now thinking that his death is related to that damage found in his car. That it was carbon monoxide poisoning."

"Really?"

"It turns out that Mike's car has the same type of damage, just not as severe, so that's why he had his car accident."

"So that's it, then? These were just accidents?"

Sam nodded. She didn't want to let on that her thinking had changed, and certainly not that she suspected Todd. "Unfortunately, yes. Some very bad accidents." She took a deep breath. If she wanted to get answers, it was now or never. "I was just thinking about that night—how after we hung out in Claire's room, I saw Mike pacing around outside. Did Todd have pre-wedding jitters like that?"

Emily smiled. "I think all guys do."

"Did Todd give Mike any advice that night?"

"I don't think so. When I got back to our room, I found Todd in bed, reading the latest John Grisham book." Emily looked over her shoulder to the living room, where Todd was watching golf. "I'm glad he's found a new hobby that doesn't involve placing wagers."

Todd's voice drifted in from the other room. "How could you miss that putt? Even I could have made it!"

Emily rolled her eyes. "Of course he still watches those tournaments."

"And you're sure he's not gambling still?"

Emily shook her head. "It's way too easy to gamble these days with all those online sites, but after he went through rehab, we put all our bank accounts in my name, and I monitor our cash flow very carefully now." She looked at Sam and smiled. "That's why we'll be able to take this trip next year. We'll have paid off all that debt by then."

Sam was about to ask if the money Todd got from that deal Brad closed on would help, too, but she saw Todd stand up from the couch in the living room, and he looked like he was about to come into the kitchen, so she changed the subject.

"How is the GoFundMe page doing?" Sam asked. Emily had set up an account on the crowdfunding site to help Claire and her parents pay for Brad's funeral and offset some of the cost of the wedding, since many of the vendors, while deeply sympathetic, couldn't refund everything. Most of them had given credit back to Claire and Mike for when they would be ready to reschedule the wedding.

Emily brightened. "Oh, it's going well. People are so generous, and we're almost at our goal."

Todd grabbed a soda from the refrigerator, and Emily gave him a hug. "And Todd is making sure that Brad's commission goes to his parents, so that will help too."

"Oh, are you talking about that Volker deal?" Todd asked. "Yeah, that was all Brad's doing, so it's only fair that his parents get his earnings from it." He stared at the soda can in his hand, rubbing his thumb back and forth, making a path in the condensation. "I still can't believe he's gone. I was a bit reluctant to bring him into our firm, but man, he was good at schmoozing the clients. I guess a guy can change." He gave Emily a squeeze. "Right, honey?"

Emily grinned as she looked up at him. "Absolutely."

39

S am went to Claire's house after finishing up with Emily. Now she didn't know what to think. Todd seemed to have everything under control, and the apparent motive she and James had concocted was gone, since he was honoring the original contract he had with Brad, even in Brad's death.

She pulled up in the driveway of the bungalow Claire and Mike shared in Hyde Park. The garage door was open, and Mike was loading supplies into the trunk of his car. After his accident, he had replaced his wrecked Mustang with a sedan, a Ford Fusion, which gave him more room for the samples he carried around. Sam figured Mike was getting ready for his next day at work as a sales rep for McHenry, a medical supply distributor. As Sam approached, he set down a can of gasoline.

"Hey, Sam. Just about to refill the tank on the mower." He glanced at the lawn mower on the other side of the garage. "What's going on?"

"Oh, not much. Just wanted to talk to Claire about something."

"She's not here. She went over to her parents to drop off a casserole she made for them. They're still pretty broken up about Brad's death." He stepped closer to Sam. "But, hey, I wanted to talk to you, anyway. After you left yesterday, she started acting strangely. She was pretty mad after you told her Brad's death was an accident last week, and she had finally settled down with what the medical examiner had determined, but now she seems upset again."

Sam waited for Mike to say more. Had Claire talked to him about Sam's new theory? Claire had told her to let it go, but maybe she had changed her mind after Sam left.

Finally Mike asked, "Did she say anything to you?"

"About what?"

"About Brad's death? That she thought his death wasn't an accident."

Sam didn't know what to say. And after talking to Emily and Todd, she didn't really know what to think. Maybe it really was just an unfortunate accident. In fact, she was talking to the person who was almost a fatal victim too. Mike's car had the same type of damage from the driveway as Brad's vehicle. She shook her head and shrugged. "It seems he did have carbon monoxide poisoning … and so did you. Thank goodness you're back to normal. But Brad wasn't so lucky."

Mike lowered his shoulders and looked down. "Yeah, he wasn't." He kicked his toe on the concrete lip of the garage floor and sighed. "To be honest, Claire and I did have an argument tonight," he said softly. "She keeps insisting that someone killed Brad, even though the evidence doesn't support it."

Sam gave a weak smile. "Yeah, I think she had me convinced for a bit."

Mike laughed and said, "If anyone wanted to kill Brad,

it would be James. From what Claire told me, Brad really tormented James when they were growing up."

"Yeah, Brad was a piece of work back then."

Mike tilted his head. "I guess if someone did kill Brad, then they would need access to his room somehow. It didn't look like anyone had broken into his room."

Sam nodded. Then she thought, no. It couldn't be James, could it? It was his aunt's bed-and-breakfast, so he could have gotten access to the key to Brad's room if he wanted to. And why wasn't he answering her texts now?

No. Stop it. Claire's active imagination had pulled her in. It was all just an accident. Carbon monoxide poisoning. That's what it was. Mike was proof it happened, because he'd been exposed too. And fortunately, he had suffered only minor injuries.

Sam took a deep breath. "Well, I guess Claire just needs to deal with Brad's death in her own way. Let her know I stopped by."

"Or you can come inside and wait." Mike motioned toward the door in the back of the garage leading to the house. "I'm sure she'll be back in a bit."

"No thanks," Sam said, backing away. "That's okay. I've got some stuff I need to do before work tomorrow."

40

Nothing made sense. Sam drove around to clear her head before she went home. She loved the trip out 35th Street to Mt. Bonnell. Maybe she could climb it before it got too dark. After passing Camp Mabry, the base for the Texas National Guard, she hooked a left, driving past Mayfield Park and its pride of roaming peacocks, then turned right onto Mt. Bonnell Road, her car climbing the steep hill into the neighborhood surrounding the park.

She was confused. Two deaths and an accident among a small group within a couple of weeks seemed beyond coincidence. But the carbon monoxide poisoning did explain Brad's death and Mike's accident. And Chris's death seemed to be an unfortunate overdose, adding to the horrible statistics these days. Maybe—but she hoped not— his overdose had been triggered by her visit to the club with James.

And what about James? Where was he? And why wasn't he answering her texts? He had said he might show up late at Emily's house after he finished meeting that potential client, but then he never did. When she texted him after she left Emily's—just a short text that read *Todd's not it, let's meet*—she didn't receive an answer.

She checked her phone again. Still no response. Once she pulled into a parking space next to the sign and the steps for Mt. Bonnell, she texted him again: *Where are you? Just left Claire's.*

As Sam climbed the one hundred and six steps up to the top, chattering and giggling from the other visitors surrounded her in the fading sunlight. She walked to the edge of the cliff, peering down at Lake Austin and the multi-million dollar houses lining the water as she caught her breath. The air was warm, but dry, and the lights from downtown Austin twinkled in the distance. Then she found a large boulder and sat, taking in the scenery.

Sam thought back to a time she'd come to the scenic spot with some friends on a chilly Halloween during her freshman year of college. She had shivered while enjoying the view. Life had been much simpler then. Looking back, she had been pretty clueless, but that was how it was supposed to be. Youth needed its ignorance. Now Sam didn't know what to do with her life and this whole tragedy. Was her mind mulling over Brad's death an attempt to give it meaning? Did she keep thinking back on what had possibly happened to give her own life purpose? Was it even really a murder?

She remembered what Mike had said. If someone did kill Brad, they would need access to his room. And James had access, since it was his aunt's bed-and-breakfast. He helped his aunt often, so he knew where the keys to the rooms were. And he certainly had motive. He'd made that clear several times.

But what did Sam really think about James? James could be crafty. He was really a jack-of-all-trades, dabbling in everything. Doing odd jobs to make ends meet. He certainly could figure out ways to kill someone. Did he do it?

The light was fading quickly now. She needed to go, and somewhat ironically as the shadows expanded around her, she wished James was there. She headed down the steps back to her car. More couples were climbing the steps as she left, to do what young couples do in the dark.

As she started her car, her phone buzzed. It was a text from Claire. *Mike said you stopped by. Let's talk. Meet me at the soap shop.*

41

D rizzle dotted Sam's windshield as she drove down South Congress, but that didn't seem to deter the pedestrians on either side of the road. She thought it was strange that Claire wanted to meet at the soap shop, but maybe she needed to talk without Mike around after their argument. The only spot Sam found was in front of the construction site where she had been spooked the last time she had met Claire at the shop. The man had seemed to be waiting for Sam to leave, not attack her, since he had come out of the shadows after she was already driving away. Then she recalled the skull on the man's back. She had seen that same hoodie before … at James's apartment.

Sam shook her head. No, she had seen that hoodie other places as well. A local band used that skull motif for their album artwork and on their merchandise. There must be thousands of those hoodies around town. Just because James had the same hoodie didn't mean that he was following her … or that he was a killer.

She looked up and down the street. Like the last time

she had parked there, it was quiet and dark. She got out of the car, and locked it, then she made sure she put her keys in the upper pocket of her purse for easy access to avoid what happened before. No one knew she was there, and she looked over her shoulder as she walked toward the bright lights of Congress Avenue.

James was still on her mind. Wouldn't that be the best way to throw someone off if you were a killer? He had readily admitted that he wanted to kill Brad, not once, but multiple times.

As she made it into the light of the streetlamps on Congress, she felt a little safer, until she reached the soap shop. The windows were still covered with paper, faintly glowing brown, probably from a light in the back room. As Sam approached, she noticed the front door was ajar.

The rain was coming down harder now, and the foot traffic on the street had disappeared into the protection of the neighboring shops and restaurants.

Sam backed away from the door, pressing her back against the wall of the adjacent dry cleaning business. The small awning over the door provided her meager protection, as the rain fell like pellets, slapping the pavement and splashing her legs. She pulled out her phone and dialed Dylan. It went immediately to voicemail. Her mind raced as she listened to the outgoing message. What should she say without sounding like a lunatic? When she heard the beep, she just said, "It's Sam. Call me as soon as you get this."

After she hung up, she stood for a moment, trying to decide what to do. The dry cleaners was closed, but she peered through the windows, hoping maybe there was someone in the back, but the whole place was dark.

A clang came from the soap shop. She let out the

breath that she didn't realize she was holding. Stop being so paranoid. It's just Claire.

Sam entered the storefront, stepping over wood scraps and other debris. The front room was empty and dark—the only light coming from the door behind the counter. She called out, "Claire? Where are you?"

She didn't get a response, but she heard a thump in the back. She stepped around the cutout in the counter. As she got to the door leading to the back room, she saw Claire lying on the floor next to the shelves, bound and gagged. A shop light illuminated her—slumped over, unconscious or … or dead.

The bright light made a strong contrast with the shadows, forcing Sam to squint. Her heart raced. She felt like she couldn't catch her breath, but she had to check on Claire.

Sam entered the back room, reaching in her purse to pull out her phone. A moan came from the shadowy corner next to Claire, and Sam saw another body lying on the floor. As her eyes adjusted, she recognized James, also bound and gagged.

He had a concerned look on his face and was trying to say something through the gag. Sam now had her phone out, and it had started buzzing, but a hand came from behind her and took it.

She turned to find the muzzle of a gun pointed at her face.

Mike stepped out of the shadows and held down the power button on her phone, then slid his thumb across the screen to turn it off before tossing it aside.

"I don't want to use this." He waved the gun. "It will mess up my plan."

Sam froze. What could she do? Talk to him.

"What plan is that?" She stepped back from Mike to escape his reach.

"To have you three die in a fiery car crash. Old friends out for a drive, losing control on a winding Texas road."

Sam looked over at James and Claire. James slumped his shoulders and shook his head slowly. Sam thought she could see Claire breathing, but it was hard to tell. "Is Claire still alive?"

"Yeah. I just knocked her out. The crash will hide everything else." He crept closer to her.

"But why are you doing this?" Sam stepped back again and bumped into something. She felt behind her. It was the marble table in the middle of the room.

"Because I had to," Mike said. Now he was almost close enough to strike her.

"I don't understand," she said. She started edging her way around the table, sliding her hands along the cool marble. If she could get farther away from him, on the other side of the table, she would be a little safer. He said he didn't want to shoot her.

"I thought I had committed the perfect crime."

Sam kept working her way around the table, but she stopped when she heard a splatter with her next step. She glanced down and saw a puddle. They hadn't fixed the leak yet.

"But then you figured it out," Mike said.

"What did I figure out?" Her foot brushed against a frayed cord that was looped through the puddle. Her eyes followed the length of the cord, and she saw it was connected to the mixer sitting on the counter, next to the sink.

"The air embolism. I didn't think anyone would figure it out, but you did."

Sam blinked. She had been right. "Why did you kill

Brad?" She put her hand on the counter, next to the mixer's power switch.

"Because he … he raped my cousin Michelle while they were in high school," Mike said as he stepped in the puddle.

Sam's finger froze and she blinked again, processing this revelation.

Mike's eyes widened, his pupils expanding so that his green irises became thin slivers. "Yeah, Michelle. After she moved here, she seemed to be doing fine, but then one day she wasn't. She started getting high all the time, and it tore my aunt apart. We finally had an intervention, and Michelle told us that she had been raped. I was pissed. I asked her who it was, but she wouldn't tell me."

He stepped closer to Sam and out of the puddle, forcing her to move back, tracking along the marble table and away from the mixer. "But that look on your face just now …" He cocked his head. "Brad assaulted you, too, didn't he?"

Sam stepped back farther.

"So you understand. He wasn't going to learn. That night after the rehearsal, when he found out I was Michelle's cousin, he came to me later and tried to apologize." Mike shook his head. "But he didn't mean it. You understand, though."

Sam's heart pounded as she blinked. She did understand … but she didn't.

"Did you know this when you met Claire?"

"No." Mike paused his pursuit for a moment. "I found out a few months ago when Michelle saw a picture I had posted of all of us on Facebook. That's when she told me." He looked over at Claire. "And it's a shame because I fell in love with her. Now she has to die too."

Sam continued the course around the table, now

wanting to draw him toward her. Keep him talking, she thought. "No, Mike, it doesn't have to be this way."

"Yes, it does. Claire won't let this go, and she dragged you into this along with James. So that's why you all have to die."

Keep him talking. "Did you have to kill him?"

"At first, I thought I would just get revenge. Make him sick. One day I scraped the bottom of my car when I went over to Claire's parents' house. When I looked under my car, I saw where the rebar had scraped, and I got the idea that since we both had Mustangs, I could just help the process along on Brad's car."

"Those holes weren't an accident."

"Yep. And when I overheard Claire talking to you, asking you to look into Brad's death, I figured if I made myself a 'victim', too, I could confuse the issue, and maybe get everyone to see that there was a possible explanation for his death."

"But it wasn't the carbon monoxide that killed him. It might have, eventually, but it didn't." She had now circled almost completely around the table, back to the puddle. Keep him talking. How much time had passed? She reflexively glanced at the screen of her watch but it was blank. "You said you love Claire. You were about to get married. Why did Brad have to die the day of your wedding?"

"Because he came to me that night. After we talked about Michelle at the rehearsal dinner, it made me furious all over again. Brad invited me into his room after he got back with that other filthy friend of his, Chris."

"You know Chris?"

"Chris is the one that got Michelle hooked on heroin. Brad said that he had forgotten about Michelle and wanted to apologize for how he treated her. He asked how she was doing."

"And how is she doing?"

"She's dead. She overdosed. So it's fitting that the same thing happened to Chris."

"You killed Chris too?" Sam stepped over the puddle.

"It was easy. After one of his shows a couple of weeks ago, I just left a couple of vials of morphine spiked with a touch of fentanyl in his guitar case. I figured he'd eventually use it. Druggies don't always think too much about a gift that magically appears."

So Chris didn't OD on purpose. It wasn't Sam's fault.

Mike moved closer to Sam, his eyes widening, a hunter trapping his prey.

Once again, she silently repeated to herself, keep him talking. He was almost to the puddle. She hoped this would work. "What happened that night?"

"I met Brad in his room. He was already pretty drunk. He had a couple of longnecks and offered me one. I told him what happened to Michelle and he started crying. Said he was sorry. That he was a different person now." Mike's face filled with hatred. "But bullies like him never change. He was close to passing out, so I dropped some benzos in his beer—some that Emily had given me earlier because she thought I was nervous about the wedding. Then I rigged his door so that I could get back into his room, and I took a walk around outside."

Sam heard a whimper and looked over at Claire and James. Claire was conscious now, but she seemed groggy. Sam didn't know how much she had heard. She pushed on. "That's when I saw you. You seemed nervous, but it wasn't because you had pre-wedding jitters. It was because you were about to kill Brad."

"That's right. I decided what I needed to do, to end this pain once and for all. I went to my car and got what I needed out of the trunk. Then after I was sure everyone was tucked in for the night, I went back to Brad's room. I knew he had seen a doctor for his headaches and had some blood tests drawn, so it seemed like the perfect opportunity. A bolus of air in the veins."

"That's why there were two puncture wounds." Sam put her hand on the counter, her finger ready on the mixer.

Mike nodded. "But it doesn't matter now. You all have to die. Claire couldn't give up on her brother, even though he was a bully and a rapist. You and James were just unfortunate that you kept digging and unveiled the truth. So now you have to go in a fiery car crash."

He stepped closer to Sam and into the puddle. She pushed the switch on the mixer and it began to whir to life with a small spark forming where the cord in the puddle was frayed. Then it stopped abruptly as the shop light dimmed briefly. The circuit breaker had kicked in. She was now trapped in the corner as Mike stepped closer, apparently not noticing what had happened.

"Time's up." He raised his gun above his head with his hand on the barrel, ready to strike her with the butt, like a hammer. Sam ducked her head, putting her hands up to defend herself.

Just as he was about to crash the butt of the gun down on her, a voice yelled, "Police! Stop what you're doing!"

Sam looked up to see Dylan standing there, his gun raised.

Ambulance and police lights flashed, reflecting off puddles and illuminating the alleyway as paramedics tended to Claire and James. Both were mostly okay, suffering only minor contusions and possible mild concussions. Once a squad car drove off to take Mike to jail, Dylan came over to check on everyone. Claire barely responded, her face frozen in a state of shock. When Emily arrived and began consoling her, Dylan motioned for Sam and James to step away so they could talk.

"I'm guessing that call to meet someone about a wedding job was a ruse to capture you?" Sam asked James.

"Yeah, it was at an abandoned house a couple of streets over." James tipped his head toward the neighborhood just off Congress Avenue. "And when I showed up, Mike surprised me and knocked me out."

"So that's why you didn't get back to me."

"When did you have a hunch something was wrong?"

"The text messages—the lack of response from you, and then the one that I thought was from Claire seemed a little strange. At that point, I still didn't know who killed Brad, or if he was actually murdered." She held back that she had suspected James, even if only briefly. "After I had talked to Emily and Todd, I was beginning to think I should leave it all alone again."

"Mike used Claire's phone to lure you here, so he could trap you without anyone noticing," James said.

"Right. And he probably thought if there was an investigation after your deaths, no one would think to look for evidence here," Dylan added.

"So how did you know you should come here?" James asked.

Dylan tipped his head in Sam's direction. "Sam left me a voice mail."

"Something didn't feel right when I got here." She hugged herself as she recalled the events. "I tried calling Dylan, but he didn't answer, so I left him a message. When he called me back, it was right as Mike was taking my phone away, so I answered on my watch."

"I was able to record most of it," Dylan said. "We'll see if it can be used as evidence."

James narrowed his eyes as he looked at Sam. "So how exactly did Brad die?"

Sam shrugged. "Honestly, I still don't know. I was waffling back and forth." She looked at Dylan. "I guess it's good that you heard the confession."

"Again, we'll see if it holds up to the DA's scrutiny."

"But to answer your question, James, an air embolism could have killed him. However, it's rare for an air embolism to be big enough to kill someone when it's injected from a peripheral vein."

Dylan gave her a quizzical look. "What's an air em—?"

"It's a bubble of air in the blood stream. For some types of procedures where we have to puncture veins, we worry about air bubbles causing pulmonary emboli, which block blood flow to the lungs and make it harder to breathe. It's the same thing we worry about with DVTs— that a piece of clot will break off and lodge in the lung. In rare cases, if the embolus is big enough, it kills the patient."

"But I thought Brad died of a heart attack," Dylan said.

"Right. He had a PFO, a patent foramen ovale, or a hole in his heart. So I'm thinking …" Sam paused as she wondered if this was getting too much into the details. But she saw curiosity on their faces.

"You mentioned something about that when I let you see the autopsy report." Dylan looked over at James.

James smirked. "It's okay. I already knew."

Dylan turned back to Sam and continued, "You said those were pretty common and that it probably didn't have anything to do with Brad's death."

Sam nodded. "At the time I didn't, but now I think it might have. The PFO could have allowed an air bubble to cross from the right side to the left side of the heart, and then block one of his coronary arteries, causing the heart attack."

"So do you really think that's how Brad died?" James asked, a worried look on his face. "I mean, it's pretty scary if it's that easy to kill someone. Just inject a bubble of air into their veins."

"Honestly, I don't know if it did or not. But it's plausible. If air bubbles get in the peripheral veins, they're usually small and get absorbed in the blood pretty quickly."

"But Brad also had other things affecting him," Dylan said.

Sam looked at him appraisingly. "That's right. It was a

perfect storm—the alcohol and the sedative along with the carbon monoxide and an air embolus—the combination of everything killed him. His heart muscle might have been starved already, so even a small air bubble decreasing flow to one of the coronaries could have been enough to cause an infarct." She shook her head. "But air embolisms are hard to prove. You have to catch them on a CT scan before they disappear. I guess we'll never really know for sure."

"But it doesn't matter now, after what just happened. Mike certainly intended to harm you," Dylan said. "And he confessed to giving Chris drugs spiked with fentanyl. So even if we aren't able to bring charges against him for Brad's death, Mike will be going away for a long time."

James looked at the ground, his shoulders sagging. "I thought he said he loved Claire."

"He hated Brad more," Sam said. "And he was going to kill all of us to save his own skin."

As the crews started to clear out, one of the other police officers pulled Dylan aside, so Sam and James went back to Claire and Emily. Claire looked up at Sam, rage replacing the flat affect she had had on her face previously. "You! This is all your fault!"

Sam breathed in sharply. She figured Claire would be upset, but she hadn't expected to be the target of Claire's ire.

Claire's nostrils flared as she spat out vitriol. "If you hadn't kept picking and digging, if you had just let it go, everything would be fine."

Sam blinked. Claire was the one who had asked her to look into her brother's death. Claire had wanted to know what had happened. And Sam had figured it out—for Claire. "But you heard Mike …"

Claire burst into tears, burying her face in her hands. After a few moments, she lifted her head, a flinty look in her eyes. "Mike told me you were going to blame it all on him."

Sam was bewildered. "But … but Mike knocked you out. He was going to kill you."

"He said you and James hated Brad. And if anyone had killed Brad, it was James." Claire glared at James as if she could punish him with her thoughts.

Emily pulled on her arm. "Claire, you don't mean this. You're upset, and everything is so confusing right now."

Claire turned to Emily. "Did you know that Sam thought Todd did it? That she and James were trying to prove it? They never liked you, either."

Emily dropped her hand and stared at Sam and James, wariness on her face.

"It's true. Mike said they would find someone else to blame. Either him or Todd. Todd with his gambling problems, he kept asking Mike to invest in different real estate deals. And with the deal Brad closed, it would be easy to frame him."

Emily frowned as her hand came up to her mouth. "What? No, it was the other way around. Mike kept asking Todd to go into these weird deals. But Todd knew better than—"

"None of you believe me," Claire said, cutting her off. She backed up, like an animal cornered, twisting her head back and forth to keep an eye on everyone. "You're all against me."

So Mike had been manipulating Claire all along. How twisted was that? He said he loved her, but did he really?

James tugged on Sam's sleeve. "We should go. This is only going to get uglier."

But Sam wanted to help. She stepped closer to Claire, her hands open. "I'm so sorry about everything that's happened. We'll find someone you can talk to, someone who can—"

"I don't want to talk to anyone! I want my life back!" Claire's face was scarlet now, her hands balled into fists at her sides. "You ruined everything!"

S am went through the proper channels this time to take a couple of days off. She figured almost getting murdered was a good excuse for missing work. She had spent the previous two days reacting to the shock of that night in the soap shop, relying on James and Alex to get through it. In fact, Alex had taken time off to spend with her, to make sure she was recovering, mainly by just sitting and being with her.

Not only was she processing what Mike had done, but also Claire's lashing out at everyone. Her outburst had drawn the attention of those who were still on the scene, including Dylan, who grabbed one of the paramedics to step in and deescalate the situation.

Emily had called the next day to check on Sam, but her voice continued to contain some of the wariness Sam had seen on her face the night before. "I'm sure Claire didn't mean everything she said last night. She'll calm down, and we'll all get through this together," Emily had said.

Sam had agreed with her, but she wasn't so sure. After

she hung up the phone, she wondered if that would be the last time she spoke to Emily.

When she did go back on Wednesday, she felt she could handle anything, even Mr. Mason.

"How is your leg?" Sam asked as she pulled over the rolling stool.

"It's fine." Mr. Mason pulled up his pant leg so Sam could examine it.

The infection had completely disappeared, as had the scab from the original wound, leaving only a faint scar. She measured both legs and found them of equal diameter.

"Have you been doing okay on the medication?" Sam asked.

"Yep, no problems at all."

"No easy bruising or bleeding?"

"No, I'm fine."

"And have you had any problems with shortness of breath or difficulty breathing?"

"No, no."

"Okay, so we'll need to keep you on Xarelto for another two months."

Mr. Mason frowned. "I'm fine now. Why do I need to keep taking it?"

Sam smiled and handed him a printout of patient information that answered exactly that question. "Because the current guidelines recommend continuing anticoagulation therapy for a minimum of three months following the diagnosis of a DVT."

"How do we know the clot is still there? Do I need to get another ultrasound?"

"A repeat ultrasound is not recommended unless you have new symptoms suggesting the DVT has increased in size or broken off to form an embolism."

"Well, I feel fine, but I would like to know if the clot is still there."

"We could do a repeat ultrasound, but because it would not be following the recommendations in the guidelines, insurance may not pay for it."

Mr. Mason huffed. "Figures."

Sam answered a few more of his questions, then she stood and headed toward the door. "I'd like to see you in a month, just to make sure you're still doing okay. Of course, if anything comes up, please let me know."

Mr. Mason followed her out into the hallway. "Thursday afternoons work better for me, usually around 3:00 p.m."

"Okay, you can let the ladies up front know when you check out."

Then he said, "You were right."

Sam stopped walking and cocked her head. "I'm sorry?"

"You were right about my company's workers' comp insurance covering my ER visit and this treatment. That medication is outrageously expensive, by the way. Over the last couple of weeks, it took some haggling back and forth between my health insurance and the workers' comp insurance. I spent ages on the phone. At first, workers' comp didn't want to cover it because I gave the ER my private health insurance card. But HR stepped in and sorted it all out." He frowned as he shook his head. "You wouldn't believe what I've been through." Then he turned and walked toward the front of the clinic.

Sam looked up to see Dylan just a few steps away. He was accompanying Mrs. Rodriguez as they followed Cynthia to an exam room.

Dylan had an ironic look on his face. "Did he just say that you wouldn't believe what he's been through?" He looked over his shoulder toward Mr. Mason. "Maybe I should tell him what *you've* been through."

Sam put her hand on Dylan's arm and lowered her voice. "He's not worth it. He's just a harmless blowhard."

She followed Dylan and his aunt into the exam room, then Cynthia gave Sam the chart and closed the door as she exited.

Sam quickly scanned Bob's notes about Mrs. Rodriguez's physical therapy sessions. She had reached all her milestones and had completed her therapy.

"It looks like you're doing quite well," Sam said as she finished up her examination of Mrs. Rodriguez.

"Yes, Doctora, I'm almost completely back to normal. Just a little bit of soreness every once in a while."

"And you've been doing fine without any restrictions?"

"Yes, I can do everything I need to do. Of course, now I'm careful when I'm reaching up high on the shelves to get boxes down."

Sam smiled. "Then I guess this is goodbye. I'll release you from care, so you don't need to come back here anymore. But as always, if you have any issues, just let us know."

Mrs. Rodriguez looked over at her nephew Dylan, who was sitting in a chair next to the exam table. "Or maybe we'll see you again? Perhaps with *mi sobrino*?"

Dylan blushed. "Tia Becky, please don't give the doctor a hard time. You know we are both dating other people." He looked at Sam. "And we are just friends."

"I consider you a friend that saved my life." Sam tilted her head. "I will say, we did seem to work pretty well solving that case together."

"And I will say, you did something no one else could have done." He looked at her sternly. "But it did put you in danger."

Sam sighed. "I know. I'll be more careful next time."

Dylan squinted. "What do you mean next time? You aren't planning to go after another murderer, are you?"

"No, no. I just meant that I'll be more careful. I've started carrying around pepper spray."

Dylan nodded. "Good for you. And maybe you could take some self-defense classes."

Mrs. Rodriguez smiled. "Look at you two, bantering like an old couple."

"Tia! You set this up, didn't you? You made sure Christina had your car today so that I would have to drive you, didn't you?"

Mrs. Rodriguez looked coy. "Oh, Dylan, I wouldn't do such a thing."

Dylan stood and opened the door to the hallway. "C'mon, Tia. I'll take you home."

Mrs. Rodriguez followed him out the door and started walking toward the front of the clinic.

"Wait, Dylan," Sam said as she lingered at the entrance of the exam room. "Can I speak with you for a moment?"

Mrs. Rodriguez smiled knowingly and patted his arm. "I'll go check out. You can take your time."

Dylan went back in the room, shut the door, and looked at Sam expectantly.

She took a deep breath as she perched on the edge of the exam table. "I just wanted to say that I'm sorry."

He raised his eyebrows. "For what?"

"For how I treated you. Back then … and these last few weeks."

He dipped his head. "Okay. I'm not sure I understand."

"Since you heard everything on the phone that night, now you know—Mike was right."

"About what?"

"That Brad attacked me."

Dylan's features softened. "I'm so sorry."

"And I finally realized why I started blowing you off back then."

A glint of understanding showed in his eyes. "That's when it happened, didn't it?"

Sam nodded, her lip quivering. "I didn't tell anyone, because ... you know. When stuff like that happened back then, everyone just said, 'boys will be boys.'"

Dylan closed his eyes for a moment, his jaw set. "But we're not all like that."

"I know, and I'm sorry. I'm sorry for lashing out at you and for making all these assumptions about you."

"I understand." He smiled. "And I forgive you. It takes guts to apologize."

"Thanks, Dylan." She went to the door and opened it. "We shouldn't keep your aunt waiting any longer."

As he followed her into the hallway, he said, "Thanks for taking good care of her. She was really worried for a while."

"It was my pleasure, although I can't take all the credit —Dr. Popescu and Bob were the ones who really got her back on her feet."

"But she said you had to deal with some bureaucracy to make it happen. So I appreciate that you went the extra mile for her."

Sam looked at him, admiringly. "She means a lot to you, doesn't she?"

"She does. She's family. And family is important."

Sam nodded as she went back to her workstation. She pulled out her phone. Family is important. She texted her father: *It's been a while. Can we have dinner tonight?*

ABOUT THE AUTHOR

Stephanie Kreml writes mysteries and thrillers after working as an engineer, a physician, and a life science consultant. *Neglected Truth* is the second novel in the Dr. Samantha Jenkins Mystery Series.

Sign up for her newsletter and receive a FREE copy of *Accidental Truth: A Dr. Samantha Jenkins Novella.*

Go to
www.stephaniekreml.com/signup
and join today!

ALSO BY STEPHANIE KREML

Truth Unveiled

Truth Promised

Coming Soon

Misguided Truth

9 781955 921015